For Nick,
I hope you
enjoy!
Jim

FEARNOCH

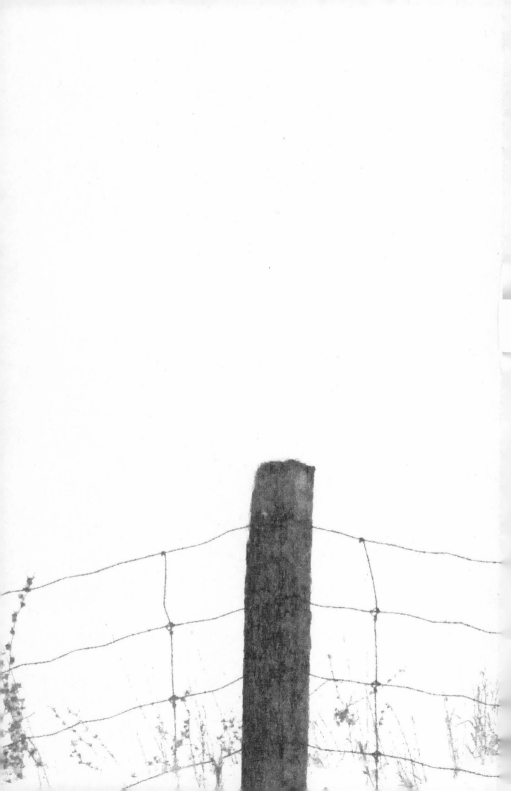

FEARNOCH

Jim McEwen

BREAKWATER
P.O. Box 2188, St. John's, NL, Canada, A1C 6E6
WWW.BREAKWATERBOOKS.COM

COPYRIGHT © 2022 Jim McEwen

ISBN 978-1-55081-941-0

A CIP catalogue record for this book is available from Library
and Archives Canada.

We acknowledge the support of the Canada Council for the Arts.
We acknowledge the financial support of the Government of Canada
through the Department of Heritage and the Government of
Newfoundland and Labrador through the Department of Tourism,
Culture, Arts and Recreation for our publishing activities.

PRINTED AND BOUND IN CANADA.

 Canada Council   Conseil des arts
for the Arts   du Canada
Canada   Newfoundland
Labrador

Breakwater Books is committed to choosing papers and materials
for our books that help to protect our environment. To this end,
this book is printed on recycled paper that is certified by the Forest
Stewardship Council®.

For Lisa Moore
who made it real

ONE

The day was done, another one done, and John took off his hat and went out and stood in his road. Sunglow slid, a pink meniscus on the hill, while he looked down at his land. Light left from the field and bush. Light left out purple and bruised and the birds left too. John was the sixth John Younghusband in his line of John Younghusbands and he lived on Sixth Line Road. He stood out there in his road and remembered that day the pigs got free.

He was a boy then under the elm trees and helping his dad fix the fence by the road. One moment there were no pigs and the next moment there were many pigs. The elm trees were all dying down the fenceline.

El-lums, his dad said. El-lum and also fil-lum were two syllables in his father's dialect, which was also dying. And the el-lums stretched their thirsty cancerous fingers up and up. It was a cedar fence with little cedar teepees every ten feet, filled with rocks. They ran three logs between these teepees, tapped in long nails and lashed it all together with wire and pliers. Bark particles and larva bits and those things stuck in the sweat under young John's T-shirt. He bled under his nails as he pried up rocks, he dragged around the deadfall, scraped himself on the wire ends and twisted the pliers with his tongue sticking out. He worried he wasn't working hard enough.

John the fifth was quiet as he worked. And then the pigs—the pigs, they made their impression on the land. An ungulate orgy descended, and celebrated, casting noise and dust; they trotted, chortled, screamed, busted the fence, knocked John into the ditch, maybe a dozen of them, grinning beasts with their ears pinned back. They were free.

The old farmhand from across the road scurried around after the pigs and was not unlike a pig himself in his movements. His great plaid stomach shook out over his pants as he emptied all his swear words onto the road. John listened and remembered from the ditch. Then he tucked his head in his knees and lay in the long grass when the pigs flocked and funnelled back. But his father caught a pig, flipped it on its side and the animal was calmer. Of course, tackling pigs had been a large part of his own childhood. He helped the farm-hand load his truck full of the objecting pigs.

You need a good fence, his father said.

Another day John remembered—he was in high school then and deeply upset about something. Maybe it was getting cut from the AA all-Ottawa Valley hockey team, or because it was his fault the hay got wet, or it was Anna Berube putting a note in the hood of his hoodie in drama class that said she was sorry she couldn't go to the semi-formal with him, but to save her a dance. Maybe it was all three of these things lined up together. He walked in circles in his socks in the basement, rubbing his head, and didn't know what to do.

I don't like it, he said, oh I don't like it at all.

Don't like it? said his dad. He was over in the tool room and thought John was talking to him.

What? said John, who didn't know he had been talking.

You're not gonna like everything, his dad said. When have I ever said you're gonna like everything? Or if it matters if you like something. He was eating a cookie. He bit it, held it up and frowned at it, then replaced it in the tin.

You like that cookie? John asked.

Doesn't matter, said his dad.

John remembered back through the dark in his field.

———

John's son Johnny, now the seventh John, was a stubborn five years old, capable of knocking over and breaking anything, and he sat himself in his mother's garden and watched an ugly old car come down the laneway to spot in front of the barn. The boy looked out at his world from under a pile of curls and poked at it all with mighty and reckless interest. Like his old man, the boy was clumsy, rough with stuff with his wee hands, and needed reminding to be careful.

The car though was hideous, and ramshackle; however, Johnny was pleased by any machine. And a man got out of the car, shadowed and gloomy by the barn roof and he personified his vehicle. He had pale blue eyes, misted and fearsome eyes like he knew something awful. Johnny knew this man, but he was busy.

Hi Johnny, the man said. What're you working on here?

The boy had a toy front-end loader excavating through the rhubarb and cucumbers. It was a fantastic garden, blooming out with fruits and flowers, because the Younghusbands always laid their gardens where an old barn had been. Splendid fat and full gardens over a centennial of animals shitting.

Working, Johnny said. He sneezed a burst of dirt and wiped his hands on his shirt. Working hard.

Yes. That's good, said this man. Good work. He never knew what you were supposed to say to children so small, and worried they didn't like him. D . . . ah . . . Do you think your mum . . .

I am being careful, the boy said.

John came out from the barn.

Mikey g'day g'day! he said. He had his hockey bag and two sticks but got tangled up in baler twine, extension cords and some antlers.

Frig, he said backing out.

Good day, said Mikey.

Johnny ran through the rhubarb to carry his dad's sticks. They walked to Mikey's shit pre-owned sedan, Johnny leading the procession, this filthy bandmaster trying to twirl the hockey sticks.

What is that, an ant? John looked down at his son and said, Are you eating an ant?

He sat the boy on the trunk of the car and hunted around in his mouth. Johnny opened his mouth wide and craned his neck upwards.

A flying ant, said John, throwing a wet bug on the ground.

On the road to the arena Mikey felt very thankful for hockey. The gift of an hour to think about nothing but pucks and sweat. Someone gets in your way and you just pile-drive them through the boards and then spray the water bottle all over your head and spit everywhere. Everything on a vicious cold beautiful hell-bending slide towards goal. And then after, after with the steam smoking off your shoulders, have a beer, leaned back against the cool cinder-block wall of the dressing room with five decades of paint on it, just have a sit and smell awful. It was September and this would be their first exhibition game, versus the reprehensible all-star team gathered from Gatineau and the Pontiac on the Quebec side that embarrassed them in last year's championship.

But here John was saying: he's got good frigging hair eh, Johnny? Great hair.

Looks like Gretzky, Mikey said, finding the perfect comparison. Like Gretzky in 1982.

Yes, said John. I love him.

Me too.

Peace said . . . she asked me—what's the best thing about having a baby? What's the best thing about a baby, what's the best thing— drunk as hell at the barbeque there. Think she kept forgetting she'd just asked me that.

Mikey looked out the window at a tiny, fat, truly silly pony that lived a few farms up from John's, which he always enjoyed looking at, but now he didn't feel very joyful.

I didn't want to say to her, John said, you know it was the . . . the transcendent love—he smacked his hand down on his dirty pants when he said the word "love," which sent a lot of dust and hay-must up in the passenger-side area. Like the love that I have that will never ever die. He looks at me and I know he's thinking that I'm the best— my dad's the best. I mean—he's wrong—but I appreciate it. So I just said his hair was perfect, I felt bad.

Mikey was quiet and tilted his head. John felt he'd been talking about himself too much and tried then to think about how his friend was doing. He tried to imagine Mikey holding a baby, a bawling baby in the night.

Do you want this Mikey? he said.

Eh?

A wife, and babies. Eating flying ants. Mikey.

Mikey stared up the long flat grey road. On the shoulder there was a rusted-out and ancient cast-iron furnace with a skid propped against it on which someone had spray-painted "Furance for sale." It was a real relic of a furance. And then farther up was a rotting billboard in a farmer's field with Virginia creeper twisting up it and it read: Guthrie Place Porn Barn Over 10 000 XXX Films.

Yes, he said. I want that so bad I feel like I'm drowning.

Oh, said John. Oh shit. And then he winced and twitched his leg when an old pain flowed into his right ball.

TWO

Anna began her days early, twisted up in the sheets, blasted to consciousness and scared to be conscious, with a sweaty sentiment of—okay what am I doing oh boy. This morning she dragged her brain drooling out of a dream about driftwood on a beach. Water like blue diamonds on volcanic sand with no weeds or people. An old log was worn smooth and pulled with the tide along the ripples in the sand. Only water, wood and sand, and an ancient serious lady narrating the dream. The lady voiced over the dream with a haughty grandeur: old log, why do you keep rolling so, on and on, in the water all these years, what do you have to tell us . . . ? Something like that. Jesus Christ, thought Anna, moving on tiptoes through the apartment with her toothbrush stuck out her mouth, that is not a suitable dream to have. Then she made a terrible face at an overstuffed and unopened envelope on her kitchen table.

Magnus's black hair spilled over his ear and Anna looked at the ear stuck out the top of the duvet, spat pink in the sink, thought about kissing the ear, gathered up her own hair, worked a hair elastic off her wrist, decided against kissing the ear and against opening the envelope at this moment. She steadied herself against the wall putting on her boots, fumbling with her finger for the little loop at the back. Then she opened the door of her Hochelaga 1½ and took all the grease and sex appeal of Montreal on the chin. She stood, the whole way to work, on the metro, on a bus, and on another bus. She held that twenty-eight-year-olds should stand if they could, while there were still world-beaten teary geriatrics swaying around out there with five Mega Dollar shopping bags and canes and legs fat with dropsy or diabetics' fat feet soon to be chopped off.

The last bus got to Anna's stop, and she debussed and slowly put one boot in front of the other, one boot in front of the other, down to a tall, pale-yellow townhouse. Dour and drear this house was, and neglected, with a noticeable lean to the one side. Moss and mould spotted up its siding and shit and feathers piled up from the pigeon activity above. It was an awful house. It was loathsome. And the smells—no amount of cleaning product could douse those smells. Anna crossed herself and focused on her breathing. The door opened slow and rusty when she pushed the buzzer. She knew there was a finite number of times she could go through this door and leave with her mind.

This house was an open custody/detention residence, the Centre Saint-Savard it was called, for offending males aged fifteen to nineteen. Inside there was anywhere from three to ten of them. They were awaiting sentencing on or serving time for a crime. They were exceptional at Xbox and drank litre after litre of silty cherry Kool-Aid. There were also two or three social workers or youth workers or community workers inside, exhausted, and wearing lots of rings, pendants and bracelets. They all spoke of "pieces": we're going to bring in the counselling piece, explore that piece and bring that piece in, work that piece. Anna was a part-time/on-call youth-care worker staff. She had trouble keeping up with all the mental health methodologies and modules that kept these particular youths out of the larger prison. Maybe they'd get killed in there. She also couldn't remember what exactly a module in fact was.

The boys were superb at hiding drugs in baseboards and vents.

The staff confiscated the boys' phones and looked at their own phones a lot, and worried about funding. The kitchen knives and scissors were locked up in a safe in the office. Sure as any house can be haunted, this one was. It remembered what happened between its walls: the hangings, overdoses, a boy stabbed up with a pencil crayon, the schizophrenic meltdowns, all the blood and shit, all the burn holes and gang signs. At night the house was alive with moans. Mice fought for their lives on glue traps, chewed their arms off, squeaking their mouse-screams. Anna felt ghosts spying on her during her overnight-awake shifts. Most of the time she didn't know why it was even a job and what she was supposed to do. Smile at the youth and try to get them to engage in a Thanksgiving collage and when they didn't, which they of course didn't, sit in the corner smiling and then record incidents on a sheet and let all hope and purpose die while smiling. She would have liked to repaint the baseboards or perhaps dig an enormous hole out back because at least that would have been something. Sometimes her mouth filled with blood and she realized on the walk home that she'd been biting her lip for hours. But she loved Ebenezer, and this was his birthday.

I want Anna to take me, Ebenezer said. Miss please.

He had his hands together and stood in the doorway to the office. For his birthday programming he was allowed a chaperoned day trip outside the house. He wanted to go to the mountain to see paths in the forest and calmness and wildlife. Anna had encouraged a mountain visit because he couldn't sleep.

A full-time staff, Miss Natalie, cardiganned and top-heavy in great bunches of scarves, looked at Ebenezer and considered, then swivelled in her computer chair to hand Anna two metro passes.

Bless, said Ebenezer. Now he was seventeen, a very little seventeen-year-old, smallest in the house, but his record was the worst. He was in love with Anna, and he said "bless" a lot. He was born in Haiti but came to Montreal one winter when he was young and no one told him or his family about winter boots. His only memories of Haiti were a goat tied to a boat on the beach and lots of empty pop bottles. He stared at Anna, the soft curve of her mouth as she concentrated on the zipper of her raincoat, then figured he'd been looking at her too long. Anna had remembered to wrap his birthday present in blue wrapping paper, not red, because he was Crips, not Bloods.

Ebenezer walked the trail over Mount Royal tentatively with his arms stuck out like how Anna might, as a young girl in Fearnoch, test a frozen beaver pond, clear black ice over bubbles and suspended leaves. Ebenezer's blue hat, blue sweater and blue pants were all looking very clean and correct.

He tripped on a root. I've never been up here quand même, he said.

Anna came here sometimes to eat hummus on a blanket and put her head in Magnus's armpit. You've never been to the enormous and beautiful mountain in the middle of your city? She was teasing Ebenezer.

No, Ebenezer said. A different Montreal for Ebenezer, a different arrondissement, for him the tenement brick and block in Montréal-Nord, uncelebrated on the postcards, not famous for bagels and bachelor parties. Every town hides its Ebenezers away in these public housing courts. Stuffed together, the shit gambrelled roofs, with plywood and cardboard in the windows, the shingles and paint falling off, rusty air conditioners falling off, little white signs saying 4B or 2C also falling off. He'd been down this way—là-bas—before but that was, for instance, to sell forty-dollar flaps of baby powder to loaded drunk men in Canadiens or Boston hockey sweaters and run into the night before they figured out what they were snorting up. He had never picnicked on the mountain.

Then Ebenezer howled and covered his head. He felt a great shadow, the percussion of wings; a branch snapped, and what he might have described as a feathered dog sat on a bough, twisted its head clean around to look at him, its eyes on fire and shuttering open and shut. What is that! he said.

That's an owl, Ebenezer, said Anna. Look, see. She pointed with a stick.

Owls are real?! Ebenezer said. His eyes were wide: he'd been living under the understanding they were a mythical beast from Harry Potter. Anna laughed and grabbed his arm. A birthday owl, she said.

Later, back at the house, there was a cake for Ebenezer with all of the icing stuck to the top of the plastic cover. Anna thought cake, hugs and owls probably weren't much relief to Ebenezer. She had to describe how socially acceptable his behaviour was during the day trip in his daily log—really socially acceptable? Eh? Really really socially acceptable? And then she saw from the entry before that Ebenezer had learned that a young man waved a knife at his mother and sister in the stairwell of their housing tower, promising to kill Ebenezer once he freed up. Anna's present for Ebenezer was a box of Nighty Night tea.

THREE

John and Mikey filed into the home dressing room at Fearnoch Memorial Arena. Their home dressing room their whole lives, back to when their dads tied their skates. The thoughtful Zamboni driver had left a storage container full of his Zamboni snow in the centre of the floor for their beer, and the walls and stalls were lacquered thick with the Fearnoch Syrup Kings black-and-yellow home colours. Kirby, their friend since kindergarten, came in late and let his bag slide off his shoulder. John, as captain, was waiting until everyone was there to give a speech. Once many years ago Mikey tried to rip Kirby's toenail off at a party. Mikey recalled Kirby as being fairly skeptical at the time.

Ahh, I dunno here boys, Kirby said.

It must come off—I can't stand looking at it! Mikey said, staring and clicking a pair of pliers together. He was drunk, with shit cocaine filtering into the blood membranes behind his nose, his face snarled and rotten. The idea of ripping off what he saw as evil had him enraptured. He'd seen the toenail a number of times now and he hated it. It was halfway there anyhow: it opened slightly, stuck on Kirby's sock when Mikey pulled it off, hinged on a stubborn purple cuticle with a fluffy milky residue underneath, and it smelled unbelievably bad. John guided Kirby into a chair. He gave him a plastic jug of Alberta Premium and went to find something for him to bite down on.

There's gonna be a lot of blood, said someone. You'll need a blood-guard, Mikey bud.

I don't . . . Kirby trailed off, eyes wide and pleading, mouth full with the rye.

Yes, blood. Mikey hadn't blinked in a while and had the pliers chomping. He straddled Kirby's legs and moved in on the toenail while John put a calming hand on Kirby's shoulder. Kirby tipped his jug to the heavens and sweated from his temples. Mikey growled as he got to work.

This, said someone else, is chaos.

Okay! said Polly, who would marry John about four years later. She made a motion with her arms, same as how an umpire calls safe. Let's just think about what we're doing here.

Cross about how the toenail was still there, Mikey went and fell against some garbage in the garage.

———

Mikey wondered if people thought about things like that when they saw him. Kirby sat next to him and yawned in his glasses and sweat-pants. He wasn't thinking about Mikey at all but rather about his piece-of-shit sump pump.

John stood then, shirtless, wearing hockey pants and flip-flops, and attempted his speech. He said this was our barn, the lads from Fearnoch and Larocque and the lads from the other side of the river embarrassed us in our barn. Pucks on net, bodies on net—we're going deep, stay out of the box—someone runs you, take a number we'll get him later, safe is death, fifteen dollars in the kitty there please. And on he went like that. There were about four Codys and three Coreys on the team. They thought about the game, which they were sure to lose, but also about jobs, divorces, if they were getting fat, why their kid pushed other kids at daycare. And over all the private hopes and troubles of these men who still thought they were pretty good at hockey and took it too seriously, the arena arched, with beer punch cards in the canteen, a Chuck-a-puck sign-up sheet, advertisements on the boards for Fearnoch Granite N Tile, Fearnoch Truck Repair, Happy Slices Pizza, Valley Rent Rite, aggregates, fertilizers and animal feeds, and by the score clock a water-damaged portrait of the Queen. The players looped around the ice stretching their groins and exhaling great refrigerated clouds.

Then the Quebecers, in their blue-and-white sweaters, put up four goals in the first period and Kirby wondered why they were in the same division. Composer of the massacre was a slick new French centre—Laframboise, it said on his sweater—and his absurd skill level humiliated the boys regarding their own skill levels, and just to make everything even more annoying for the Fearnoch bench, Laframboise ripped through their defence in white skates, white gloves and ringette pants. John caught his own skate in a rut by the Zamboni gate; he felt sick, felt his femur threatening to unhook out of his pelvis. Mikey sent John what he thought was a very clever and cute pass, but it was soft as muffins and a Pontiac forward picked it off and then scored with a very fancy-Dan bury. Mikey hit the post and the crossbar and knew it was not a night for glory. His hockey pants were in tatters, like he sat on a bomb, because after a game once someone dropped a cigarette into his hockey bag and started a small fire.

What am I? he shouted, scrambling to cover someone much better than him. Left wing? I'm right wing? Who in the fuck is play-ing centre?!

I don't know. Fucking . . . just play hockey! John said, and got whistled for slashing.

Kirby scored a goal: as shocked as anyone else when a shot from the point sang in and deflected off his penis and in, and he celebrated by lying on his side in pain. That made it 7-1. By then the puck was largely forgotten and the game veered into cultural warfare. A French forward cross-checked John into the boards from behind and Mikey got angry—this was his captain after all—so he gave the forward a tap on the ankle and shoved him when he turned around, and Mikey got the only penalty on the play. Once he got out of the box, he hacked at the French goalie's trapper just after the whistle went. This was unsporting of him, sure, but he was frustrated.

Désolé, he said. Pardon uh—uh toute suite.

And was promptly struck from behind by a cross-check of such magnitude and significance he imagined later that night, wincing as he got into bed, its energy had originated on the Plains of Abraham and gathered ferocity along the centuries, waiting in the dioceses and patateries of Quebec for a chance to come across the river and find the proper Anglophone recipient. He wheezed on his knees by the net and felt his kidney had exploded and was draining into his abdominal cavity. A giant from the Pontiac defence stood over him.

Kirby wanted to help his friend. On the drive home he thought he should have cross-checked the defenceman. It would have been the right thing. But he didn't really want to hurt anyone and anyway he froze looking up at this exhaling mastodon Québécois blueliner. John did not freeze and pushed past Kirby and cross-checked the defenceman. The man turned and dropped the mitts, and John dropped the mitts, and they both fell immediately on top of Mikey, who hadn't yet figured out if he could stand or not, but was endeavouring to because as he'd been taught, hockey players never stay down. Kirby picked up the gloves and sticks off the ice and skated them over to the penalty box.

When the game was over, 9-1 it was, both teams shook hands at centre ice. The big defenceman patted Mikey on the chest and said, You will never beat the Dark Side.

John said to Larocque, the French captain: sorry I called you a

Peasoup. And a Gatinese. I was angry.

Larocque offered his regrets in Gatinese for all the things he called John. They knew each other from midget hockey camp. Then they had their beer and drove home all under the same moon that spilled onto the only real intersection of Fearnoch.

———

Kirby dug around in the freezer for a frozen bag of hash browns to put on his privates. His partner Peace showed him her progress on her beadwork. She was finally pregnant again. She had peed on the stick and danced out the bathroom naked from the waist down. But it was too early to tell anyone and her miscarriage from last year still loomed over their bungalow. They lived on Wind Chime Crescent in the newest Fearnoch subdivision, just behind the Younghusband farm, back where the fence met the tracks. It wasn't their home-steader idyll with a windmill yet—it was their starter home, for to build equity.

You shouldn't play hockey. Peace pointed at his privates with a sewing needle. I need that for more babies! More! She sang and con-ducted with the needle. Kirby sat beside her on the sofa. The thawing hash browns started to make his lap wet.

No more hockey, Peace whispered to her stomach, holding it.

A tractor pulling a hay wagon rattled past the living-room win-dow, the farmer probably loading bales in the middle of the road again and ripping even more empties into the ditch, Kirby figured. John's cows were making an awful mewling racket and then a donkey contributed its ghoulish heehaw. Peace had never got used to this place and she looked out the window alarmed, toying with her nose ring. Kirby stared at the carpet and thought how in the morning he had to get up early to drive an hour into town and pretend he knew what he was doing at his lucrative government job with Human Rights and Complaints Authority Canada. He prayed for North Korea or somebody to explode the internet or for the green socialist revolution to begin overnight.

———

On the other side of the fence and across a cornfield and a soya bean field and two fallow fields from the socialist revolutionaries, John the capitalist patriarch was watching a children's movie with his boy and his dad. John's dad now lived in the small cottage down behind the farmhouse. Sitting on one end of the chesterfield, John was one full head taller than his dad because his mother had been a giant. A real towering Richmond beauty, is how his father said it. The younger Younghusband siblings had moved away years ago now, sensible enough to see the future.

Mercifully the film about robot anime puppies ended. The actual dog, who was named Busty, stuck his ears up when the robot puppies were howling. Busty just showed up one day, got himself stuck in a raccoon trap, and became the dog. He was ancient and lousy, with one bottom canine missing. He was very calm but despised thunderstorms.

And John's dad was asleep. His face folded smushed and grey into his chest, and a butter tart with one bite out of it in his hand. He looked vulnerable, even like a child. John touched his shoulder to wake him and when he did wake, he couldn't find his hat.

Forgetting about the hat, he said: Goodnight, goodnight, patting his grandson who was asleep too on the floor and breathing in tiny whistles.

In the dooryard under the light and moths, John watched his dad shuffle down the lane to the cottage. He sure didn't look it now but once this man was a great amateur boxer of Fearnoch. A famous son of Fearnoch, with extensive coverage in the *Fearnoch Valley Press*, a now out-of-print newsletter that had been about three-quarters obituaries. The story goes that he hospitalized two fellows from

Smiths Falls after they came after him with pry bars when he used to work the railroad. John couldn't imagine that, although he liked to when he was younger, even though his dad said, don't listen, it's not true, it wasn't quite like that. It was a different time, John, he said also.

Now the old man's pants were always up high, higher and higher, so that about three-quarters of his body was pants. He spoke slowly and quietly, very Valley and olden, pulling his words from deep out of the Valley. Soft and low then with his hands in his pockets, shrugging and flapping like an old hen, staring ahead, swaying almost like he was surfing, everything but the piece of hay in his mouth. It was a little strange. But that was how he went about it.

Peace found it very strange and John's dad helped her with some stump removal when she first came to Fearnoch. She noticed he said straw-burries not strawberries and said words such as tool and pool with such a loving lingering delicacy they were sung more than spoken. Like he was trying to push a large fragile flower out of his mouth intact.

The water will pooooool here. I'll get my tooooools.

The old man had a dead-earnest look, a look so long ago and forgotten it almost seemed a mild assault to be looked at like that. He'd look at you and look at you—with his good eye now, the other knocked sightless by a puck when he was a young fellow on the outdoor rink—and still he'd look at you waiting for you to speak first, until finally he'd stand up and say, Well, I've got work to do.

Peace was a little suspicious as to what this was all about but she did like it when he pulled up and inspected a great old log, wrapped in tremendous moss and mushroom growth, and said, well, it's more alive than dead, really, and so set it down gently in the bush not the burn-pile.

John wasn't ready for his dad to get old and forgetful with the bottoms of his eyes sagging open and glistening blue-pink. John Sr.

walked down the lane fiddling with his hands and trying to remember something he needed to tell John.

———

Across Fearnoch Road and close by the Fearnoch Convenience and LCBO, where people bought their beer and cigarettes and crosswords and ham, and you could still rent DVDs, and beside the barn where the farmhand hanged himself during the Depression, Mikey used the side entrance and climbed up into the loft over the garage at his parents' house and got into bed. He shifted his weight off his deflated kidney and pulled the quilt up to his chin. He slept on an ancient horsehair mattress it was said a great-aunt of his with Down Syndrome died on. His parents said he could stay in the loft so long as he continued to see a therapist. They were not wealthy—his mum was an administrative assistant at the Granite N Tile and occasional cleaning lady, and his dad a lineman for Hydro One till he got hurt— but they worried about their boy and paid for the therapy. Mikey had a stutter that wasn't as bad as it was when he was a kid. Words that started with "d" could be tough when he was nervous or excited to say them. Overall he was undistinguished. He was also a labourer at the dump.

Mikey decided to get up and re-tape his hockey stick. Sitting on his bed, he ripped the puck-marked tape off the blade. God hockey sure does rule, he thought.

He wound the new tape on carefully, ritualistically, snipped the excess and waxed the curve. His alarm clock sat on its face on the night table, as Mikey did not need to be reminded about time spinning into the future and out of reach. His cat, Mrs. MacPherson, was dead, and his one plant was dying. There—beautiful fresh white tape-job, right to the toe like Ovechkin. His plant, name of Robert Plant, had moist, velvety, delectably moist soil, but was dying. And you couldn't say Robert Plant was overwatered because Mikey hadn't watered Robert in a month. He was positioned in the sunniest quadrant of the loft.

You gotta frigging dig deep here Robert, Mikey said, putting a finger in the soil, and picking up three brown leaves.

He stood and rubbed at his kidney in timid and inquisitive circles. Mrs. MacPherson had really been a battler. Through the curtains came the yellow buzzing light over the barnyard where he found her.

It was a rotten windy chilly shit of a day that he found her in the puddle, in the mud out front of the barn, this abandoned runt barn-kitten sneezing out blood with her head down on her paws. Her brown tabby-cat fur wet in the rain and eyes full of white shit. One eye worse than the other but both looking very bad, as he remembered. Her mouth was stuck in a tiny soundless bawl and she was trembling. Mrs. MacPherson was blind and bloody in a blind world that didn't care and she bowed under all the pain of trying to continue being alive. If she didn't matter at all—what did the smallest, last, shittiest of a litter of five inbred barn kittens matter for anything?—well why was it so painful? Mikey thought. Cows walked by, people walked right by, and she shook her little feet, trying to lift herself out of the mud.

The recollection stuck and it always hit Mikey right there in the sweet spot, right in the jaw, the pain and bravery of this creature too innocent to know even that she was abandoned. Mikey couldn't square it with the universe. He couldn't rationalize it off into a corner of his head where it could be understood, like he did with the death of old, unhealthy and nearly forgotten Great-uncle Alvin. That was sad but made sense and folks gave the life, what little they knew of the life, a little dignity, their styrofoam plates and cups and stories behind the church and a beautiful sort of Celtic fiddling woe to the afternoon. Mrs. MacPherson didn't get any less sad with time.

Which made Mikey think about Anne Frank. And he thought— no, don't look, but then he had to, so he got *The Diary of Anne Frank* down from his bookshelf, and the book had four pictures of her on the cover and more at the beginning of the book, which he looked at.

A story that's sadder and sadder, forever, he thought. He had trouble explaining himself to people.

After he pulled Mrs. MacPherson from the mud, he took her to the vet in a towel, wrapped her up shaking and bleeding away with her ears flat, and she got better by degrees but never forgot that her heart belonged to the barn not the house. Because of the inbreeding, or traumatic events prior to meeting Mikey in that puddle, her eyes were permanently half-lidded and her tongue hung out. And if the barn cats had a fight out in barnyard, one of their profoundly violent, eye-gouging, ear-removing affairs, she ran, puny and gallant, into the fight, not from it. Maybe she was just truly unintelligent. But these features Mikey adored. He played with her, dragged around his finger or a skate lace for her to attack, and if he forgot to play with her, or was too tired, she'd wait in the place where they played last, wait for ages, hoping it was time again soon.

Mikey thought it was hilarious to yell Mrs. MacPherson! at her when she did something bad. She howled to be let out so she could be free and kill all those mice, birds, bugs, anything living, and she bit and clawed at everything, particularly plastic shopping bags. Always purring, licking and gnawing into old Loeb grocery bags. Mikey didn't see why cats had to treat small animals the way they did—the slow and gleeful toying, really dragging out the demise of a dissociative field mouse or chippie. He tried to save the mice from her wrath; he caught them with a pail and a flattened cracker box and let them outside demented, dopey and dozy, moments away from a heart attack. Probably he should have dropped a rock on these mice but he wasn't tough enough. Anyhow Mikey liked when Mrs. MacPherson was calm, purring in a rectangle of late afternoon sun on the quilt with her eyes closed in perfect tight feline symmetry because she had trust in him and his loft.

Now Mikey wanted to watch videos while he fell asleep because that way he wouldn't think about anything in the dark. Burn his brain out on the acid-blue midnight glow. He thought about Cassie, his old girlfriend, the one he'd liked the most, of course he did, but then thought, no, Jesus enough of that. Maybe his future wife was out there in the dark somewhere, in Quebec or Winnipeg or Bessarabia, also debating putting on a YouTube. That was a nice thought.

No, we should not watch videos in bed, he concluded, I doubt Teddy Roosevelt or One-Eyed Frank McGee would have watched videos in bed. They had too much to do. I should act as if I'm camping. I should try to be a more interesting person.

The quilt kept coming up and making his feet cold. He found some classical music on the computer, something with harpsichords and powdery baroque jewelled ladies warbling, which he set on low volume, and thought this was more suitable than hockey highlights. And he got out his great fat book about Ireland and fell asleep with his face stuck to a page about elderly lifelong celibates on the rugged coast of County Mayo. He woke several times in the middle of the night, exasperated to be conscious again.

———

West then along Fearnoch Road, past the elementary school, the shuttered chicken farm, past some bloated pigs lying around flapping their ears, nearer the river now, one road in, one road out, where historically the criminals and the Catholics—then just any poor people, now poor and rich people—lived, trailers with rotten lattice between stone-masoned mansions, Anna's mum pulled the cord on the lamp by her bed and thought about when she might have a grandchild.

And far from sleepy Fearnoch, over the border into Montreal, Anna flipped her pillow and watched city light fan through the curtains and slice on the wall. Above the Centre Saint-Savard the pigeons tucked their heads in and bunched up fat together on the roof. Inside Room #7, Ebenezer pretended to be asleep when the night staff opened his door to check that he was there and alive. He was looking at a naked picture a girl from his old high school had printed off of herself and mailed to him and this was electrifying but contraband. Maybe there was some weed or pills left in the new hiding spot under a tile behind the toilet or maybe the other boys had taken it all. It was four in the morning and he drank his cold cup of the Nighty Night tea. He thought about his mum and his sister.

FOUR

There is little you could say that would distinguish Fearnoch from any other small Eastern Ontario town. A Great Fire licked across it and the Great War took half its young men. It wasn't prominent, wasn't built in the bones of a War of 1812 outpost, like nearby Guthrie Place. The town had its brawls in the beginnings, like all the others, the collision of tribes. An assortment of folks the rest of the world didn't have the time for and marooned away up here. Scotch, Scots-Irish, Irish Catholics, Orangeists, Anti-Orangeists, French Canadians, all coming down the stagecoach trail, all raising and drinking their rums, another toast, another toast, filling pre-industrial taverns and hotels with their oaths, then going outside and beating each other with sticks. They bloodied one another over canal-dredging jobs until it didn't matter who was who and besides you needed your neighbour across the fenceline to help get the goddamn hay in, no matter what starving Old World shire their genes came from.

There was a church, then another church, a schoolhouse, a slaughterhouse for a while, a community centre with an outdoor rink. Silos and rogue white pines salient from the thickets. It was a small quilt out on the line—Fearnoch Road, Fourth, Fifth and Sixth Lines running east-west, Archibald A. McHugo Side Road and Guthrie Boundary Road cutting them north-south. People enjoyed hockey, bingo and euchre no more or less than any other town along that stretch. Old men in their trucks, with their seatbelts clipped on the seat behind them, stopped in the middle of the road to talk to each other until someone honked behind them. Every summer more cyclists than the last, coming out from Ottawa in packs, all the gear, not getting over onto the shoulder enough. Farms and bungalows were laid out from the one intersection—with a streetlight now, and angled parking spots—that had on its four corners: a plaza with a gas station and convenience store, a defunct cheese factory, a field, and a field. It was a one-hour drive east to Ottawa, but they were going to put in a new highway, which would change things. John loved Fearnoch, got very romantic about it. Kirby was embarrassed by it. Mikey was trying not to think anything bad about anything. Anna was afraid of it because everyone there expected her to be someone important.

In some places there are kinkajous or narwhals or ocelots. Or bioluminescent atoll skinny-dipping, or mounted falconers hunting golden foxes with golden goshawks, or walking boardwalks and holding someone's hand, feeling the rings and the sweat-suctioning, looking at this hand, and maybe you'll fuck tonight, sweat everywhere with your clothes together on the floor but, that is, after ice cream at Coney Island.

Fearnoch is not any of those places. Although the sun and moon still visit, like in all the other places and to all the people and creatures in them farming, falconing, swimming, crying, fucking. And also there are many places just like Fearnoch, with swamps and dead farms and dead elms hanging over the rusted Quonset huts, and lawns uncut around ancient satellite dishes and umbrella drying-racks. But Fearnoch is still a place, a piece of the planet, even if no one knew where it was, and even if Peace once called it a cousin-fucking colonial cow-shit-hole.

—–—

But before any of that of course, for ten thousand years the whole place was covered in a glacier and then for the next ten thousand years it was a little part of the great hunting grounds of the Algonquin people.

Samuel de Champlain, he of the Canadian grade 10 history textbook, was the first European to see any of all this, or at least said he was, and this was in 1613 or possibly 1615. The French explorers desired beaver, and they imposed themselves into an old war between the Algonquins, river people, and the Iroquois Confederacy, farmers to the south, and they gave the Algonquins firearms if they converted.

Champlain, Kirby whispered in class back then, was a piece of shit.

Mikey had to do a project on the French and the Algonquins for the class, and he struggled with it. He tried to imagine what Fearnoch township would have looked like at the time. The bush on steroids, he figured. The great white pine stand still dominating both shores. Concert of the pines, empire of the moose, and wolf, and dragonfly. Algonquin warriors warning of Iroquois attacks and taking old sun-fucked malarial Champlain, who must've been dreadful at paddling and portaging, up the river in their war canoes.

Champlain's group camped on an island where Champlain figured mosquitoes must have been invented and wrote so in his field notes. He scratched at himself, eating his slumgullion, and about nine kilometres behind him Fearnoch was waiting, a spectacle of bush and insect. And from the river, looking out at the valley, well what did he think? wondered grade 10 Mikey with his pen. Probably, he thought it was one big awful vast nothing. Nothing special. No permanent settlements on this stretch at least. Not good farmland like down south. But certainly a lot of space. Now where's the beaver pelts . . .

But the Algonquin would have seen it differently. Their river— their highway. Trails through the woods with bent trail-marker trees, places to gather in summer and hunt in winter. Mikey tried to imagine.

They saw it differently, the bush, because surviving all those Ottawa Valley winters with no modern infrastructure engenders a certain humility towards the bush.

———

Mikey went over to ask John for help with his project.

Voltaire said Canada, the whole place, was just one big bother and he wished an earthquake would hit it, Mikey instructed John. He said it was boreal bullshit. Barbarians, bears and beavers.

Who?

Voltaire, said Mikey, and showed him the library book.

Well fuck him anyway. Look at his hair!

And, continued Mikey, flipping ahead, look—England tried to give Canada back to France but Napoleon said fuck off.

John's dad came into the kitchen from the fields and took his boots off.

Dad, you ever know any Algonquins around here? John asked him.

His dad sat down, held his cattle-cane on his lap, and thought. No, I never . . . I never did. I did hear—when I was a boy I did hear, the old-timers said sometimes they'd come and trap on the creek. That would've been at least oh fifty years before me.

The creek? asked John, pointing out the window.

Yeah, said his dad. They said it was their land. And I guess, you know, they were right.

And off he went.

———

But in Champlain's day Europe wanted more and more beaver hats and so the Beaver Wars turned Eastern Ontario into a killing zone. That alongside the smallpox that came off the pigs and chickens from France. An Iroquois army of fifteen hundred men, armed with Dutch guns, overran the Algonquin and the French, and the Huron tribes got caught in between. For a century it was a very dangerous place to be.

And in the last of those vicious 1600s there was a great slaughter, that almost everyone had forgotten about, just up the river from what would become the Fearnoch intersection. A mad and starless night and a war party of French and Algonquin snuck around behind and slaughtered a war party of sleeping Iroquois, who were planning on how to slaughter them. The mighty Iroquois never woke up, knives stuck down into their dreams and the sand filled with their bones.

Mikey stuttered throughout his presentation, said I can't imagine several times, and received a D.

Then by the 1800s, timber replaced beaver in importance and now the British sent lumbermen to buck the great pines, float them down to the Quebec boom, and hew them into masts for warships to fight Napoleon. Retired officers got land grants to settle the valley so that the Americans wouldn't get it. When that wasn't enough, the Crown sent boatfuls of poor people—they promised good, cleared farmland and free supplies to people from places with names like Skibbereen, Wigtown and Haghill. Troublemakers from the Scottish Highlands and tubercular Irish Catholic famine orphans. Just clear them the frig off the old continent. And, because of course the land was abysmal and uncleared, and probably should've never even been farmed, and there were no free supplies, and taking into account also the temperature swings, the astounding isolation, and bugs, historians still bicker, not only about how these destitute settlers settled, but why.

The Algonquin had seen enough. Their river clogged with logs and Loyalists, beavering and lumbering interests, boat after boat of strangers. Most left, to the mission down in Trois-Rivières, to the north and west, deeper into Shield country.

A Frenchman had a store and trading post where two wagon paths met at an abandoned British supply depot leftover from the Revolutionary War but he disappeared and then there was a post office and a cheese mill there. A sign on a post read "Fearnoch Corners," in honour of a diseased fish-drying hamlet in the Highlands someone's second wife cried for as she died of typhus during a winter colder than anything Scotland had seen in 250 years.

And none of these people could have guessed that one day the town would swell to a thousand souls, Anna would catch a catfish with her bare hands on Champlain Island and present it proudly to her mother, who screamed, and skidooers would drink and piss in the trees there; the French Canadians would conduct more slaughters, in the hockey arena this time, built in the same sand that held the Iroquois bones, and in high school Mikey and John would ignore the *Speeding Costs You . . . Deerly / La Vitesse, Ça Coûte . . . Cerf* sign with the deer on it at the Fearnoch intersection as they piloted dark Fearnoch roads, spilling their Max Ice in a Dodge Omni field car with no licence plate.

———

The first of the John Younghusbands was the seventh child of a failed Glasgow hardware merchant and haberdasher. At age fourteen he was told, like the others, he had to leave home because there wasn't enough food. And like the others, he boarded a boat. His boat would go to the Province of Canada, which made no difference to him. His employer, one of the lumber barons, paid for his passage and he'd work it off with five years' service in farms and lumber camps. He saw Scotland from the sea for the first and last time, watched the hills lie back in the fog, did not cry, but went below deck to steerage and got cholera. After a month and a half on the boat and a year and a half on a quarantine island in the St. Lawrence, he made it up to the Ottawa Valley. His employer recalculated his service then to seven years, due to the delay. He thrashed in the summer, shantied in the winter, he lost two fingers on one hand, one on the other, and was terrible at the fiddle. Maybe in Glasgow they were walking to the shops, putting coins on the bar and talking to girls. But John was sunburned or frostbitten in the alien bush thinking about shops, coins and girls. He didn't ask a whole lot from life, he knew better.

———

An old and maimed man in the lumber camp, Mr. Cecil Munro, brought salvation down for John and all the future Johns. In the bunks one night during John's seventh winter in the shanties, the man next to him was caught in a violent dream and gave him a savage kick on the kneecap. John slid away and rubbed his knee. He lay on his back on the pine boughs, watched his breath rise and heard wolves singing to the cold. Then he rolled over to look down where Mr. Munro sat in front of the wood stove. He held his face in his hands and studied the old man. Many years ago now a felled tree had hopped and crushed Mr. Munro's shoulder, making one arm hang useless ever since. The cook had pity and had taken him as a helper. Mr. Munro stared into the fire and produced a bottle from his pocket before looking about, suspicious. He held the bottle up in the firelight to see how much was left. After a great wet cough he allowed himself one small drink.

Ah, he said. Ah God . . . then he spoke some Gaelic softly and coughed again.

Mr. Munro had worked the bush since he was ten, and now he was dying; everyone knew it, most were tired of his coughing. John thought how nice it would be to have a drink, then the man next to him kicked again.

Next morning the teams of buckers and sawyers shouldered their axes and cross-saws and walked to work with their beards frozen. The snow whined, coming for them through the trees, collected and whipped up under and over. John tucked his chin and sank to his hips. The man walking alongside him, a man new to their shanty, had a moustache of ice and, John noticed in shock looking down, the old man's bottle peeking out of his coat pocket.

Maybe this is a different bottle. No, this is the same . . . Mr. Munro's bottle. The injustice sat poorly with John.

He thought about the bottle and this new man all day, and concluded he should not have the bottle. This new man takes drams from a dying man and also, John thought, I don't get any drams.

John sawed, squared, hauled the pine, and tried to lead the horses through the snowdrifts. He knocked tobacco out of an old cigar end and chewed that in place of the more expensive chewing tobacco. Yes, I hate this man. And that's all I can make of that, thought John dropping his axe in the snow.

Then immediately he sought out the man, located him having a break in a tree-well and hit him, knocking all the fluffy snow off the tree and down onto the two of them. Fights didn't rouse much alarm with the lumbermen, and no one rushed to aid a new man. John took up the bottle. The man reached for it and John shoved him back in the tree-well.

It's Mr. Munro's, said John.

The man with the ice moustache said nothing.

John narrowed his eyes in the falling snow. You're nae Scottish are you, he said.

John snuck one drink before getting back to the hauling. For a minute in this big white new land, old Scotch whisky glowed in his guts and behind his eyes.

———

Later John held the bottle in his bunk surrounded again by snoring men sleeping in clothes they didn't change for months. The smell of the shanty was unpardonable. It existed as more than a mere smell and hung in auras or hauntings over the stove. John felt for the bottle. He had decided to keep it, he liked it too much, and he would ignore the old dying man. But he saw Mr. Munro down by the fire as always, done for another day with all the porridge, biscuits, beans and salt-pork-fat cubes. This defeated skeleton, he cracked with coughs, his limp arm shaking around. Mr. Munro knew death was at the door and spotting his handkerchief. Soon the door would bust in and admit a blizzard and he'd be dead and all he asked was his little bottle to ease the end.

Fuck, thought John. He couldn't endure the eyes on this man. Blue and beaten on the fire. He climbed down the rough pine ladder and handed Mr. Munro his bottle. The old man spoke in Gaelic to John with his eyes rheumy blue and John rolled away in his bunk wishing he still had the bottle. Two nights later and Mr. Munro was stone dead, frozen and smiling with his eyes open and the bottle empty.

The cook had a piece of paper from Mr. Munro for John.

Cecil said for to give it to the man who gave him his bottle, the cook said. You are this man? He got some supper beans from his hand on the paper.

I am, said John. He tucked in his shirt and pulled on his suspenders.

The cook handed the paper to him. John couldn't read, so the cook took it back, held it at arm's length and frowned at it.

Lot 4, Concession 12 . . . It's a deed, he said. You have been deeded . . . he tightened his eyes which made his mouth open. One hundred acres. In Fearnoch, down the line a piece. You know where this is?

Aye, said John. He did not. It could be anywhere; he was very happy. Never had a Younghusband been able to measure his land by the acre.

Well, good lad, the cook said. He watched young John float away dreaming into the snow and remembered all the times the auld man had said even an Irishman wouldn't want his stake of shit in Fearnoch.

———

But one hundred acres.

The next summer John made it to his acres. He beheld a great dirty rhombus of uncleared bush and swamps between exposed bedrock, dropped on his knees and rolled onto his back and laughed. The back of his shirt and pants got wet in the swamp and he shook and breathed thank you to the thorns and milkweeds. Up into the cloudless sky he submitted some very fond words about God, the people in Glasgow and Mr. Munro with his bottle.

John set about clearing his acres straight away. He had no ox or horses. He hacked into the bush by himself, burned the stumps and he spaded the thin earth and planted potatoes and wheat.

My land! Mine, all mine! he sang out and he swung his axe.

In what came as a minor scandal for Fearnoch, he fell in love with a Catholic girl and she loved him back so fuck everyone else and they got married at a ceremony with four people at it and lived in a wee eighteen-by-eighteen-foot one-room shanty with moss and clay chinked in between the logs. This girl was wandering the township in rags trying to sell a lame old cross-eyed billy goat and came up to John's acres. When she opened her mouth the Connacht accent that came out was so strange, a series of songful bleats, he thought she was playing jokes on him. Her goat's ribs and coccyx tented though its skin and it sat in the mud. John bought this goat and it died soon after.

And by the time he was old and sat down in his field and died himself, John Younghusband I had roughly thirty acres cleared, one son who survived infancy, two cows, and one horse.

The second John was a cheat, a liar and a drunk; he cleared few acres, enjoyed the dance halls, nearly lost his land in a wager with the McHugos—Kirby's mincing Presbyterian forefathers—survived the Great Fire by hiding in a well while his wife and children and animals ran for the creek, and he died relatively unmourned and soon nobody was quite sure where his grave was.

The third John lied about his age, went to Flanders at sixteen, saw his friends showered down onto the earth in little pieces, returned home incommunicative and prone to screams and long walks with his weary dog, and was just another veteran who limped through town, scaring the children or making them giggle.

The fourth John cleared the remaining acres, expanded his barns and his herd, considered ingestion of turpentine to be the cure for every ailment from insomnia to tinnitus, and the only nights he didn't spend in his own bed, as he never wanted to be far from his cows, were when he had to go blow up U-boats.

The fifth John worked his farm, he boxed, went to Saskatchewan to become a Mountie, didn't and came back, was quiet, rarely drank much or swore, was kind to people and animals, enjoyed reading, privately wished he had more friends he could talk to about reading and ideas, and was inching closer and closer to a possible psychotic collapse, with his hippocampus deteriorating, but hadn't told anyone he felt off, and he could not remember for the love of Jesus what it was he'd been meaning to tell his son.

And the sixth John inherited the one hundred acres at a time when all small farms were dead or dying.

FIVE

The Fearnoch Community Association held a meeting in the parish hall attached to the St. Andrew's Presbyterian Church just up the road from the Fearnoch intersection. They were filling the locals in on what they knew of new land developments and potential government assistance packages. Land prices were jumping, with all the new rich high-tech people from town looking to rusticate and make everything too expensive. Peace sat on the board of the Community Association and helped draw up some of their more ambitious plans. The board recommended that locals restrict wood-stove use and keep outdoor fires under two feet in diameter—recommendations that were unanimously disregarded. Which roads were and were not getting paved was the topic that attracted much more interest, jealousy and suspicion.

The old farmers came out from their lands, they filed in and sat on those old metal and wood stackable chairs. It was chilly for September and they wore sweaters and coats and fussed about a frost. The hall had fake-wood panels lining the walls and long, thin windows with dead bees in them. Needlework and quilts commemorating Jesus and the wars and the harvest hung off hooks and wire, over folding tables and over the piano. There was a kitchen full of teacups and saucers with roses on them that didn't match and generally a musty, geriatric inertia throughout.

These were secretive, independent, tribal folk, hard-to-know country people forever suspicious of the government. The arthritic, plaid-shirted heads of the old clans: the McKenzies, MacKays, Mulrooneys, Doolans, Cheesemans, the Younghusbands and McHugos. They knew every truck, who was having beer in whose garage. They held all the secrets of agronomy for the region. They tacked Back Off Government signs to fence posts and trees along their property. The only thing they wanted to do, regarding the government, was to vote Conservative, which they did, and would do until they died, no matter what, like how someone might cheer for a hockey team. Little was forgiven or forgotten, and grudges spanned down the decades. Something they did forget though was that most of them came from people who wouldn't have made it through the first winters without government immigration-assistance provisions like blankets and biscuits and forks. They grew up without electricity and their grandparents warned them to mind the faeries, out in the hawthorns with their mischief, frigging with the butter churns. Now the faeries had departed deeper into the bush.

These people could be generous and charitable: give away old trailers, a ladder, or eggs. They helped each other in the needy times, opened the door into the parlour with beers and buns on the tablecloth, but not if they suspected some form of outside authority might come in. Proud farmers, left behind, and if anyone noticed, truly noticed them past their ratty barnyards, they'd see they were accountants, engineers, veterinarians, horticulturalists, breeders, machinists, mechanics, weather-people, marketeers, labourers, worriers and entrepreneurs all at once. Their sons and daughters had left for cities, no interest in getting out of bed before the sun and cow-punching.

John was an outlier. Anyone like him was all dead, or dying. When he was a boy his father got him to bring an old milk stool over

JIM MCEWEN

to the McKenzies across the road as a gift. Mrs. McKenzie saw John and said: if you bring that cursed milk stool over any closer I'm going to burn it. The Younghusband milk cows had an udder disease back in the fifties and she hadn't forgotten. But she gave John a muffin after he dropped the stool. The McKenzies, grey and sleepy, sat with the others, crossing their arms above their stomachs and awaiting whatever loon-shit fate the Community Association had in store for them. John was the only one under fifty in the hall and he sat with his dad, nervous and as sad as the fake-wood panelling and teacups.

——

And now, out parked in the potholed parking lot, Peace sat with Kirby in their SUV. She held her purse on her lap and didn't want to get out just yet.

It'll be all right, look—I promise, said Kirby, twisting to kiss her. People do change, they do. Eh? he said.

Peace came from a town in BC that didn't have a Conservative candidate. She'd figured conservative farmers were something for the old books, like Ostrogoths and Minotaurs. So she was not well equipped to process these old-timers pushing their hats back and smelling like pigs at the Fearnoch plaza. And they probably weren't quite sure what to do with her either. She taught their grandchildren or great-grandchildren, part-time, at the daycare and kindergarten at Fearnoch Public School.

——

The day before, John yelled at her for her teaching methods with the young lad. He yelled at her over the fenceline when he saw her in the garden—he thought about not yelling at her but in the end yelled at her.

Peace was having some difficulty getting nature to do as she said—the evil and insistent roots and vines going all over and driving their prehistoric vendettas. Everything committed to killing everything else. She thought she'd hacked and ripped and killed everything but under her feet the roots carried on. Her overalls were filthy, and the beastly rooster was after her again too.

G'day Peace, said John. A great fifty-metre-long tail of baler twine dragged behind him from his pocket. He held half his property together with baler twine. Peace reminded him that she needed young Johnny's permission slip and he dropped his mess of baler twine down in the pasture.

You need to back off about twenty per cent on all that, he said. You teachers!

What?

John squeezed on the rusted barbed wire with both hands. Around and between the two neighbours grew the groves of lamb's quarters, weeds peerless in their invasiveness which John said were demons from hell and Peace said were nice on salads.

You teachers, he said. What happened to teachers? You're supposed to teach, not . . . you know, frigging . . . and he took his hat off. He wasn't pleased with how clearly he was expressing himself but he was upset and worried about his boy, and annoyed in general because Peace had notified him, twice now, that she'd contacted the MPP to discuss John's carbon footprint, and check that he was paying the correct carbon taxes and fuel taxes.

What are you talking about? Peace said. She stood up and walked towards the fence with sweat and dirt stuck on her forehead.

Okay here so Johnny's crying today, John said. Yesterday too and day before. He said the world was going to die, he said we killed the planet. I'm killing the planet. John pointed a dirty thumb into his chest and got angrier.

Well there are a lot of children suffering severe climate anxiety, said Peace. Not much time left.

Until what? We're all dead.

Yes.

You told the children they're all going to die.

Yes.

No please don't tell him that—why would you say that to a child?! He doesn't know you don't actually mean it.

I mean it! All the scientists mean it!

He comes home with drawings in his school bag—now these are very troubling drawings.

Johnny's doing very well in drawing.

And he called me a "once-ler." Whatever the shit that means.

Peace looked delighted and laughed.

John stared at her and then said: You think whatever you want. Just don't go taking the young lad on your Earth crusades. Let him be a boy. He was happier about how that came out and he leaned on the fencepost and addressed the clouds thoughtfully. John had transitioned directly from young man to crabby old man.

Peace was calm because her cause was just and long ago she'd figured out John was an idiot. Johnny has finally been attentive in class, she said. And he's interested in climate justice and climate action. We need the permission slip so we can go to Parliament with our demands—whole school's gonna go with our demands. She slapped her gardening gloves on the fence.

I don't think children should go to that, like I said. Not Johnny.

He's interested in climate action, she repeated.

He's five!

He's the future and you're giving him a shit planet.

It's a good planet!

No. Shit.

John closed his eyes. Peace exhaled and made her hands into little fists at her sides. Both of them were angry now, both knew they were right and had been wronged. Both their worlds were dying on either side of the fenceline.

This is insane. That's it we're done, we've finally gone insane, John spoke with his eyes still closed. And then he opened his eyes. Isn't school supposed to be two plus two, don't hit, listen to grown-ups . . . eh? Maybe, maybe curb the tantrums. Now we're taking them downtown and encouraging tantrums! I should have put him in the goddamn Catholic school.

They both continued to yell at each other for a while about a world neither one knew very much about until John turned and walked away slow through his field. A calf then let out a woeful waning five-second-long moo of such sorrow and frustration it served to exemplify John's condition. John sighed and turned back to Peace, who watched him with her arms crossed.

Sorry about the calves, he said. They miss their mothers. And he walked away.

———

Sometimes when she was falling asleep Peace could smell the Pacific and the wet mountains and felt them pull at her. Back to that plush mossy bounty of oxygen by-product. And the ferries in the fog, cedars in the rain, pulling her tenderly by the leg, pregnant and prone, away from the hay and pigs. But if she had to be here, at least she could help people help themselves and make Fearnoch a better place.

A better place, Peace mumbled and swung open the door of the SUV.

What kind of hat is that you got there? Kirby asked, and Peace slammed half her massive skirt up in the greased SUV door as she got out. Her hat, a new fashion choice, sat somewhere on the spectrum from beekeeper to pheasant-hunter.

Peace strode into the hall smoothing out her sweater with what she felt was a warm and compassionate look and her skirts swirling. She noticed John with his dad and then a lot of ghostly people with glaucoma and bright white hair. It looked like some of the old fellows were having a competition for who had fewer fingers. Several folks were enormous; one, instead of a leg and a foot, had a skinny metal tube stuck down into a cushy senior's shoe. Many of them wondered privately and wearily when these city people would just frig off. An old lady, with her head hunched down so far it seemed to be growing out her chest, waved up at Peace like a child might, perhaps thinking she was one of her grandchildren.

Peace helped the Community Association with the presentation. Kirby got up and turned the lights off and Peace pushed play on the PowerPoint. She switched the slides at the correct intervals because no one else knew how to do it. There were a lot of exciting opportunities on the slides. A new park with a play-safe playground, federal subsidies for windmills and solar panels built over unused pasture. A large Eco-Wellness Hospice put in the old wetlands. There were plans for a new café, something called the Pussy Willow Cottage that looked quite sweet. Peace continued pressing click and the seniors' white poofy haircuts and glasses and farm equipment hats lit up blue and green under the images of bike paths and wetland boardwalks slated to replace the land they could no longer farm.

After the last slide, Kirby turned the lights back on and said, I work downtown at HRCAC and if anyone has any complaints or questions I'd be happy to sit around and just talk. He said this like everyone knew what the acronym meant. He was wearing sandals.

Wherever there are folks down on their luck there's always someone who shows up in sandals and thinks he knows how to fix them, thought John.

Well, said a Mr. MacKay, all ninety-three years of him popping and creaking while he rose from his seat, I'm glad I'll be dead before I see any of this.

My land's going to be a golf course, I think, said Mr. McKenzie.

Paintball course, said Mrs. McKenzie.

At least it'll be some money for the young lad, said the old lady with her head in the middle of her chest, whose name was Ada Honeywell. She patted Mr. McKenzie on the shoulder and tried to dig her cane out from under the seat in front of her. Ada looked like she might be crying, but maybe her eyes were always filmy and leaking like that.

Wish we'd gotten in on that gravel pit, said a lady still seated, looking forlorn and like a teapot in her wool sweater.

Pussy Willows Cottage? Eh? What? Goodness.

And so it went and they all left the hall without saying very much to Kirby who stood by the door with his sleeves rolled up and his hands on his hips, nodding and trying to make eye contact. The locals knew their culture was dying and they just wanted to go home and enjoy what little of it they had left. All cultures die in the end and what can you do? Have a Labatt 50 in the garage and go to bed.

Angel Mae, a caretaker from the Philippines for old Mrs. Mulrooney in the wheelchair, stopped in front of the dusty picture of Jesus and put a hand to the tiny crucifix on her necklace.

Let's go Angel—you got plenty of pictures of the Lord at home, said Mrs. Mulrooney, and she wheeled towards the exit.

Angel Mae was embarrassed and followed her client. She got mocked for this piety to baby Jesus but if you hadn't seen your five children in years and if your husband had a new girlfriend back home but wanted you to keep sending the money and so you scrubbed the shit stuck deep in old ladies' skin and hurt your back helping them into the bath and the old ladies were kind and well-meaning but could lay off a bit on talking about immigration and how much spice you put in the food, and if the only time you remembered really that you were human was the one or two nights a year you could put on tight sparkly sequinned jeans and go dancing with your girlfriends, also caretakers, also from the Philippines, in the Market downtown, even if you felt old and used up and it was your faith that was the only thing stopping you from strafing everything with a .50 cal, then you might pause in front of a picture of your Saviour too. Besides, everyone protected some type of god—they refused to question the high reign of some type of god.

Kirby then walked over to where John was still seated, with his face in his hands. John rolled his face off his hands and said, I'm not in the mood Kirby buddy. He mumbled incoherently about government, city people and fuck off.

Kirby sat down and slid his hands in his pockets. It's a good look for Fearnoch, he said. The government will help . . . we can fix some of the problems.

I don't want the government to help. I don't wanna castrate myself for the government dole. Then I'd already be dead. Government takes ten years to put in a culvert.

Well fuck, Kirby processed that and glared out a window with a fantastic spiderweb in it. I didn't castrate myself—

You take this place for granted, said John. You'll remember one day.

Why don't you just work in trades or government like everyone else . . . any normal person would have stopped farming eons ago, said Kirby and he left very sour.

Peace hugged him in the parking lot.

That was not bad! she said. I think they get it. I thought someone might throw an egg at me. Then she said Brrrr and pulled her sweater collar up over her chin.

Kirby was still angry at John for the castration comment. He bore a bellicosity unbefitting a pacifist, and when someone touched his shoulder from behind he made a fist. He turned around and saw it was John's father who'd touched him.

Kirby, John told me about the—the baby last year, he said. I didn't know. I'm sorry. He nodded at Peace and put his filthy hat back on.

SIX

When Mikey was in a bad mood, a sour, sour mood, when he drove through fields awakening in purple and dew, spun full of wet spiderwebs, and the barn swallows dipping around, flirting with each other with the sun rising up their wings, the long shadows stretching off the bales, while he himself was on his way to sweat all day at the dump, he tried as an exercise to remind himself of all the other people who had, as he saw it, been through much worse. People get spina bifida. They get attacked by pirates. Mikey considered pirates.

He took in his surroundings and tried to be thoughtful. There on the fenceline was a rogue pine, which was an old white pine too deformed for the loggers. They would never be good planks or masts and were left alone to remain delightful, enormous and peculiar in the pastures. They danced slowly, this slow samba, Mikey thought, celebrating their survival and strangeness and sending their great feathery boughs in every direction for centuries. That was great. Then an old ranch and pancake house, a place for hay rides and sleigh rides, no longer operational. Mikey remembered they had a bison, but he got hit with a lightning bolt, and also Clydesdales, and he loved Clydesdales. Now that was a glorious and honourable animal, quiet steady work-beasts with the magnificent woolly boots, thumping and jingling, great harnesses of bells. He read they were going extinct, but he thought there was one last lonely Clydesdale in Fearnoch, although he couldn't see it from the road and hurt his neck twisting around.

It was a left turn at the scorched foundations of what had been The Country Mouse, a bar on the old highway. The parking lot taken over by thistles and giant hogweeds, of course the lamb's quarters and mulleins, and the sign, now only two posts and an empty steel rectangle, may as well have read back then: The Country Mouse—Drinking and Driving Is Fine and We Endorse It. He found a human tooth under the table at the Mouse once, with John. After that another field, and the old simpleton Doolan's trailer retired to the back, left to decay with the hay grown up long around it. There, he thought, it's a good example. Been through much worse.

He thought about Doolan more then, and did not do so un-emotionally. Foolish old Mr. Doolan stacking wood in front of his trailer and waving at every car.

People used to whisper a lot about this man. He was cow-eyed. They said both his parents had the last name Doolan. Never trust a Doolan, never turn your back on a Doolan. To be fair, a lot of these people quick to judge might not want to go digging around in their own intertwining ancestries. And they said a barn door fell on Doolan when he was a boy, and/or he had rickets. His eyes pointed outward, looked away from each other, this dazed bovine look, full of cud. But he was simple and friendly. He wandered Fearnoch doing odd jobs, none of them very well, enjoyed beer and talking about beer, and also skidooing.

Years ago, his rowdy years, Mikey woke up with one shoe on and so he drove back to the river where the party had been to see if he could find the other. He tried to keep the car in a straight line with his bare foot on the gas pedal and his face hot and greasy. Fearnoch Road ended at the river, not so much in a beach but broken asphalt and gravel tapering into a grass path then more gravel and broken glass culminating in the water. This was before a township fundraiser to put in a black rubber floating dock made from old tires. Along the shore a grove of willows bowed over a pile of scuttled concrete water-breaker blocks. These willows and concrete blocks made for great climbing when Mikey was a child, but his mum would holler at him, a large woman, from her towel on the grass with her Diet Pepsi.

Mikey, quit your monkeying up there! She worried about broken beer bottles and condoms from the teenagers. Mikey listened to his mother and came back out of the tree in his bathing suit using his feet like chameleon pincers on the branches.

You'll get some kind of disease back there, she said. He checked his stomach and the bottom of his feet looking for spots or signs of the disease.

But then when Mikey went looking for his shoe, he found Doolan sitting in a rotting recliner chair and fixated on the remains of the bonfire.

Doolan said G'day Mikey.

As happy as ever.

Mikey blinked and vaguely recalled a drunken fraternity with Doolan by the fire the night before, an arm around the shoulders of the man thirty years his senior, pretending he knew plenty of things about Yamahas and tractor-pulls.

I'm looking for a shoe? said Mikey.

What's it look like?

Like this one.

Ah.

I'm gonna peek around, said Mikey, hopping on the one foot.

I'm not gonna lie to you buddy, Doolan said, pulling the lever to recline and closing his eyes. I'm thinking it probably went on the fire.

He'd been through worse and he didn't complain. He sat on the old chair and the willow wept over him.

———

Ten minutes more down the old highway and Mikey arrived at the scrapyard, or dump. The scrap and garbage started to sweat off the frost. He worked with the steel in the back, in a rusty swamp of I-beams and channel iron. His job was to blowtorch the steel into pieces smaller than four feet by two feet, heave these pieces into the backhoe's bucket and drive them to their corresponding piles, either Plate & Structural or Number 1 Steel. He didn't really know or care what those piles meant and everyone called it a crackhead's job anyhow.

His colleagues had the outlines of their hats and helmets permanently sunburned into their heads. Many had bare or sparse gumlines, here and there an incisor hanging on. As do most labourers, they favoured peeing in the gravel, dirt and pavement using their opened truck door for privacy. They said things such as "good we're puking right along here" and "just puke all those down into there, Mikey." They quarrelled and squabbled, in their toil, and they all enjoyed a good cough around the scale house, while inside the calendar of women holding gas saws half-naked was still stuck on April. Anything unsavoury in their lives—an angry wife, a daughter's diabetes meds not covered anymore, a bad leg that stopped working, frozen up again "cock-stiff"—this was ceded imperturbably, near spiritually, as the way she goes. They made a motion with their hands like they were breaking a stick when it was break time. They were dreamers and storytellers, disciples, drunks, and dissenters, but more than anything they were bonded by the holy promise of "shutterdown." Together always and endless under the hope of shutterdown. This the song of the labourer, their deity, and they the stewards, four thirty the beautiful hour, tools down and shutterdown. And then move the cooler from the bed to the cab of the truck and drive a hundred kilometres down whichever Forgotten Junction Road homeward to Lanark County or Renfrew County and have about three calm quiet pints on the way.

Many at the dump could not read well. The concrete slab where they kept the oxygen and acetylene tanks for the torches was organized into two sections: with FUL and MT spray-painted on the ground. There was PTSD Ed, Don, Pete-buddy, but Mikey's favourite co-worker was Mumu-bou, who was Congolese. Mumu-bou mainly kept to himself in the back of the rusty swamp but he wasn't negative or hungover all the time and he encouraged others to cheer up, cheer up!

Is Mumu-bou your real name? Mikey asked him once he figured he knew the man well enough.

No, said Mumu-bou. He threw an old barbeque high up onto the cast-iron pile.

Well what is it?

I have eleven names, he said.

Oh. Eh?

Mumu-bou is good boss, Mumu-bou said, patting Mikey on the back with his work glove.

PTSD Ed and Pete-buddy told Mikey that Mumu-bou smuggled himself out of the Congo in a shipping container and ate rats and had killed people during the civil war. Mikey was dubious but didn't ask Mumu-bou about his life previous to the dump. He saw that Mumu-bou took great pleasure from online poker, smoking, and WhatsApp video calls with his sons. The internet said the Congo was the poorest country in the world. In any case, working at the dump was not difficult for Mumu-bou and he would have liked it if everyone just cheered up a little.

Every day there was something new to cut that the crane had added to the swamp: a hundred beat-up dishwashers, a nest of two-inch-thick rebar, a new mountain of manifolds, four old escalators, once an entire Harvey's restaurant.

Strange and occasionally frightening men dropped scrap at the yard, the strangest and most frightening being an old man who looked like he had died and been reanimated, with grey whiskers growing off in every direction like a cat's. He brought a truckload of rotors, struts, leaf springs and compressors back to the slab and got out of his truck smelling unmistakably of urine. The other labourers referenced the man as Mr. Darling, same last name as Mikey. The urea mist coming off him made Mikey's eyes water. He found out later through his mother this man was his estranged great-uncle Alvin.

Oof where do I come from? thought Mikey.

The finest day Mikey ever had at the dump was when he unloaded an eighteen-wheeler of obsolete computers.

D . . . uh . . . Do I have to be gentle with them? he asked the foreman Don.

Oh no, said Don.

Mikey smashed monitor after monitor, glass to dust, keyboards, esc and alt keys all down in the mud. He was the sole perpetrator of a mass grave of old computers. He laughed, was a boy again for a day, happy without being drunk, and an ancient joy rode out inside him.

But normally it wasn't fun like that; it was undeniably smelly, uncomfortable and tiring. One interesting morning Mikey walked to the back, same as usual, dragging hoses with his torch over one shoulder, but this day there was a tapping sound. Mikey stopped and looked towards the big excavator claw that was piling a mountain of refrigerators. Pete-buddy was working the claw and waving and beating on the glass in front of his little cockpit area. Mikey squinted at him. Pete-buddy was certainly very frantic. Then Mikey seized up and felt like he was being strangled, like an invisible force was ripping his respiratory system out. He bent to the gravel and retched without sound or air. It seemed his lungs were congealing, that he was drowning on land. Mikey tried to describe it to John later: like someone poured engine coolant down into your lungs. Pete-buddy got out of the claw covering his face and helped Mikey hobble back behind the claw. He'd punctured an old refrigerator with his claw and then Mikey walked right into the invisible leak of freon and ammonia. Pete-buddy told him at lunch that every breath he had of that mess was about the same as smoking ten packs of darts.

PTSD Ed offered his wisdom: this job is a piece of shit Mikey. People don't realize. You get union and you can get good money but it'll fucking make you miserable. He picked up his hard hat.

One thing Mikey did enjoy about working at a dump was how you could litter wherever you pleased.

———

But there was a new person at the dump. This was surprising. It was morning and the sun was huge and uncompromising on the horizon. Mikey was cutting some sandy steel plates. You had to manipulate the dials on the torch to get the correct ratio of oxygen and acetylene, spark it up, concentrate it on the steel until you got a little white-hot bead and slowly coax this bead along with the torch to achieve a cut. The sand from the plates would alight and fly up in little hurricanes to funnel down under his work gloves. He paused to straighten his back and howl, and then saw a beautiful girl with braids and a clipboard walking towards him with the sun behind her. Her outline burned into Mikey's brain.

Sweet Jesus who is that and what is going on around here, Mikey thought.

Because it was already so hot she was wearing her coveralls wide open with a sports bra underneath.

This is a mirage, he concluded. I haven't drank enough water. Or this is an acid flashback. I am having a mirage-acid-flashback at the dump, thought Mikey.

Hi! the girl said. I'm Stella. Mumu-bou said you're Mikey. She stuck out her hand.

Yes, said Mikey. His safety goggles were fogged and leaking sweat condensation. She had bangs and braids and freckles and one dimple was a little bit bigger than the other when she looked at Mikey. She had a white hard hat like the other engineers or scientists or whatever they were who visited the dump sometimes.

Oh God, he thought. He said something abrupt like: What are you doing here? Or: What can I do for you?

I'm doing my master's at the university. I'm taking soil samples, Stella said, and held up an expensive looking stick-device instrument. The university, she said again, when Mikey was quiet, staring at her then the stick.

The university, he said slowly. He took his blue hard hat off.

Stella only looked at him.

Mikey said: Well it's nice to talk with you Stella, sorry, my torch is frigged.

But it wasn't.

He went over into the empty water tank with a rectangular door hole blowtorched out of it that served as their equipment shed. He sat up on the damp steel workbench and let his workboots swing under it. Sweat fell off his nose and landed in dots on his pants. Rust hung in stalactites and grew around him as a soft orange fungus.

Phew, said Mikey. Phew.

The thing you gotta understand about these people, said Pete-buddy later, meaning the white-hats, is they're fucked in the head. Eh? They don't work for a living. I don't know what they do.

Pete-buddy's arms were bigger than his legs. He'd been a labourer for thirty-two years and his lunch was cigarettes and Timbits. Whenever he was exasperated or his task was especially laborious, like lifting a cast-iron bathtub full of rust-bits blowing all over him, he routinely made a "bbbppppppppth" sound like a horse, flapping his mouth around everywhere, which would be very odd to anyone new.

White-hats and blue-hats each thought of the other as Unter-menschen, Mikey summarized to himself. They had an eighty-gallon plastic drum of water by their water tank-shed that used to be full of black olives for some reason and still had a few waterlogged purpled sliced black olives in it and from this eighty-gallon plastic drum Pete-buddy splashed water all over his head and the back of his neck and smelled like brine.

They could at least bring us coffees, Pete-buddy said. Coffee and muffins. A carrot muffin. Bpppppth.

It's four thirty, said Mikey.

Shutterdown, said Pete-buddy in solemn ecstasy.

SEVEN

Anna liked to ride the metro alone at night. It was romantic was what it was, and she imagined she was in a movie. She felt this was what it meant to be in the city, the light and noise of the city coming in shafts, this neon loneliness, the music or cadence of the city grumbling up into her private parts. Anna wore a big toque and sat there reading *Anna Karenina* trying to feel smart.

This is how people think, she said aloud because she was alone. He knows how people think, I think.

Then she was thinking too much herself and dug her bookmark back in the crease after only two paragraphs. Her copy was from 1956 and soft brown old pages were escaping the spine down onto the metro train floor. She squeezed the fat book in both hands and slapped it against her knees.

Inside the unopened envelope, heavy and presiding over her kitchen table, she was sure, was the latest rejection of her book. If the last dozen times were any precedent. Years of email attachments and checking in and following up and touching base with professors, agents, writers, publishing houses, anyone she could imagine who might know how this frigging thing worked, and then figuring she was bugging people, she was being impolite, but everyone told her you gotta bug people, you gotta hustle. Now Anna thought printing it out nice-nice, ink and A4 borrowed from the Centre Saint-Savard office in the middle of the night, and tucking it then fresh into the soft seductive envelopes, maybe this was a nice touch. Someone, whoever and wherever they might be, might enjoy touching the words—away from the carpet-bombing of emails, the breached in-boxes of burning pixels, they could open the envelope and slide the paper out. So they could ignore it in that way too.

But she would wait until she was ready to rip open another disappointment. Anna had written a mystery novel but the twist was you never find out who did it: because we don't deserve the truth! She was adamant about this plot feature.

Maybe she should work on being a more creative person, a more sensitive and highly unusual creative person. She should explore the fabric of who she was. Her rare and significant identity. Short punchy sentences too. Edgy staccato sentences. The fabric. Of who she was. So many periods she couldn't breathe. Oh here, come and read along. Find out how to be a better person like me. Because I know.

We don't know, Anna thought. I don't know. We must leave room for wonder.

Anna took off her toque and puffed her cheeks out, and acknowledged she was really just jealous. She was being peevish and, worse, untruthful, which, she said while looking at her reflection in the black glass, wasn't good for her writing. She'd love to explore her complex significant fabric and tapestry actually, so she couldn't be too righteous and so, this was unsatisfying and troubling. And also the success of her unsolvable mystery novel wasn't the only index of her value as a human being on the Earth, she tried to remember, though that was very difficult to remember. But still, lonely and quiet on the Orange Line, never too far from her failures and going nowhere, Anna sat, her mood incorrigible.

How many books can we say absolutely need to exist? Like ten, maybe even five, she thought cruelly, watching a passing train scream out from a tunnel. Not many. It's certainly a lot of fluff—we cannot subsist on fluff!

If asked, Anna wouldn't say oh yes, I am a writer. But she did see words everywhere, floating in the street, and she mumbled to herself and walked straight into irritated and gorgeous Montrealers on rue Hochelaga, rue Saint-Jacques or rue Saint-Antoine Ouest. Then at home she would put all the foraged words on white paper and now she'd hate how they looked, all lined up like that. She didn't read enough, she didn't keep a journal, she didn't drink much tea, dipping the bag, pensive and blowing on tea. But writing was her attempt to prove that despite the last eight or ten years, she was not a fool. She worried everyone would find out she was a fool and additionally the act of writing made her feel like even more of a fool. All she really had was a good memory, that was it, and she wanted to remember things and find a home for little moments so they didn't get lost. That was just the way it all came out for her. Get it however it comes out and make up some shit-ass justification later. Anyway, she stole all her stories and cute babied sentences from other people who were too busy with their own interesting lives to document them and who ran around on Xans and fucked everybody and got internships in Barcelona.

But no, Anna thought, no, back to the count here.

Levin here—Levin who she was tired of and wanted to get back to Anna—he was trying to read a book about heat and electricity but his mind was sliding away to his cows and dreaming about the future: *Splendid! And I and my wife will go out with our guests to see the herd come in* . . . Levin said.

Yes, doesn't it go just like that, Anna agreed, then thought about a bear. The bear memory was summoned out and it hit her right between the eyes in an empty metro train car with an empty pop bottle slowly rolling towards her feet just before midnight.

This bear was a young black bear, a pleasant young bear full of berries. He had a playful energy and he trotted up out of the berries onto the road like a dog greets a car coming down the laneway.

Anna was eighteen then and already always running to the next thing as long as it wasn't Fearnoch and this time it was tree planting up near Fort Nelson, BC, where no one thought someone so young and sweet would last longer than a week in the bush. The sun came up at 1 a.m. There were wolves, bear, moose, someone saw a cougar. Anna saw a large snake whipping its tail around with a frog sticking out of its mouth, and she jumped and unspooled a great length of blue flagging tape to signify the snake's dangerous lair. And an hour later she was back with more trees in her planting bags and saw the same snake again, with more of the frog in its mouth, the frog ribbiting blood and still not ready to die.

This is their place, not mine, she thought.

She found out what it was to be tired, vomit across the hood of a F-250 Super Duty tired, sleep with an inch of ice-mud in her tent tired. She fucked her knee, her back and her fingers, her brain pounded into her skull wall with the dehydration. But she wouldn't stop. The temperature could go deep into the thirties with the ruthless northern sun, but then it would snow on Canada Day. One of the other girls had—in quick succession—a panic attack, a seizure and hypothermia and needed the helicopter.

The bottoms of Anna's feet were hard enough to put cigarettes out on. She lost nine out of ten toenails that summer which made the pedicurist start crying when this sweet young girl put her feet from hell in the pedicurist's lap at the end of the summer. However, Anna found a certain freedom was afforded by not checking your email and shitting in the woods. She felt it was the only time in her life she'd truly worked. And she proved everyone in the woods wrong regarding her resolve, she made sure of that—and she tried to remember it on the days her pride took beating after beating from the city and real life.

When the hot days found their merciful ends Anna would sit in the dirt by the road, a thin vein cut through a continent of muskeg that curled over a corner of the globe. She found the perfect seat once, the sandy ditch fit her lower back and hamstrings exactly. One brave fat little cloud covered the sun for a moment just for her. And in the five minutes before the truck came to pick her up she thought: before, she might have been bored to wait for five minutes by herself with nothing to do, but now, just how lovely it was to have five minutes to do nothing, how perfect to be bored, half-asleep in the dirt.

After the season a convoy of trucks and campers headed home back down and across Canada. On the third day of straight driving, and they had only barely got to Manitoba, a young man who'd never been off Cape Breton Island before all this and hadn't said anything since about Moose Jaw, he looked out over the prairie and said quietly: Terry Fox was out of his goddamned mind.

And that was when this bear trotted out like a happy dog and Anna loved him and put her hand up to the window and then he was absolutely creamed by the truck behind them. He cartwheeled like a teddy bear along the middle of the road and came to a stop on his back with his tummy zippered open perfectly from neck to bowels as if a surgeon had sliced him. There were berries all over the road from his stomach that didn't exist anymore and his intestines, now outside of him, moved, writhed like a pile of snakes. Planters ran out of the trucks and everyone thought he must be dead, but then he raised his head up and put his paws up, covered his face and said, Ohhhhh, like a human would. The young man who drove the truck that hit him held the bear's head in his hands and cried, the ears sticking out between his thumbs and pointer-fingers. The bear swallowed and died bravely. It was like watching a man die. After a while, a foreman said, we probably shouldn't be on the highway too long, and the young man and his friend dragged the bear to the ditch and crossed themselves, T-shirts smeared in bear's blood.

The metro door slid open and Anna walked out and up, the empty metro station a mausoleum, the life rolling away from the bear's eye.

EIGHT

Kirby forgot something as he left the house, so he swung around on the heel of his shoe, went back inside and picked up what he'd forgotten, then walked back out to the laneway and remembered he'd forgotten something else, and also he'd picked up the wrong thing, so he swung around and went back inside again. He considered punching a hole in the drywall. Through the field he could see John out in the hay. Then Kirby's phone went off again, rumbles and beeps in his pocket. On this government-issued phone there were now nineteen work emails since he woke up. The emails all described talk of reaching out, further to the above-noted matter, I refer you to the action plan, etc., and ended with cheers or regards or best.

It was quite a thing to watch John when he was in the hay. John was off his tractor and bucking squares up onto the wagon, fat green bales, carrying two at a time and sending them up in high, ferocious arcs. No hay hooks, slugging the hay away with baler twine for his belt. He was working hard for so early an hour and it was impossible to watch him labour without being reminded of your own capacity for labour.

Another example of this is John gave Kirby some old plywood for Peace's chicken coop. It was a few inches too long at one end to fit under the whole operation for to collect shit and feathers. Kirby went to fetch the Sawzall.

No look—here, John said and leisurely he busted one end off the inch-thick plywood like it was a cracker in his hand.

My God, he's a beast! whispered Peace. She looked at Kirby.

Mikey would have felt the same. When he and John were young and throwing the hay, up into the loft, up to the ceiling, he asked if they could take a minute so he didn't barf and black out.

How am I supposed to do this all day? I'm seeing d—I'm seeing d—ahhh, I'm seeing double here. Mikey sat on a bale and slid off it onto the floor.

I don't know, John said. He stopped and rubbed his nose with his farmer-glove. You just . . . give 'er. He shrugged, and he didn't want to make his friend look bad.

Now Kirby looked back at his phone when it started making more noises. He pushed and clicked away at it to make it stop. How these messages and meetings did anything to address issues of oppression, he'd like if someone broke it down for him soon.

Kirby wanted to help people. This his covenant. His world was in the shadows of bullies.

In grade 7, when the French teacher, Mme MacLean, asked what will you be when you grow up, Kirby did not say NHL player, or fireman, or veterinarian, he said—help people. Aider les gens. Instantly he said it and lowered his eyes.

And he was a small, pleasant boy, who'd worn glasses since he was two, and had the same flawless hemisphere of mushroom-cut on his head then as all the other boys, except for those whose hair was too curly, like Mikey.

Mme MacLean said, Ah, comme un . . . peut-être un diplomate, Kirby?

Oui Madame. He would be a diplomat then. If that meant someone who welcomed dying, crippled, faceless skeletal forms in rags, these babushkas and orphans, fed them boiled potatoes with a wooden spoon, held them in his arms as he was not afraid of their sores and disfigurements. He would hide them away from Nazis, polluters and his father. He would change a few things about the way things were.

And then John, out there in his tractor, wanted everything to stop changing. He was, and he was always supposed to be, a farmer. Not a coder, not a social media marketing coordinator. His progeny should farm on into forever, farming the dead farm with the fences needing to be tightened and the barn collapsing with the next snow and no milk quotas. He was a remnant and a bygone, bringing in the last of the measly second cut. A hundred years ago there'd have been tall tales written about him. He could raise a barn and then get shit-drunk with the shiners at the stills and ride out to a jamboree or dance hall. Dance across the logs each spring in the drive and tell the government to frig off, if he ever saw it around. Maybe he'd come across a postman or a country reeve on his horse once or twice in his life and that'd be all he knew of any government. He'd be on his own. He could be a farm-king, a lumber-king even, famous among the hedges, and lord of the sugarbush.

But no, of course, those days were dead. And John's farm was grown up in bush and coyote song and he stood in it useless. Like someone had reached in, through and around his crops and cattle, and ripped his dick off. Take a good long look because he was the last one.

Peace had told Kirby to tell John to stop using fertilizer.

Well, no, John said.

It's cross-contaminating into her garden, Kirby pointed at the raised beds by the fence. She can't say they're organic at the market.

No one can say their shit is organic around here, said John.

Kirby looked at him.

I can stop using fertilizer but the fertilizer from the McKenzies,

John pointed across the road, is gonna blow over onto my crops anyway. So they're not organic. Same with hormones and shit with the cows. The cows ruminated and slowly looked over at Kirby and John like they knew they were being talked about. They got back to their chewing, one of them standing up on the wagon.

Like your fertilizer blows into her garden, said Kirby.

Yeah, said John. And if there was no fertilizer at all, my crops would be dog shit and I'd be even more fucked than I am now. Which is fucked, he added.

She just doesn't want it in her garden. That's all I know.

John looked exhausted. There were old salt lines from sweat on his hat and bits of alfalfa stuck to his shirt. He lived his life bestrewn with hay bits.

Does she want to sell organic gourds at the Sunday Farmers' Market?

She does, said Kirby.

Well. I got work to do buddy, said John, and he got back to his bales.

Kirby stopped at the Fearnoch Convenience for a big dirty styrofoam cup of coffee because Peace had forbidden all coffee. He plunged on the big thermos and it just coughed and pissed a tiny stream of rusty water, then stopped. He set the cup down in dismay.

Think I'll skip that, said the old-timer behind him, pointing at Kirby's cup. This was Mr. Mulrooney, with his great beard and rubber boots clumped heavy with his labours. They're a little slow on the bit here today, he said.

Kirby agreed.

———

At work there was a meeting and then another meeting, and his boss Mrs. Tremblay came down from the floor above to tell Kirby and Kirby's team their project was being put on ice. They'd move to a different file for the time being. Several co-workers threw their pens in the air and sighed, but Kirby was secretly relieved.

We're gonna have to switch gears with the election, Mrs. Tremblay said. We'll circle back to this file. Tall and imposing, with giant shoulder pads in her mauve blazer, she went on a smoke break.

Kirby got the job in large part through the clout of his sympathetic uncle, who was a high-ranking public servant. During the interview process he was asked questions such as: describe a scenario in the area of communication in which you excelled. Describe a scenario in the area of communication in which you faced challenges. Describe your satisfaction with this current conversation.

In a year he was bridged in, off probation and he'd pretty near have to murder someone to get fired. He thought his salary was ridiculous for what he did. If he wanted, he could sit and look at his fantasy hockey team and complain with the others then leave at three o'clock. Which is not to say everyone there was lazy; the hardworking and the creative were the most miserable, stuck in the mud, another project dissolved, another million and another million spent on not even sure what.

Sacrement, make sure you're spending enough, Mrs. Tremblay reminded them often. I want everyone thinking about the budget. And she'd make the sign of the cross.

He didn't want the job because that was selling out. But Peace had a good counter-argument. He remembered she was wearing an apron with big pockets and she put her hands in the pockets and sat on his lap.

Maybe you can change the system. Maybe this is how it works, Kirby, she said. From inside. And she reasoned furthermore: now we can live in the country. Kirby had inherited some McHugo lands.

Kirby thought about his dad, bared his teeth and then said yes. They couldn't scare him out of Fearnoch. They could rusticate, they could leave the treeless boulevards and city landlords of Vanier, or

South Keys, or Baseline Road.

I'll plant carrots! said Peace. I'll have hens. We can go off-grid and have windmills. Oh God.

But so far Kirby had not found a way to effect any change at the government. He comprehended so very little of what was going on. He tried to find out more about his work without betraying the fact he didn't know more about his work.

Shoot an email to the new RO4, said Mrs. Tremblay. And an email to the RO3. Is this about the PCC on Friday? I'll shoot an email to HR.

Kirby had no idea what she was saying.

I feel like I'm not being very helpful, he said.

Mrs. Tremblay was beating away violently on her keyboard.

Don't worry McHugo—we can put you on the bench for a bit, while you get caught up on the new file. Take some mental health days if you need. You look awful.

———

John liked to take his boy for tractor rides, sometimes on his grandpa's International 434, and thought his boy liked it too. He put Johnny on his knees and let him steer along the lane.

I think I am a good dad, John thought. Is this what good dads do? Jesus I am fucking tired.

A country-Western song played on the portable radio that was covered in spiders in the tractor and it was a very bad country-Western song. It was all about beer, chicken, good dogs and old jeans you really like. John put his chin on the top of Johnny's soft head for a minute. He was embarrassed that the song perfectly described all the stuff he cared about. He was simply singing one long shitty sentimentalist country ballad. Just shoot the thirty-aught-six and talk slow leaned on the fencepost and have beer by the mailbox and boil sap. All that. And the real sap, not the fake city shit sap, but the real

Fearnoch township floating-dead-squirrel-in-the-sap ass syrup.

I'm desperately passionate about all that, thought John.

And he took his son around his dominion. They circumnavigated the Younghusband rectangle of the earth that had grown now six Johns.

———

John's father was out in the northeast field with the cows. He was always frigging around with something and had no idea how to sit inside and age by the wood stove. They had thirty-three head, which wasn't very much. Most of the yearlings were sold off, they kept a few heifers and steers and separated the calves from their mothers to get them off the milk. The calves and their mothers watched each other through the fence, making long mournful moaning consternations back and forth that continued to drive Kirby and Peace insane. Now an ancient cattle pen had finally rotted right apart and a bull from the next farm got in with the calves. Cows breaking out was common. Johnny was clutching a grimy potato and pointed towards his grandpa with it.

Their farm was laid out in long, thin fields. Thin ribbons of land was the Younghusband way. It wasn't great land for farming, not deep and loamy like around Guthrie Place. A frail skin of farm stretched onto the dirty rocks, those great dirty folds of Devonian limestone that formed four hundred million years ago when the Ottawa Valley was underwater and smushed up against Northern Europe along with the rest of the North American plate, and armoured fishes big as school buses patrolled the globe. One spot in the centre of the property, which the cows flattened and ate to the roots and to the rock, and everything canopied by these whorled-over hardy sickly bastard trees, this always reminded John of something from the Bible. Like a garden in the Holy Land for lambs and sermons.

And not that anyone driving past lost on their way to pick strawberries would think about the Bible—they wouldn't think about shit; and they'd forget what they'd seen five seconds later because it looked just like everywhere else. Still, like everywhere else too, the acres had their sermons if anyone could hear, the dead watching, the ghosts and spectres out wandering, the past proximate.

If the lost strawberry picker looked further they'd see an untidy and unplanned community of buildings on the farm. Among the barns, gates, posts, a single right angle they would never find. John and Polly's bungalow close by the road, only thing built since about World War Two, with the one healthy elm tree left blooming and magnificent over it. Then the modified three-season cottage down the lane where John's dad lived. Several outbuildings, a silo, a grain hopper, barns and sheds, a hideous shack someone plastered with fake brick asphalt siding which earlier Johns used at times to house guns, pelts, fuels, and friends who'd drunk too much. And a pighouse, chickenhouse, icehouse, all ancient and bowing back into the ground; inexplicably, a caboose near the back. A chronology of retired, rusted-thin hay elevators and hay rakes and disc harrows. Brambled-over outcrops of piled rock and old timber visible in the hay and corn. The foundation of the first John's shanty, or what it was agreed was the foundation of the first shanty, dented a small rectangular depression in the pasture, by an intermittent creek, a row of stones peeking out from the long grass, an old refrigerator and a tree growing out of the hole, close by a cattle-feeder wheel and a hay wagon with a broken axle. Everywhere these old tubs, old pumps, ruins of abandoned horse-drawn machinery—someone would put a large spool of fencing in the ditch, forget about it, then eighty years later there it was still, rusty in the cattails. And back by the train tracks, watching over everything, a skull sitting up on its knoll, was the old brick farmhouse John's dad was born in, far away from the road it predated by many decades. The ghost-house, or the ghoul-house, John called it when he was little.

And John and Mikey and Kirby had investigated every acre of the farm when they were boys trying to have adventures. It made for good exploring. John took them to the ghost-house at night, the wind and shadows playing tricks through the bare hollowed rooms, and Mikey's imagination got the better of him when he saw an old wooden wheelchair in the corner, and off he ran on pure animal adrenaline, a little Ichabod into the night.

They built a fort that coyotes later took as their den. They threw snowballs at chickens, pigs, porcupines and then felt terrible. They had fistfights and once Kirby fell and cut his shin open and John decided they should camp there for the night as their friend could not go on and began trying to construct a bivouac until Mikey convinced him they should just go tell his dad, who, really, was just over there by the barn. John enlightened them on what he knew of French kissing and they debated trying it on each other before trying it on girls.

I'm gonna frigging French kiss you Mikey right now and get it over with! John caught him by the ear.

No! Mikey cried and swung his arms.

These activities always involved climbing over a series of fences, something that was never Mikey's strength. He'd get stuck on the fence, John on one side, Kirby the other, both of them laughing, another pair of Mikey's pants ruined on the barbed wire.

But now here John's dad was trying to separate a cream-coloured calf from the bull. The calf was headstrong, insistent on going under and trying to nurse from the bull. The formidable, beautifully muscle-contoured bull looked around, indignant and needing an explanation.

John's dad fell over and the calf evaded him. The old man sat with his head hanging between his knees on the stubbled field and kept his head there when he waved to the boys on the tractor. His shirt was ripped up. John offered his arm out for his dad and brushed his back off. His dad had a laugh when he got up and gestured at the calf.

He thought he found the best udder around.

Carefully and together they handled the bull, who was a good bull, back through the cow pen to his side and wired it shut. John slapped the unruly calf on the back, and it jumped and trotted in a circle. Its enormous beguiling brown eyes were new and innocent to the world, with prom queen eyelashes.

You frigger, he said, little frigger. What a gorgeous calf it was. He remembered when he was a boy he saw a calf such as this, creamy and perfect, but lying dead and abandoned against a shed with flies landing in its eyes. The other cows grazed past and around it unaffected, no time to mourn. John told his dad in a panic and then started crying.

Don't look, his dad said, don't look at it. John put his face into his dad's plaid coat that was wet and covered in burrs.

Very early in life John began to understand the look in the bull's eyes when he smelled where a lady cow had peed, he understood the harvesting of lambs, he understood farms for what they were: fenced rectangles of sex and death. And shit, of course. Good for a young lad to get comfortable with shit-smell. He had trouble dividing childhood memories from childhood dreams, such as seeing the dead calf's head on the path.

At night after Johnny had settled, John and Polly would have long serious talks up into the darkness. She'd sniff and then the pillow would be wet and he knew she was crying.

I will sell once Dad dies—I will. I can't do it while he's alive, John said. He rubbed Polly's shoulder blade over the comforter. And I'll look into the school-bus driving job.

You'll be sad forever, said Polly.

And John then remembered to promise again to follow up with the doctor about the ultrasound on his ball. Polly was exhausted with John complaining about his bag and reasoned that if there was something bad growing up in him, he should find out. It was just a dull and quiet ache, when he sat in the tractor wrong, or got out to pee in the ditch. Like one ball was spun around backwards on its tube, like a tetherball, or was hanging wrong, horizontal: imagine a tiny and painful blimp. John couldn't find any lumps in the shower and it hurt all the more from squeezing on it and hunting around for something pulsing and evil. He wasn't even sure what the little tube hooking around the ball was supposed to feel like when it was being normal but it sure didn't feel good. He couldn't get comfortable, then found a potato under his pillow and whispered: frigging Johnny.

NINE

Also Anna and Magnus were having serious talks. Or trying to have serious talks but perhaps letting it die without a serious talk. Anna had only ever been dumped; she had never dumped anyone. I wonder what that's like, dumping someone, she thought. Maybe it's harder. Sometimes. Maybe I'll try it one day—I should try it. She thought of old relationships, where she was gun-shy, wading in slowly and trying not to slip on a rock. Darren or Darrell or Jean-Luc would say, come on Anna, it's fine! It's great.

And she'd breathe and say, okay here we go, and he'd take her hand lovingly and help her up over a wall, and then she'd fall down and plummet towards a bunch of poisoned sticks.

When she met Magnus he made her feel like she might be okay in the city. He knew how to offer his arm and navigate the glowing beast. He kissed her at a Christmas party under a balcony where they were smoking because it was snowing wet and horizontal. It was surprising and exciting and they both had their hoods up. The snow slid through the cracks in the boards on the balcony and wound around their mouths and cigarettes. He was small, sweet and just balding a little bit. Anna could put her face against his nice, well-fitting shirts and feel calm for a minute. But that was all two years ago. He did not enjoy any talk of the future. He was thirty-four and never said dating, only hanging out. And he was the worst snow shoveller she'd ever seen.

No, that wasn't fair. Magnus was usually very nice and they did all the nice things—they slept in, they rolled up the hems of their pants and went to gallery openings, brunch, out for bubble tea and soup dumplings. He contended that capitalism and climate change had fucked everything anyway so why bother. "Paradigm" was a word he used regularly. He said New York would be under the sea in ten years. It was cruel to have kids at this point. Anna wanted kids but she kept her mouth shut and considered her chequing account and also the effects of Adderall on babies.

Well then maybe they can build dykes, said Anna, on the topic of New York sinking. I want to go to New York.

And instantly, in the kitchen holding a cold wet dishrag, she submitted to an electric fuchsia fantasy about kissing someone in the rain on Broadway and then felt bad because the tall shadowy stranger she was kissing definitely wasn't Magnus.

He offered advice on her novel, but he was skeptical about a mystery that is never solved. Anna frustrated easily on the matter.

It's because everyone says they're looking for the truth but they're not, everyone is untruthful, everyone is unbelievably full of shit and it's commonplace now and accepted, she said without looking up from her computer. Everyone.

Okay, said Magnus, rattled. But I think people read mysteries to find out who did it.

Sorry can't have it. Not that easy. Anna looked at her Word document and wanted to cry. Just sitting there with her words again. She stood up, stuck her arms out, and rotated them in violent clock-wise circles.

Grrrrrrrr, she said, at her computer.

Jesus Christ I'm tired of frigging with words, she thought. You frig them around so much they don't mean anything. She could look at a word, like "fulgurate," or even a nice little one like "milk," until it fell apart, the letters rolled away from each other, and she thought maybe she'd been tricked and these words had always been fake. You could use a thousand words to say nothing so easily and the clichés are always sneaking back in. Fall in love with a precious little word like "yesternight" and just have to get "yesternight" in there somehow and then ruin the whole page.

I know I've asked this before, she said, but please for the last time, what in the hell is hermeneutics? A hermeneutical lens.

The writing was slow, just sitting and sitting until something shit out reluctant. Bleeding, bled out, nothing good unless she took the long horrible pain the right words required. But sometimes, when there was no one up but her and the moon, or the mice, and she crossed her eyes and entered some sort of surface-tension, drooling, highly ephemeral, blessed fugue word-limbo where it felt right, and she knew it was right, it was perfect, and she felt drunk even, and she'd go outside into the night listening to rap on her headphones like she was heading to a party. Outside a lonely street with a lonely dim streetlamp, hills of old grey snow by the Jean Coutu, but on the inside—in her nothing but deep, individual and ferocious joy.

Later she said sorry to Magnus, sorry if I was mean.

Why don't you ever take me to Fearnoch, he said.

You don't really wanna go. I don't want to go.

I wanna do something honky-tonky!

Anna sat on the floor, spread her legs and tried to see if she could still touch her forehead to the rug. She would have liked a cat to sit on her back. Nothing could prepare Magnus for the all the bootcut jeans and sheer amount of hunting gear adorning Fearnoch. Hope he liked the smell of two-stroke.

Well, nothing ever happens there first of all, she said. Drinking and driving is like a religious denomination. I guess there's inbred people if you're into that. Then she remembered poor old cow-eyed

Mr. Doolan and felt mean. She puffed and blew her hair out of her face.

Magnus reminded her about the poetry recital he was organizing. Anna thought about six undergrads on antidepressants speaking about themselves at a café, and wondered when did she ever get so mean.

———

Anna also worked at a diner but her French wasn't too strong, and she got embarrassed a lot. It was called Café Plus. There was a lot of eggs and beans, everything very wet and sliding around on the plates, a serviette dispenser for every small table, the laminate finish of the tabletops corroding under the constancy of quarts of Bleue Dry. Pie, entire or a great creamy wedge, was popular among the patrons. The cook yelled and the manager yelled and she'd just stand in her apron covered in sauce and take it. Once she dropped one of those old bulbous coffee pots and wasn't prepared for it to detonate like a bomb on the tiles. Glass shrapnel propelled in a generous radius, and the diners adjusted their hearing-aids, looking at each other in terror.

One of the waitresses had been in the industry almost fifty years. A half century in her orthopaedic shoes covered in ketchup, the broom and dustpan, stoking the coffee makers in the same spirit as the stokers did the boilers in the bowels of the Titanic. Then, exhausted, she sat on the overturned grease bucket by the dumpster at 2 a.m. smoking darts.

She was Yvette: never to be fucked with. Tales of a former life were tattooed in birds, names and greening roses that wound up both arms, up and lost into the sleeves of her black polyester V-necked waitress-issue blouse. She had a small silver flower studded into her nose and spread makeup thick on her face, which had been tanned and entrenched with cigarettes. Yvette carried herself straightforward and proud through the thankless universe, her pencil behind her ear, her heart disease, glasses on a chain, licking her thumb and stabbing the receipts on the spike. She had the same portion of emphysemic kindness waiting to be ladled out for everyone, a blind ninety-year-old pensioning regular who'd be leaving this life soon or an oxy-spiking drywaller on the pogey stamps. Anna didn't know much about her past but imagined drugs and motorcycles. Yvette called her H'Anna sometimes. H'Anna take my h'arm, when she was tired of trying to pronounce the English right. Anna did know that Yvette wished her daughter would reconnect.

There was a new girl at the café Anna was supposed to help train in. Her name was Maria-Jose. She was very small and gorgeous, she had a ponytail coming out one side and just bounced around the café with perfect skin, her hands behind her back and a warm interest in everything. She had tiny feet and was slow to answer questions because it seemed like she put most of her efforts with her mouth into smiling.

She is: pulchritudinous, thought Anna chewing on the word, not sure if it was a good one to use or not. No maybe not, but—maybe this is a new friend? How about that!

But Maria-Jose missed a shift, then another, and the manager licked his lips and fired her. He loved a good firing. And then Maria-Jose was just another person who was gone forever.

Then there was a newer girl, Océane, who from the first day was cruel to Anna. At least that was what Anna had concluded. Something about tips, or maybe Anna had said something, or maybe it was just something to do. I'm a pretty easy goddamn target, she thought. Océane was tall, also beautiful, but with a severe and officious ponytail, not a playful one like Maria-Jose's. Nothing about Océane was out of place, not one hair, and she was comfortable to return Anna's questions with silence. She'd stuff her notepad into the pocket of her apron, irked and precise. When she did speak, her French slid out breathy and aromatic and superb. It sounded like every one of Océane's sultry syllables was attached with thin mouth-polymers and Anna thought she could string them all out like a garland and hang them on the Christmas tree. Anyway, maybe she was just beautiful and icy to everyone.

But Yvette noticed Océane wouldn't tell Anna what on Earth was happening with Table #3 and said, Suis-moi, Océane, and took her to the closet behind the bar where they stowed the vacuum and the coffee filters and all the little blue and white Bonne Saint-Jean ornaments. Whatever Yvette said in there, a different Océane came out of the closet, eyes like she'd seen a horror movie, and Yvette followed, blasting four cataclysmic coughs into her fist. Océane was different to Anna then, and maybe there'd be a new friend after all.

———

Yvette said: H'Anna you drink Lowenbrau?

Non Yvette. It's beer?

Oh I had one. Tiens . . . open up a Labatt's Blue on your workbench there for one, two, three day, she counted to three on her thick pale fingers. Puis uhh, puis drink it. That is Lowenbrau. And she swallowed in disgust.

You see, there is poetry everywhere, Anna thought to herself.

Yvette said she'd like to meet Anna's mother. Which made Anna think about her mother.

I would say to her you are this . . . Yvette paused and looked at her phone, then read out: conscientious. She grinned up at Anna, like to say: that wasn't so bad getting that ridiculous English word out.

Anna didn't know if anyone cared about Yvette. She didn't think the world noticed Yvette. The old woman was invisible, people looked past her, through her, on their way to someone or something else. But she is the backbone of this whole shit, her and people like her hold it all together, and nobody knows it, thought Anna. She wanted to put her hands on Yvette's tired shoulders, on the old polyester, and say that she mattered very much.

TEN

Sometimes John would get hit by the premonition that Mikey'd just killed himself. He'd take the dog up to get the mail or look around for some twine or eat a jam jam, and he'd intuit it through a change in the breeze. That's it, I'll bet Mikey just killed himself just then.

Because when they were little Mikey had to go to the outpatient psychiatric wing at the hospital in Guthrie Place to talk about his feelings and problems with a doctor or a group of doctors. His parents, the teachers, the guidance counsellor and the priest were concerned. John was too, and he twisted up his hat and looked down at his feet in the guidance counsellor's office because it wasn't enough that his mum was sick, now his best friend was going to hang himself.

Mikey didn't know what to say and got upset with everyone who got upset at him for being down and not saying anything. He only felt that he was shit, but he wouldn't kill himself and he didn't know what to say other than that—is what he told his mother. He was a sad person. Her lower lip shook and she set down a large plastic glass of homo milk and Mikey said sorry.

Whatever feelings and problems he had, he made good and sure to see if the booze and drugs helped, starting in about grade 8. Being fucked off drugs and beer was finally a little break from feeling that he was shit. And he always had a headache, there was always too much noise, always too much information firing in and around from the moment he woke up until bedtime and everyone talking and talking, but not if he could just push off pleasantly into beer and coke.

When the premonitions came rolling in, John would call or drive to Mikey's house to make sure Mikey wasn't hanging somewhere spinning slowly.

I didn't kill myself John! Mikey shouted once from behind the woodpile, where he was sitting. Jesus!

On the lonely days, John thought about his friend. When everyone else was asleep or on vacation but he didn't have vacations because he was a goddamned farmer in a country that a hundred years ago was ninety per cent farmers and now was one per cent farmers, and he'd work every day all day until he was dead, he remembered old Mikey stories when he was out making the turns in his tractor. The tales seeped out of the furrows, his friend's chronicles kept him company. Sometimes he could only laugh, and he laughed to himself, grinning and shaking with his plaid shirt tucked into his jeans, wondering at what point he'd crest up over the laughter and burst into tears.

He recalled when they stuffed him into the back of a lady's car, as John tells it, at the quarry pit. Mikey was in an unmanageable condition and the lady was not excited about it. Through a hospitalization-worthy level of rum refreshment and corn spirit, Mikey had unlocked a secret self within himself which had always been waiting there, drunk, but no one had quite had the pleasure of meeting yet. Most knew him up until then only as a shy but pleasant stutterer who sat with John and his lunch out front of the library at the school, where they talked about hockey scores. Now it appeared he was actively trying to give himself alcohol poisoning. He smoked an entire cigarette backwards without noticing, ripped the whole thing back, which Anna witnessed, spellbound and silent. He bellowed strange things, spooky things, like "full pin—full pin, mon homme!"

and listed old hockey players like "Bill Ranford!" to anyone who'd listen and cackled to himself like an old witch. Then he got tired of yelling "Bill Ranford!" and lay like he'd been shot, with about four per cent of his brain working, supine in his underwear by the fire. Somebody's mum came to pick up her daughter from this demonic pit of shadows, and nobody could have been too excited to have their sons and daughters at a party down there. And they thought it was Mikey's mum beating the horn and headlights into the quarry and as well Mikey looked like he could use some attention. So four drunk boys carried the drunkest boy up to the car and stuffed him in the back seat, where he lay half-naked, wet and unresponsive. They folded his legs in, slammed the door and went back down into the pit, ignoring or not hearing this lady.

I don't know this person, I don't know this person, what is this?!

John shook in his tractor. Maybe he shouldn't laugh, but Lordy Mikey.

Other stories didn't make him laugh. For instance, some years after high school when Mikey went over to John's to watch an Ottawa Senators game on a sleepy and minus-thirty Tuesday with a bottle, and he drank the whole twenty-six ounces for no reason before the third period was even over, and there was absolutely no change in his demeanour from before he'd started drinking the bottle which, to John, was alarming. This was not good. Mikey remembered this night, this bottle, he wanted to stop, but it was cold and the Senators were awful and drinking more was much better than not drinking more. That night the microscopic effervescent sweet li'l rye-nymph-bubbles sparkling off his cup and telling him it was okay were just too much.

And the drugs: there's always drugs everywhere if you look, even in Fearnoch township, coursing under the surface of quiet hardworking old people, sleepy pigs and fallows, and when Mikey found out, well he could be a monster. He gobbled, snorted, smoked anything:

cocaine, MDMA, Xanax, ketamine, dihydrocodeine, T3s, even crack, never as far as smack but once rat poison, although that was apocryphal. He put a bill up his nose in every other garage this side of Archie McHugo Side Road and took potent combinations of pills and went on unique voyages, a pioneer in a new dimension. Troubling visions accompanied him sometimes, once a giant extraterrestrial octopus attacking the town of Arnprior. John got angry at him because this was too much, all the drugs he was snorting, and then he spilled a big splash of ranch on his pants and looked at it, and Mikey said, you spilt some ranch, and John said: Yeah well you wanna snort this shit up too Mikey?

And Mikey only lay on the floor in the basement at someone's house and screamed and everyone was yelling at him to shut up and he thought yes someone is really making quite the racket and yelled at them to shut up too without understanding who it was doing the screaming. He snorted more till he snarled and padded around like a tyrannosaur.

John then remembered a party at a hunting camp down there near Ompah or Plevna and two older boys readying a mountain of drugs on the card table by the stove.

We're gonna feed young Darling drugs until he goes insane, one of them said, matter-of-factly.

Mikey bumbled over, put his hands behind his back and pigged out on whatever was on the table then went missing in the woods for several hours. The next morning he returned and asked John what happened.

I woke up in a duck-blind, Mikey informed his best friend.

I've never seen anything like it, said John, who was trying to see if any of the wet lighters worked for the fire. You weren't Mikey anymore. You looked like a ghoul.

A what?

A ghoul.

Oh boy, said Mikey.

You talked about Cassie a lot. Then you tried to snort coke through a fucking, a fucking rolled-up thing of old you know, luncheon meat. And—you also ate a lot of raw pork steak.

Mikey held his stomach. Was Cassie here?

Mikey talked about Cassie a lot, the one girl from high school he thought he was in love with, or as close to love as he knew how to feel, and then he'd promise John to stop talking about her.

Cassie, tiny and outspoken, with her hair up in a knot and her jeans with the knees ripped out, in the smoking section at the school, telling the teacher to go fist herself. Whose dad put everything, his whole family, down the coin slot at the VLTs in The Country Mouse. Who'd take Mikey's arm and take no shit from anything. Before too long she'd informed him she'd take none of his shit either. She said he was spineless and marched away and this word spineless followed him, orbited him like a lesser moon. Don't worry about Mikey, she said looking over her shoulder, he's spineless. He missed trying to make her laugh on the phone.

But before this spineless comment, when Cassie had said, okay Mikey I'll go out with you fuck it, he was shocked she wasted no time in taking off all her clothes, getting in his bed and lying naked next to him, just like that. Small and soft in the bed, her hair hung across the pillow. It was incomprehensible that someone might think he wasn't shit at least for a moment. He nobly allowed that he'd give up drinking and drugs, his tortured ways. She probably just wanted to bang a few times before moving into Ottawa or someplace but there was Mikey, crouching and kissing her eyelids like a Romantic poet.

I'm spineless, Mikey said to John, babbling and drunk when she was gone, thereby reaffirming that he was shit. I'm like a vampire. I don't think about anyone else's needs, I just sucked happiness off her like a vampire—my love is vampiric.

Frig off Mikey, John said. He looked at the moon, enormous and close and yellow.

There are child-slaves on Earth, said Mikey also noticing the moon, which looked to be coming closer, and I pout because someone wants to fuck someone else.

C'mon now Mikey we're Fearnoch lads! We've got that Fearnoch charm about us, said John.

Maybe you ah dddo . . . I'm just some quiff with a broken brain—and Mikey, not without a good sense of timing, threw up everywhere in front of the Petro-Can.

Mikey now was embarrassed. He didn't want to talk about boozing, it was embarrassing, what he meant was he needed amends. This was his atonement now, his monastic loft-life with the boring books, the no-more-than-four-pints policy, his cat dead and his plant dying. The shame for a decade of making people worry, believing he was a saint of Fearnoch if he could drink a two-four, opening beer cans by smashing them off of his head, figuring himself a dreamy dark complicated boozer drunk again out among the ice shacks or lost in the rhubarb or blacked out at a bonspiel. Many Christmases he did ruin. He fell off buildings. He did E and ran down the median of the old highway on E and by the grace of God managed to skip out of the way of a cement truck, such was his mischief.

Mikey felt he was doing pretty good now with the boozing, better with the boozing, but still he got frustrated that people couldn't understand how it made him feel like he wasn't shit, the creepy power of just one sip and the liquor's charming vapours swimming up into his head. How good it made you feel. If his blood alcohol level was rising his happiness-receptors were happy; if it plateaued or dipped he was shit. It wasn't so complicated. When, for example, PTSD Ed undid his pants and sucked his stomach in, tucked his shirt back in and did the pants back up while discussing his breakfast beers, with his white boozer hair especially thick and lustrous, Mikey got the shivers because not too long ago he would have thought this was hilarious and great. Just the amount of piss and barf and stomach distension, the infinity of lager, required of a true boozer was horrific.

You can't take me anywhere, said PTSD Ed. He showed Mikey a plastic sleeve you could pull over a beer can which made it look like a pop can.

Not just for the drive home, but picnics, the cinema, not bad, not bad, he said.

The origins of Mikey's no-more-than-four-pints legislation remain murky with intoxication and lore.

John said: it was when you went to the dentist Mikey.

Mikey went to the dentist drunk. He slept at John's house, he didn't remember much of the night before except telling John's dad he had to go to the dentist at nine o'clock the next day and also eating his coke off a CD case in the rain because it got too wet to snort. John's dad woke him up, said: Wake up Mikey, rubbing his shoulder, remember the dentist?

And Mikey fell over trying to get his shoes on, knocking down the Younghusband coat rack with his stutter out of control. He could smell his own mouth. He felt terribly sorry the dentist had to go anywhere near his mouth when he opened it.

But Kirby said: I thought it was when you went to the vet.

Mikey went to the vet drunk too, Mrs. MacPherson was sneezing blood out again, it was an emergency, and security cam footage of Mikey swaying around and peeing in the parking lot in the middle of the day came to light. He apologized, he was penitent, and he kept his head bowed and accepted his ban from the clinic.

Mikey said, no it was all of those times and more, but mostly it was the time I saw the gerbil-mouse.

He was getting his piece of shit phone fixed at a mall, a greasy old mall, or mews, and he wandered over to the pet store and looked at a hamster or gerbil-mouse or something like that, he wasn't quite sure. The poor little bastardly gerbil-mouse was scratching for all his life against the glass in his small rectangular domicile, which was only four walls and some wood shavings and pellets and a $15.99 sticker on the glass. The gerbil would stop for a second, fix an eye on Mikey, then resume the chaotic scratching. Mikey watched him and thought, what the fuck are we doing with gerbils here? $15.99. And he watched him some more and felt he had to make some changes about how he did things. The four-pint cap was a start.

Four pints is still quite a bit, said Kirby.

No it isn't, said John.

What about Christmas?

Yeah. Jesus.

Okay, said Mikey. Four pints one night a week on Friday or Saturday . . . if needed. Not during the week. Unless it's hockey, then it's, oh, two, he said, making the amendments in his notes with his tongue sticking out.

However, one day a year in late September, he could invoke the notwithstanding clause and get drunk as hell with John because nobody's perfect. John had taken to calling the blessed day St. Mikey's Day, as in I'm getting fucked this St. Mikey's Day don't anyone even try to stop me.

And mercifully St. Mikey's Day was coming right up.

———

Now Mikey sat in his car in the Fearnoch Convenience and gas station parking lot. He had a gas station sub on the passenger seat. The shit, the absolute shit people paid good money to eat at gas stations in rural Canada was concerning. Likely it was a core Canadian value to pay too much for something too shitty and not only not complain but like it a lot, and a lot of it. He hoped no one he knew would see him eating a gas station sub in his pre-owned sedan with the one door that didn't work because of the snow plough. A round hay baler knocked out its bales in the field behind the store. This was a Cheese-man field, and Mikey helped with the haying when he was a teenager, but it was the smaller, square bales then, which you had to buck by hand. He remembered scratching hay out of his hair on the walk home and blowing it out of his nose in the bathtub. He looked back down at the sub. The plastic wrapping on it was puffed up hard. Puffed up like a fake tit, Mikey thought. A violent gas whined out when he tore the plastic.

This is grim, said Mikey. The sub said: spicy country-style chicken-strip sub. It contained chicken product and also chicken-flavouring agent.

Albert Cheeseman came out of the store. A true beast of a man who'd always spooked Mikey. Great chieftain he was, of those fields behind the store down to the river. He held the door open for an old lady and the stuffing from his plaid coat hung from under the arm like an old mall-Santa beard. Albert loved to put young lads to work, bark at them from the tractor, and prove no one could slug the hay like they did when he was a young lad. Mikey got good and rattled when old Albert bellowed at him for putting the hay in the straw's spot or the straw in the hay's spot. And for picking up a bale wrong so it busted from its twine, and for throwing up in the loft. The loft was a dark hot piece of hell and Mikey had never seen anyone so angry, with a face so red. And the bales just kept coming up the elevator and in through the hay-hole. Albert would begin each day with Labatts 0.5 beer but, inevitable as moon and tide, at a certain point he'd say fuck, and rip into the box of his forbidden secret real beer, which he kept around in strategic areas such as the backhoe.

Though when the haying was done and Mikey was laid out, shaking in the shade under the hay wagon, Albert came over in a great mood and extended twenty dollars, a very cold beer, then a handshake down into the shade.

Albert's son, who everyone called Mush, followed his father out of the store, also wearing a ripped-up plaid coat also with Santa-beard stuffing escaping it. He too was a giant.

Mush Cheeseman and his exploits were a big topic for people in Fearnoch. They talked about him like this: Oh . . . Mush . . . fuck. Maybe with a beer halfway to their mouth.

Mikey didn't know why he was called Mush. He was older but failed a lot of classes so he was in Mikey's class sometimes. Mikey figured he was in about grade 15 then. Mush sat in the back, eyes hemorrhaged, his great face bloated up like he'd been stung with a blowfish. Stoichiometry or King Lear didn't bother him too much and besides, soon he'd be making lots of money working in snow removal and septic. He was full of confidence and advice.

——

Once John and Mikey both got dumped over the same weekend.

I'm done, said John. I'm done!

Mikey only stared into the hills.

They paddled to Champlain Island and unfolded their camping chairs out on the sandbar. In the rippled sand and zebra mussels, they revelled in their sadness, poured it all over, argued about who was sadder, let their beer cans float away to the sun. Then they were silent awhile, defeated and out of applicable words. And then one of Mikey's chair legs buckled and snapped and he was pitched onto his side in the river. He lay just as he'd fallen, motionless and resigned in an inch of water.

Just leave me here, he said.

John made no indication he'd even noticed the change in how Mikey was seated. He watched the horizon with his beer on his lap then got up, walked two steps away and arced a mighty and long piss towards the ripped-up sky and sun that died and bled in the river.

At this time Mush floated around the point, directly in front of and very close to John and his humongous piss.

Great, said Mush. He was winding in his fishing rod and it appeared he was sitting on a very small or even invisible boat, or that his pants were, in fact, a boat.

What is that, said Mikey. He sat up in the water and put his hand over his eyes. Are your pants a boat?

Mush kicked himself out of a camo floating chair with hip waders built into the bottom of it. It was a chair-pants-boat for anglers. He moored up his pants-fish-chair-boat, came ashore and took some of their beer. He drank many of them, and then shared his advice:

This is what you have to do. Meet a girl you really like . . .

Yes, said John.

. . . you spend time together and it's great and nice . . .

Okay, said Mikey.

. . . and you both really like each other eh and it's going real well, then . . .

Yeah, said John.

. . . then you just fucking dump her.

John and Mikey were quiet.

Outta nowhere, fucking dump her bud, said Mush in his indefensibly bad sunglasses, emitting urgent greedy suckling sounds on the beer can.

What! said Mikey.

But that's all that I want! said John.

I'm sorry—you gotta dump her. Nothing is better for your confidence.

That, to Mush, was the way forward.

Mikey made a splash lying back in the water. He thought he'd leave his head there in the mud and weeds for a while.

Pontoon-pantaloons, John said, smiling at the pants-boat.

It got dark and still they were on the island.

———

Now Mush and his father spotted Mikey in the parking lot and came over to say G'day Mikey.

Hi—hello Mush, said Mikey, working on his sub. He thought about the new girl Stella at the dump and tried to hide all evidence of the sub. Probably she has a boyfriend who has a condo, good shirts and he's better than me at hockey.

And then an older woman, small and trembling, appeared on the other side of Mikey's car. The parking lot was frigging abuzz today and no one could sit and enjoy a secret sub.

Could you . . . uh could you . . . excuse me, she said. She moved a balled Kleenex into her pocket. Mikey noticed she'd been crying. Her nose was red and she blinked a lot behind her glasses. Maybe something terrible had happened. She had a short fluffy older lady's haircut common to Fearnoch, fluffy as chicken-down, with also layered dyed parts and a frond of bangs insistent on her forehead. The wind was coming cold through the corn and messing up her new haircut. She then held up a gas cap.

It broke off? Mikey got out of the car.

No, it won't go on. I thought you could do it maybe. It's always falling off, she said, and sniffed.

Let me see. Mikey inspected the gas cap. It said on it: twist until clicks three times, and had a little clockwise arrow.

The mechanics they sold me the bad one, the cheap one, she said. They know I don't know anything about cars. But I can bake pies, cake . . . she hovered over his shoulder as he looked at the cap then the hole on the tank.

That's also important, Mikey said. I think you just . . . He lined up the little nodes on the cap and tank, pushed on it and reefed on it clockwise and it clicked three times smartly.

There, he said. The cheap little gas cap sat snug on the tank.

Oh! she said and slapped him on the shoulder. Oh!

ELEVEN

On the Friday night Kirby and Peace invited John and Mikey over for supper and a movie. They were trying to be friends. Polly didn't want to go and stayed home with the young lad.

I don't wanna watch you and Kirby pretend to be friends, she said. It's sad.

Polly was tough. She was from the sticks: further up the line. Small and hardy, proud, with big defiant dark eyes and an impressive farmer's tan, she'd been a champion barrel-racer when she was a girl on her pony, and the *Fearnoch Valley Press* bragged that she never tipped a barrel. Sitting still was never for her. John said she wasn't one for leisure. She grew up on a farm too but wasn't romantic or hopeful about family farms in Fearnoch, and she was just too busy for politics and positions and totalities. Polly knew what was coming, for farms and for John and Kirby. Mikey had always liked her and he liked to think about the time she drove past his place very pregnant with, curiously, a calf in the back seat of her car, and she gave an embarrassed little wave, or once too pulling Johnny in a toboggan along the road directly into a blizzard, frozen and annoyed into the irreligious snow, pockets full of mittens because Johnny always took off and dropped his mittens, but doing the same little wave. A nice thing about the country, Mikey thought, was the little waves you get from people.

Everyone saying g'day. That and you never had to look for a parking spot.

Kirby's my friend, said John to Polly.

Okay.

We've been friends since we were four. You've been—we've all been friends since we were four.

Can you take Johnny to bug camp tomorrow cause I'm looking after him tonight? Or is it sports ball . . . she looked at the calendar: no, bug camp.

Yes.

———

No one seemed too excited about this evening, except maybe Peace, who'd chosen the movie.

Imagine owning a house, thought Mikey in front of the door, owning a house. He decided he didn't want to say very much tonight. I will ask people about themselves, that's how we're supposed to talk to people.

John left his rubber boots out on the porch and tried to brush the hay bits off himself. I'll be nice, I'll be nice, I am nice, he said to himself. He stepped over Peace's gourd collection in his socks.

Kirby opened the door a little unsure why he'd arranged all this, but he was a conciliator and would make sure it was a nice evening.

We're gonna do make-your-own pizzas, he said.

John handed Kirby a box of beer. Outstanding, he said—do we have to talk about class struggle? This was meant in humour but was not received that way.

Yes, called Peace, who'd heard from the kitchen.

Mikey thought: So, we have a conservative farmer, and these, these activism-hosts, and whatever I am, a weasel, a wastrel, and we're together for supper and a movie. Something was afoot. But they sat at the same table, children from the same god, busied with pizza construction, getting flour everywhere. Peace and Kirby had put out bowls of exciting things like pea-shoots, prosciuttoes and pears.

I am really going for it over here, said John. He had flour up in his eyelashes. I mean I am really givin' 'er on this one. Eh Mikey. What do you think here Mikey? John's pizza, obese with meat, sagged when he moved it onto a tray.

Me too, said Mikey, creator of pizza worlds, looking down at his firmament and threatening another mittful of cheese. Thank you Peace, and Kirby, he said and looked up at his hosts just as Peace spun towards him with her arms wrapped around a large book. It had a padded dark-green cover with a leather strap and *Palmistry* written in gold on it.

Before Mikey could say how are you now Peace, as he was planning, she said: Mikey. Can I read your palm?

Uh, he said. Uh it's got a lot of cheese on it.

She held his hand gently on her knee and consulted the book. Mikey's hand was cheesy and also singed and bubbled by blowtorch sparks. He closed his hand without thinking and she cracked it back open.

What's your astrological sign? she asked.

The one with the bull.

Do you have any Chinese heritage?

What?

She blew flour off the pages. With one finger she traced along Mikey's palm and the other she traced along the words. This says you should be Chinese. She thumbed through the pages and wrinkled her forehead, mouthing the words then flipping back, annoyed.

I'm just a white guy, Mikey said.

But what's your ethnic heritage?

I don't know, Ireland. Wales I think. And Lanark County. Places like that. I guess maybe someone was Chinese at some point. Mikey was puzzled, having long assumed while the Chinese were off inventing writing and gunpowder, his Darling ancestors were covered in mould and moss, shitting behind rocks in a part of the world with mists the sun never punctured.

There's a new girl at my work, he said. He had not meant at all to say this. He just sat back and felt the words fall out and thought oh boy here I am saying something.

A girl! said John.

Is she pretty, asked Peace without lifting her head.

She's so pretty it's offensive. This is offensive to me. Mikey glared at the wall.

Are you going to talk to her? Kirby said.

I don't know. No.

A girl, said John again.

Peace continued her inquiry of the hand, squeezing it against her billowy pants that had elephants embroidered on them. There's goddamn pus and blisters all through your line of heart, she said. I can't read this right now. She gave him his hand back. Then Mikey, who was starting to feel maybe okay about talking tonight, for the time being, had an idea.

Kirby, he said, you still work with the kids at the community centre?

No, said Kirby, looking out the window through the bush towards the community centre and remembering for a minute a time when he felt he was helping people. But it paid thirteen dollars an hour.

Do they need volunteers? said Mikey.

I could ask, said Kirby. Doesn't Polly work there? He looked at John.

She does, with the Women's Institute, she does everything, John said, nodding along in a rocking chair.

You want to volunteer Mikey? Kirby asked. With disadvantaged kids?

Well, he said, I helped someone the other day you know.

Who?

I helped a lady at the gas station with her gas cap. I put it on. It was great.

Okay. Um, that's good . . . Buddy some of these kids are profoundly damaged.

Sure. Mikey got quieter. Alls I do is cut steel and sleep above the garage. And Mrs. MacPherson is dead.

Talk to Polly. Sure they need help. You need a criminal record check and I think there's a drug test.

Mikey stared at the ceiling with sauce all over his chin and recalled an altercation of his with a moose when he was a dishwasher snowboarder cokehead one winter in the Calabogie highlands. And then all those cold nights in the drunk tank using his shirt as a pillow.

I don't do drugs anymore, he said. I have a Labatt 50 after hockey.

We are shit at hockey, said John.

But how are you though Kirby? Mikey said, remembering to ask how people were.

I'm good, said Kirby. He wanted to say his fucking sperm had finally done its job, but it was too early yet.

———

Peace had chosen the film because it featured one William Wasserman, from whom she'd taken an acting workshop when she lived in Vancouver. It was set in a smoky future world of planetary apocalypse and geopolitical strife. They sat full of pizza in the dark focusing on all the explosions, subterfuge and sexuality.

What the hell is going on, said John after another car bomb went off. I thought he was already dead. Are we in the past? Where's Wasserman?

Shhh, said Peace. That group is murdering all the rich people. I think. She tucked her toes under her blanket.

Where are the North Koreans? whispered Kirby. The ones at the beginning.

Do you know, said John, Kim Jong-Un or whoever's assassins murdered someone by smearing poison all over his face at the airport?

Poison-smearing, Mikey said slowly.

Shh! said Peace.

On the face! said John. Imagine that—you're jet-lagged and hungover like in Newark and you take a big smear of poison on the face.

I swear . . . said Peace. But then yet another explosion lit the room orange and she said: Oh they got another one.

This is a hateful movie, John said. In fairness he might not have hated it if they were car-bombing communist dictators or terrorists instead.

You can't say they don't deserve it, said Peace.

Rich people?

Rise up! Death to the fascists! She was picking on John and she raised one fist out from under the blankets on the sofa.

You are the rich people, said John, forgetting he was going to be nice.

What? said Kirby.

If you want to car-bomb the rich people we should all car-bomb ourselves. If you take the whole world and history.

I mean the fabulously wealthy. Like the banks, said Peace. The oligarchy. She loved to say this word with contempt, to snarl it out. It felt good to be angry. Peace was very comfortable in her anger.

Yeah, that's you and me, said John, also feeling it was good to be angry, but sometimes he thought if he kept getting angrier he was going to give himself brain cancer and certainly testicular cancer.

Kirby pressed pause and said: First of all this is going to be a nice evening. And second we are not the fucking rich people. Kirby pressed play and felt very good and angry.

John wanted to say that Kirby got paid 80K a year of taxpayers' money to check his email, but he held back and considered how much of his pizza he'd just eaten. Instead he said: So we murder the ten evil billionaire oligarchs who are ruining everything and take their money and then everything's perfect forever for everyone.

Okay, said Peace, giving John a sinister grin.

Mikey, forever walking the lonely lands between these two poles, thought he should try to change the conversation so he said to Kirby, almost in a whisper: My plant is dying.

Not Robert Plant, said Kirby.

It's so simple and superb, said John, still pink in his ears. The perfect idea. You could also put anyone you don't like on trains.

Kirby forgot about Mikey's shitty plant and pushed pause again.

John you know the system is utterly, utterly broken. I know this is just a shit movie, he said, and Peace seethed, but don't tell me it's fair.

Well who gets to decide what's fair? Who's gonna put Mikey and me and Polly on trains? said John.

The less privileged will decide this time, said Peace.

Mikey remembered when he was told it was rude to talk about politics, which seemed very long ago now, and also wondered why he had to get put on a train too. And then, thinking about getting put on a train, he recalled the great grievous World War Two book in his loft which he'd abandoned halfway through a chapter on the Eastern Front, this chapter of inestimable horrors that documented forests of frozen cannibalized bodies, a girl who'd escaped the butchering of her whole town and had lost the ability to speak, her eyes insane, and the fate of a million Soviet POWs, a million marching yellowed skeletons, and good Lord now Mikey felt off, and cold, cold like Russia, and he'd eaten too much pepperoni. And John, he didn't notice Mikey shivering and gave in to the teasing he told himself he wasn't going to do.

Well it's nice to know Fearnoch will finally be a utopia then, John said. After all our hard work.

Fuck Fearnoch, said Peace. She was exceptional at confrontation and never backed down from her aggressors. She took the remote from Kirby and pressed play and then threw it across the room so the batteries busted out the back of it.

John looked at Mikey and Mikey was silent. You people just wanna rise up because it feels good, John thought. But then he reflected on all the things he did because they felt good. He left it: he was supposed to be nice. One battery rolled slowly into the kitchen.

And then Wasserman finally made his appearance. He was a policeman in a police car on an overnight stakeout eating a bag of chips. The house he was watching exploded and Wasserman said "fuck" and "shit" and set down the chips.

That's William! said Peace.

Wasserman! cheered John. Sets down the chips!

Wasserman screamed into the radio and fishtailed out of his only scene in the movie.

———

After the movie Peace was in a rotten mood and went into the kitchen to make tea for herself.

So, North Korea wins the war? Eh? What? John hadn't been following too closely.

Oh yes, said Kirby.

Then a mug smashed and Peace shouted. She'd poured her tea quickly while angry and scalded her hand. She held her hand and bit her lip. Kirby got the broom out. John looked at her hand.

Here, he said. Put it under cold water. He touched her hand, but she pulled it away. A rosy discolouration in the shape of a peanut spread at the base of her thumb.

I'm fine John. She sniffed. I'm fine okay.

Thank you for the pizza, said Mikey, breaking his silence.

When John and Mikey left, Peace said with her hand under the tap: Do you hate John? I think I might hate John. Really. And Mikey's fucked, you can tell.

In small towns, friendships are based on geography, not common interests, Kirby thought.

Later Peace said: That film was pretty shit though.

———

John didn't want to go home to Polly and Johnny yet and asked Mikey if they could drive around for a while and just smoke.

Every time I say I'm gonna be nice and well, it's as you say Mikey, you see what happens. Let's go to the forest at the end of Fourth Line there. Do you have any fucking Cinquante in here? he said. He turned and rooted through all the dump-garments in the back seat of Mikey's pre-owned sedan.

Now by the dark forest and freed from Kirby and Peace, John could fume a bit and he spat out his words on the bush.

Does the whole world just love bullshit now? Is that movie the kind of shit people are into now? We are fucked eh Mikey, what do you think? He booted a small log into the distance and drank his Labatt 50 and got a soaker.

Mikey considered an old rap song and after a while he quoted: I ain't a shot-caller just another motherfucker in the crew.

John sat on the edge of the forest, then lay on his back in the wet clover with his beer up on his knee. He put his hands under his head and surveyed his township between his knees. The fields were silver by the moon and rolled plaid down into the river. They were alive with moon and whispers, the crickets and frogs. This bare geometry of road, fenceline, power line and row crop. Dark branches held the moon up and cattle lowed and John could have cried. Mikey watched a woolly bear, orange and black, inch up John's leg.

Our ancestors worked in these fields with no teeth and their fucking spines bent in half, John said in a softer tone. Just a bit of gratitude. He pinched off and held up a single stalk of hay.

My grandpa Darling's job at the castings foundry was to push a button at nine, drink rye, push this same button again at five, then go home, said Mikey, studying the woolly bear intently.

Gratitude, John repeated. He tasted the delicate forgotten word. You know what I mean Mikey? he twisted to look at his friend.

Gratitude, said Mikey. The woolly bear inched up along John's side. Mikey had a spasm of self-loathing and felt he couldn't concentrate on anything well until he got laid again.

Yes what happened to gratitude? Oh no, we gotta rise up—rise up Mikey! And he tried to hand him the hay stalk. Mikey didn't say anything.

You used to talk a lot more, said John.

I was drunk all the time, said Mikey.

Well. Don't be too hard on yourself.

I drove drunk everywhere, I delivered pizzas drunk, I fell off buildings and shit John, more than once—I should have been shot!

John took a huge performative drink out of his beer. Well, it's as you say, he said.

I didn't say anything, said Mikey.

John sighed.

What do you want me to say? asked Mikey. I don't know anything—that's what just about everyone should be saying. Just say I don't know. But that won't stop them, everyone just talking and talking like they know everything. I try to think: Is this—what I'm about to say—shit? And usually yes, it is shit, so I try not to say it.

I'm lonely, John said. I was friends with Kirby. Now I'm a pig racist land-rapist, or whatever it is that I am now.

Everyone is only trying to do the best they can with what they have, said Mikey. He was thoughtful and looking up into the ribboned indigo galaxies and worlds and Oort cloud over the field and bush. We all just need a little more grace I think, he said and held his 50 solemnly with two hands.

Thank you Mikey that's inspirational, said John.

It's true. You and Kirby are each of youse more and more right because whatever you believe in makes you feel really, really good . . . and you'll never agree on anything until something big happens. Like war, and pestilence, or like a big fucked tsunami.

You sure about that?

I'm not sure about anything, ever. But I'm reading about it. All your squabbles will disappear overnight but you'll have each other. All the horseshit will get ripped away one day and you'll have each other but no horseshit. Or maybe humans really just need a big fight every so often, frig I dunno. John—watch the woolly bear there.

John had sat up to do a big spit and knocked the woolly bear off. It hit the ground and rolled into a black and orange ball and lay there motionless, maybe now fated never to become a not-very-noteworthy moth.

What?

The woolly bear, said Mikey, pointing. He fell off your back.

Oh. John picked him up clumsy with thumb and forefinger and put him in his palm. A fuzzy-wuzzy. He poked the woolly bear, who didn't move. Maybe he's hibernating. Sorry.

Mikey was displeased at the fate of the woolly bear.

Do you think Peace will put a hex on me from her witch book? John carefully set the dead or hibernating woolly bear down.

Probably.

Mikey wandered down by an old lime kiln and found a plaque on the path in the forest. He studied it in the moonlight.

This plaque commemorates the swamp fire of 2012, he read. What swamp fire? I don't remember that.

John looked at the plaque. Four acres of wetland burned in the

fire started by lightning on August . . . He stopped reading. Who . . .
gives a shit?! Did they think there's never going to be lightning and
fires? No, this forest just has to stay perfect forever. Welcome to our
perfect forever forest!

Mikey then found another plaque.

Oh is that one to commemorate the three voles that perished in
the great swamp fire of 2012? John asked.

Yes, said Mikey. I think there's a statue of those brave voles around
here somewhere.

Voles in the swamp fire, said John. Is anything worth a real
plaque happening around here?

Jesus. You should think why you're so mad. All we did was
watch a shitty film and have too much pizza, said Mikey, thinking
about what his therapist might add. Mikey knew when he was mad,
it usually came from some personal deficit—like he was jealous, or
fat, or lonely—rather than whichever issue under discussion. He
wanted to say this but stopped because he believed he hadn't said
anything interesting, smart or appropriate in years.

Sorry, yes, you're right, said John.

And John thought and had trouble remembering why he was so
mad, it had been so long.

I guess . . . I guess, it just makes me feel like I'm nothing. That's
it. I'm nothing, I'm not worth anything at all—I'm a fool.

A what?

A fool!

Yeah.

And the ingratitude—that would make anyone mad I'd think.
I'm scared about Fearnoch.

Fearnoch is just a place, everyone has to come from some type
of frigging place, John, you're relying on setting too much. And
nostalgia, said Mikey.

Well, said John, everyone has to remember something fondly for shit's sake.

He had a vision of his barn finally slumping over, returned to the earth, the farm conclusively grown up in bush, and a middle-aged Johnny, fat, staring into space with pleated khakis and a goatee and an ID badge on a lanyard, surrounded by humming glowing photocopiers in a business park.

Nothing's perfect, maybe in the future all farms will be, oh like internet farms, he said. Farming the internet. Crops of servers.

Yeah internet farms, said Mikey. Probably they already have those.

Is there gonna be a day when Peace and Kirby and everyone say okay that's it everyone, pens down, everything is finally perfect?

C'mon here, I'm not talking about that, c'mon here, said Mikey.

They just keep fucking with it. Busybody piece-of-shits—just go away for the love of Jesus! More rules more rules. Oh just a new tax here, new rule, um, owl-tax now, gotta tell folks to do shit, everyone has to have owls now, or tax. Just to fuck 'em off.

Mikey laughed. Just making sure everyone's got owls here.

My wife thinks I'm a xenophobe, John said.

Are you a xenophobe?

I don't think so. I hope not.

Your wife is wonderful, said Mikey. He was jealous. He thought about how great it must be to sit in the living room listening to a record with your wife. Let's put on a record please my love.

I know, said John and he rubbed his face. I should tell her that. Maybe we should all just be quiet for a bit.

Yeah I like it! said Mikey. He brightened up. Everyone just work down in the mine and shut the Christ up, he thought.

———

When John got home he remembered he had to go check on the calf, the cream-coloured one, who was now sickly. He walked down the path to the barn with a flashlight and thought about Peace's burned thumb. He flicked the light on and the calf was at the back of the barn alone and blinking. The other animals ignored it. John readied a pail of pablum supplement, stuck his finger out for the calf to suck, then transitioned the calf from finger to pail. He scratched its chin as it drank. The calf drank desperately, pulling and stamping, and pablum mix ran off its chin in streaks onto John's hand.

Polly was half-asleep and mumbling gibberish to John in the bedroom. Mmm-hmm North Korea and Kirby . . . yes, she said. Yes the tomatoes . . . Johnny's sick.

You're wonderful, said John.

And immediately Johnny announced himself at the door, naked and crying, with barf stuck to his chest.

He's been like this all night, said Polly, now fully awake.

Okay come on, Johnny, said John. He took his hand and brought him to the bathroom. He wet a towel and cleaned the boy's chest. Johnny stood naked on the closed toilet lid and coughed till he peed. Dad you sleep in my bed, he said.

John got into Johnny's tiny bed because Polly had done it the night before. He dragged the tin Ottawa Senators garbage can over in front of Johnny and let his feet hang cold off the end of the mattress and a plastic toy lion stuck into his back. Johnny held his dad's hand between his own filthy warm wet little hands and continued to cough.

—

Mikey's Ireland book was finished so, with courage, he took up again the struggle with the even fatter World War Two book—someone had to remember this shit—and was careful to skirt around the Eastern Front chapter. But now he couldn't read more than a few sentences without his head slipping away to wives and record players and then he'd forgotten what he'd just read.

Jesus, he thought, I'm fucking trying to be a good reader and get the transference going here but I don't need to know about each and every cocksucking tank formation in Sicily. This long-winded author couldn't have imagined how lonely and bored Mikey was. Or maybe he did know, truly, he knew Mikey was the only person in the world reading his book at this moment and his book was a way of saying, don't worry Mikey, I'm just as bored and lonely as you are.

Mikey had a book about the fall of Rome and other empires that he picked up when he got tired again of all the World War Two slaughters, but there were plenty of slaughters in the Rome one too. He clicked off the light and was proud he didn't look at any pornos.

TWELVE

There was shit Anna had to clean off the toilet during her brunch shift at Café Plus, and then there was shit waiting for her to clean off the toilet when she got to her evening shift at the Centre Saint-Savard.

Tabarnak, said Yvette when she saw the state of the stall where Anna was on her knees scrubbing away.

Anna stood up to stretch her back and made a big frown. How do they get it up around behind the toilet tank?

I think we serve the shit food here, said Yvette hobbling away with her large and exhausted ass heaving and pitching under the knot of her apron. She went to find the manager to say stop making Anglo Anna clean all the shit always. Océane smelled the stink from across the restaurant and kept well away.

Non non non tabarnak osti, she said.

The shit at Centre Saint-Savard was all over the seat and down on the floor. Anna almost laughed. What a world, she thought. She figured it was a form of protest because the workers had found and destroyed the boys' drug stash. When you have nothing else, you can still weaponize shit and shit all over the place. She was so used to picking up shit she didn't gag at all and almost forgot to put on gloves.

———

And then Ebenezer had gotten in a fight. Miss Natalie asked Anna to check in and follow up with Ebenezer and then fill out the critical incident report, because no one else wanted to go anywhere near him.

Why . . . why? Anna was cross. She crossed her arms over the critical incident report binder. They're gonna send you back to Lac-de-C you know. They're itching to send you back and all you gotta do really is not get in fights. She meant the larger and horrible youth jail.

Ebenezer said nothing. He tried to smile like it wasn't a big deal, he was tough.

Miss Natalie said it was awful. Why? Anna asked again.

He's SA anyway, said Ebenezer. SA meant sexual assault.

Why Ebenezer.

Ebenezer looked up and said directly: He said I was a faggot and he was going to fuck my sister. She's thirteen.

Oh, said Anna, and paused. Then she dropped the binder and slumped down next to him on the floor against the wall. Just the size of him—Anna was always amazed at how small he was. He was just a boy with basketball shorts on under his pants and his whole ass out of his pants and his ears stuck out under his hat. His narrow shoulders, skinny arms, a child with awful tattoos home-poked on his arms and hands, like one of a hideous mouse, Anna thought it was supposed to be, with "Haïtien" written under it. And then there was all that he had to carry: all that luggage on his tiny frame. He was like Marley's ghost. Anna thought about that for a minute. Chains double-ironed, wrought in steel, long and wound out like a tail, dragging everything he'd done, and been accused of doing, and everything that'd been done to him. Anna could only imagine little pieces from what Ebenezer told her—Jamaican patties and pop for breakfast, getting a good beating because he fell asleep during an overnight shift in a crack house. But really Anna was only imagining. She herself fussed about her boyfriend not just getting on that frigging end of the snow shovel and working the frigging thing, and not eating her out, and getting rejection letters.

Shit, she said. Well still is it worth it to go back to Lac-de-C?

Ebenezer thought he was going to die soon anyway. He looked at his hands and brought his knees up to his chest. It's not fair, he said.

———

Earlier, Ebenezer had been in a counselling session in the counselling room with all the Kleenex boxes and soothing posters of palm trees and sand dunes. He held his counselling notebook and all his jail-school cahiers and Duo-Tangs on his lap.

The clinical psychologist said, I think you are finally showing some remorse. This is progress, Ebenezer.

Miss Natalie touched his knee and said, you are sorry Ebenezer.

Yes, he said.

For what you did . . .

Yes! he said.

Talk more about how you're sorry, said the clinical psychologist, leaning back in his chair. Talk about . . . um—he looked at his notes—Mr. Bachmann, he said. He renewed his gaze at Ebenezer.

I'm sorry . . . I'm sorry.

Mm-hmm, hmm.

I'd talk to him, said Ebenezer.

I don't think we can do that. I'm sure he doesn't want to.

Ebenezer thought about Mr. Bachmann, and he was really always thinking about Mr. Bachmann.

When he left the room, the older boy, who was SA, even though they weren't supposed to know that, but everyone did, said: You're crying? Then he called him a faggot and said he knew his sister and was sweet on her and she wanted to fuck him.

Ebenezer was much smaller but knew some important things

about fights. First is protect your chin. Most people will talk a lot then start shoving then fight. Very few expect you to fight right away. Once you're going, count on an immediate right haymaker from him, which will happen most of the time. Try to kick his knee back because he's going to be looking at your hands and head. And punch for the jaw not the head, where you're going to hurt your hand more than you hurt him. Also don't stop because you don't want him getting up. This was what he knew about how to fight.

So the older boy was still talking about his sister when Ebenezer dropped his notebook, cahiers and Duo-Tangs to the floor, and cracked him in the jaw in the hallway. Then he kicked at his kneecap, trying to snap it back. The boy staggered and crumpled and Ebenezer kicked him in the ribs, then the head. He hurt his toe and switched feet. He steadied his hands against the wall and kicked the boy's ear when he covered his face. He didn't stop until two staff put him in a restraint, one on each arm.

Are you crying? he said to the boy as they dragged him away down the hall.

———

Anna's mother fed the birds every morning, if it was forty below, if there was an ice storm. She was out there pouring the seeds from an old coffee tin in the breathless cold and whine of the skidoos. Entire migration routes recalculated to visit her feeder, which was a sheet of plywood on a post. Several smaller bird feeders were strung up in a circle around the plywood. She frigged her back putting sacks of seed in her trunk at Fearnoch Farm Supply. Five-, ten- and twenty-pound sacks, a fifty-pound sack even, of black sunflower seeds, striped sunflower seeds, niger seeds, all-purpose birdseed with corn and millet. She was a retired hairdresser in old dirty jeans who didn't fuss much about makeup or new recipes or wine, and she drove around loads of birdseed for all the chickadees, nuthatches, and hopefully, one day, a bluebird. Maybe she would wear makeup if she got invited to a wedding, but other than that it really wasn't her business.

She broke her day into chapters, and bird care was a lengthy one. She focussed on the little things, like leaving cookies in the mailbox for the mailman and his family at Christmastime. Sometimes she cut people's hair at the kitchen table—old ladies talking about the Almanac while she coiffed their hair to lambswool, or young fellows gripping action-hero figurines and not sitting still. She watched the birds from the kitchen window with a notepad. She looked at job websites for Anna. She ran a birdwatching newsletter and pondered the ethics of letting the cat out.

The chickadees were always there. Fearless, they'd land on her hat, with their perfect little faces, tiny inquisitors who had to inspect everything. A dozen mourning doves, a little more tentative, landing in a clump with their noisy wings after she went back inside. The red-winged blackbirds with the handsome epaulettes came back every St. Patrick's Day on the day. And those blue-jay bullies, and grackles, American goldfinches, evening grosbeaks, sometimes an enormous pileated woodpecker. At Christmas, the fat cardinal lording with his missus. Crows and ravens who lived over on the barn. She knew them all. She wanted more orioles and barred owls and whisky jacks, not so many wild turkeys coming in like a dinosaur herd, not so many squirrels. She talked to Anna on the phone with her notepad ready for any new bird activity.

How's Magnus? She tapped her pencil. She had met him and liked him. He seemed harmless and polite, Magnus.

He's okay, Mum, said Anna.

Is there any news about his job?

No, he says he's still waiting for some old professors to die.

Oh. How's your book then?

It's not a book yet . . . I like it one day and hate it the next.

I guess that's how that goes eh. Can you tell me who did it? I won't tell.

No, that's the point. Nobody gets to know. I don't know.

I think it was the heiress who did it.

It's a pretty narcissistic thing to do—write a book.

Anna you have to—

Everyone stop and listen to me—I know what I'm saying—

Anna you've always been good at writing. Every teacher you ever had said.

Thanks, Mum.

You need to use your contacts and get it published.

Yes I know, said Anna. If she wasn't happy her mother could always divine it off the telephone line. If she spoke she knew, if she was quiet she knew. Anna tried to call only when she was upbeat. She didn't want to make her worry, but not calling made her worry even more. The unsaid bubbled away always: please be happy so I can be happy. And come home and have a baby.

Are you gonna come home for the Corn Boil? Or Swamp-Fest? The Bird-Watching Committee has a pavilion this year.

Oh . . . maybe. Tell me about the birds, Mum. She lay on her back on the carpet with her calves resting up on the bed and her mother regaled her with chickadees, hairy woodpeckers, downy woodpeckers, starlings and flickers.

———

Anna's father left before Anna's mother even knew she was pregnant. Anna's mother had spent a lifetime wondering why he left, and on her better days she thought: I won't ever understand and that's fine and fuck him all the same. On her bad days she thought maybe it was because she was poor, needy, ugly, boring, dirty. Maybe he wanted more more more—more women, more life and things to do. If he stuck with one woman who didn't wear makeup in a nowhere town in the Ottawa Valley with sunflower seeds and old ladies' hair stuck to his socks, he'd rule out all the others.

Maybe he got to fuck and leave all different types of sad women all over Canada—Edmonton, Newfoundland, Wawa—in living rooms, hotels and back seats. Fucking them with no condoms, holding them after with his carpenter hands sliding over their hips down along their legs, laughing and kissing their ears, eating from their cupboards and bowls, then soon enough gone down the dark eight thousand kilometres of Trans-Canada Highway.

Maybe he had a spectacular life exploding along in lustrous bursts, green and blue fireworks up into the dark. Laughs, sex, money, maybe tango dancing, bisexual foursomes, doing cocaine and creating art. Anna's mother imagined him tearing with his teeth at all the things she could not offer a partner.

Maybe he got all that, but he never got to see what his daughter looked like sitting on the heat register in the kitchen eating her porridge. Anna sat on the hot air vent on the cold kitchen linoleum on cold mornings and her mother brushed her thick blond hair. Her little bottom on the grate, tiny back straight and sure, she'd lean back slightly as her mum tugged away at the knots, but she didn't spill her breakfast. He never saw the frost coming through the windows and the static pops of Anna's hair as she peered into her bowl. She was a quiet and careful child. Then she'd pull down her balaclava, making sure not to mess up her brushed hair, and wrap her scarf and brave the cold up to the school bus. Little determined steps in her snow boots.

He never got to sit on a small desk at Fearnoch Public School while the teachers year after year, some of them close to tears, would say: The brightest student I've had in forever, just a pleasure, a joy you know, shy, and nice as pie, and after so many rotten kids between you and me, Miss Berube . . .

He never got to see Anna fourteen and blundering into the world of makeup, phone calls and worrying about your tits.

No Mum, this is how you're supposed to do it, she said. Stubborn and poking herself in the eye with the mascara brush. A big dusting of rouge or concealer or something, eyeliner, opening her mouth wide and painting it with purple lipstick. She tried to look sexy in the mirror. Maybe the girls at school would leave her alone now that she was trying to look like them. What she looked like was a heartbroken prostitute getting on the boat for New France.

Oh Anna, I don't think it's supposed to look like that . . . But what did she know? Anna's purpled bottom lip quivered and she turned and went into her room.

And Anna's father never got to see Anna come down the laneway with the makeup washed off and the school bus pulling away through the trees. Anna's mum was raking leaves and dropped the rake and Anna hugged her and cried into her neck for a long time with wind and leaves in her hair. Only Anna's mum got to see that.

———

Now the turkeys come every day after breakfast, eat everything, even the compost pile, you know. Anna . . . Anna?

Mmmpf, said Anna. Sorry Mum I fell asleep.

That's okay.

It was a nice thing to fall asleep to, said Anna, falling asleep again.

———

There was a meeting in the Centre Saint-Savard office concerning Ebenezer's latest incident.

The only reason, the only goddamn reason, said the program director looking around the room, that he's not going back to Lac-de-C is because he's freeing up soon. Then we're done with him.

Three fat binders containing Ebenezer's extensive file sat on the desk. The program director packed up his briefcase and scowled at the binders as he left.

He's a child, Anna sputtered to Miss Natalie after the meeting.

He's not, said Miss Natalie.

You know how many people—they're saying they're going to kill him.

I know, Anna. Whatta you want me to do here? She strained to lift Ebenezer's file back onto the shelf.

Anna went to tell Ebenezer. She knocked softly on the door to Room #7 and found him hiding under his cot, asleep.

THIRTEEN

Mikey stopped taking his depression pills because he worried about his serotonin secreters depending on them and as well he fretted about his dick falling off. And as he stepped back into life without the pills, he wondered if this was what going crazy was. I'm crazy, he thought. I'm villainous. I'm the villain in the story. And everyone's looking at me. He visualized his mind piloting a thin highway of sanity, spooled from cerebral fibres, and crashing offline into a dark corner of his skull.

In the office at the scrapyard, which was an old shipping can, there was still one of those old punch-in clocks. Mikey found his card and punched it just as the clock struck eight. He turned his workboots upside down to let the dirt pour out, put them on, opened the door and ran face first into Stella. She had braids and bangs and freckles and her brown eyes were deep and severe. He'd been avoiding her.

Have you been avoiding me, she said.

He thought this was a very direct thing to ask someone she'd only just met.

No I'm not, he said.

I wanted to ask you . . . I forgot my lunch.

Well, said Mikey, uh—you can have some of mine? He revealed that he had a tin of meatballs and gravy and a can opener.

No. Take me somewhere. Where do you go to eat around here?
She crossed her arms and held her shoulders.

Mikey thought. We could go to the fries wagon there by the river
and have fries.

Yes let's do that, she said.

———

And so at noon Mikey drove them to the fries wagon and they sat
down at the picnic table, across from each other with their fries
platters mountainous. The river was languid, mute, in no hurry at
all, and the clouds piled up fat and lazy. Stella was quiet, wiping the
grease and vinegar on her pants and surveying the river.

Mikey tried to think of something to say. Are you finding any
good soil samples? he asked.

Oh yeah, she said. Oh yes, the scrapyard's fucked. Her eyes went
large and she speared at her fries with a toothpick.

Yeah, said Mikey. What's it for? The soil samples.

It's my master's, my field work. I have to test for pH, nitrate
index, magnesium, manganese—she noticed Mikey's eyes cloud up—
at waste management facilities . . . anyway it's boring. But, she said,
all the tailings, and the amount of boron and barium they just
dumped in there from the old sawmill is really, really not good for
Fearnoch.

The dump is the highest point in Fearnoch township, he said.
He opened his pop up. He thought she was beautiful, beautiful, but
there was also a little sadness to her, a quiet gloom or longing, like a
mermaid that wasn't in the sea. Mikey couldn't figure her out.

Stella looked at him and didn't say anything for a while. She kept
looking at him and didn't break eye contact to look at the river or her
fries. Mikey then became conscious of the issue of what to do with
your eyes during a conversation. I'm staring. Should I be staring?
Once, on an unfortunate date with a girl from the city, the girl and

Mikey were downtown and she yelled at him for staring at everything and everyone and Mikey said I'm from a small town, I frigging stare at people and unusual things—of which there were many examples of both around.

But this was like going on a nice bicycle ride and then remembering oh but of course I don't know how to ride a bicycle and instantly flipping over the handlebars and eating shit all over the pavement and bloodying your knees. Did we learn back when we were *Homo habilis* or *erectus*, or whatever we were, where and where not to look while talking? Maybe it was involuntary and natural until we talked to someone whose bangs and nose and chewing were all just too much. Mikey looked into her eyes for as long as he dared, remembered about blinking, broke away to look at the river, squinted and looked at Quebec, looked at his pop, then tried her eyes again and still she was looking at him. He looked at her ear when she tucked a strand of brown or possibly auburn hair behind it, and in the end decided to look down between his feet and just wait this one out. His eyes stung and he hoped lunch would end soon before he made a mistake.

Do you have any pets? she asked from out of nowhere.

I had a cat, Mikey said, looking up and rubbing his eyes. Mrs. MacPherson. But she's dead.

Who's Mrs. MacPherson?

My cat, my dead cat.

You named your cat Mrs. MacPherson?

Yes after my secretary in elementary school, Mrs. MacPherson, she helped me when I barfed on the bus in grade 1, then she got transferred to the city. I liked her, I thought it was a fine name for a cat.

Oh.

Mikey watched to see if Stella cared at all about this and when it seemed to him that she did, he continued: Also Mrs. MacPherson, the secretary that is, she made zucchini bread at the Christmas party

and no one ate it so I felt bad and told her, you know—it was great!
But it wasn't, it's zucchini bread. But she gave my mum the recipe
and I just had to eat so much zucchini bread for a while.

Oh. That's nice.

Stella bent forward to tie her boot under the table and her hair
hung very close to Mikey and the smell of hair, the conditioner, the
forgotten scent of girl was so overpowering he thought he might have
to say: You gotta back up I—I'm gonna black out here.

What are some things that you like? she asked. She certainly had
a very direct way of speaking.

Uh, said Mikey. He couldn't think of anything. Not being hungover? That sound of an orchestra warming up? He had no hobbies.
Regarding his interests, he was not noteworthy.

Reading? he said after contemplation. I try to read and not look
at the internet.

What about movies?

Sure, I like movies.

I like horror movies, bloody gory dirty fucking greasy horror
movies, said Stella, trying to make a horrifying face with fries in her
mouth.

I like hockey, said Mikey, remembering he actually did like some
things.

I love hockey!

You, said Mikey, like hockey? It was dawning on him that she
was perfect and it was terrifying.

Yeah I'm from Thunder Bay for Jesus' sake. I play, I have my gear
here, do you play—can I play?

Um, said Mikey. Well, I could ask John.

Stella put down her toothpick. You don't have to . . . if there's
room, you know. She looked down at her hands in her lap. A tractor
drove past them with a jostling hay wagon which left cow shit and
straw all over the road.

Mikey tried out the questioning. What are some things you . . . ah d-d-d . . . ah d-d-d—he really had to take a running start on the word and his face seized up and he almost screamed it when he finally got it out—don't! . . . like?

Having no friends in a strange small town, said Stella immediately. What don't you like?

This Mikey had answers for.

Well, he began, I think people get too excited about baked potatoes. It's just like a ball of ground you know? And when people clap when they laugh. And snappy abbreviations and how bright the high beams are on new trucks. Also iPads. And I'm tired of Tibetan prayer flags. Mikey had been wanting to tell someone these things he didn't like for a while.

This was a lot of negativity and Stella considered with her nose wrinkled.

I like Tibetan prayer flags, she said.

————

Mikey drove them back to work, up from the dusty river road and up the hill, and now they saw the sky had a black rectangular hole ripped out of it. A black rectangle, exact as math, on the horizon.

Oh great, thought Mikey. Maybe it's the birth of a black hole. I've been waiting for this.

Both Mikey and Stella were aware of the hole and looked at each other to confirm they were seeing the same hole, then looked back at the hole. Mikey drove them closer, closer to the vector fields from the beyond, or the end of all things, or whatever it was he was driving them towards, both of them frozen with their mouths open.

Stella was first to address the new feature on their world.

What, she said pointing her finger, the hell is that? It was getting bigger.

Mikey didn't know how to respond. What was there to say

except: Now our world has a hole in the sky? Science must present some answers. He watched the hole, watched Stella watch the hole, still pointing, and still it got bigger.

Instead of being swallowed, they got close enough to see what the hole was. A massive banner hanging from a hot-air balloon.

Oh, said Stella, exhaling. Oh I thought it'd be more interesting than that.

The banner was an advertisement. *Future site of Edenia,* it said, *Pastoral Peaceful Affordable Detached Family Homes.* And under that— *Edenia Outlets: Over 75 Stores. Living Green.*

Well frig, said Mikey. I wanted a black hole.

Yeah fuck outta here Edenia! Stella cupped her mouth and shouted out the window.

Mikey looked at what would become detached family homes and over seventy-five stores. A creek cut a soft looping gully through overgrown fields and briars and a derelict wind pump squeaked in the distance.

It's so nice as it is, he said.

Yes, said Stella. It is.

I guess people gotta live somewhere, but Jesus, said Mikey.

What's your phone number? She pointed at him with her phone and Mikey told her.

———

When they got back to the scrapyard, Stella said: Can you not ignore me anymore? I don't know anyone in this place and I'm here all semester. She undid her seatbelt and gestured with her hands at the mountains of old appliances and cars. All I know here is this dump.

I'm not ignoring you, Mikey said.

Sure, said Stella.

Stella got out of the car and walked off into the dump to gather her scientific gear. She was gorgeous and direct and loved hockey.

Mikey sat in the car holding his work gloves and tipped into a true unmedicated hole of sadness.

Wow, this is feeling, he thought. An acute absence of happiness molecules. Those pills had some power.

I don't want to ignore you, he thought. But I don't know what to say. Do I have to fake confidence? Do you have any idea how old and poor I am? Are you interested in my horsehair mattress, the nightmares, or my one frigged up nostril from drugs? If he didn't like himself, but she possibly liked him, then how fucked was she?

He wanted to get into the hole in the sky with her, shutterdown with her, and slow dance and get pizza at midnight and discuss hockey statistics. He wanted her to come back once he'd done something magnificent and they could talk about that. He wasn't ready for this yet. But mostly he wanted her not to figure him out, to see him through the dump fumes. Not to feel along with her fingers and discover he didn't have a spine. And he knew she would soon enough.

FOURTEEN

The floorboards in Johnny's room were warped and water-damaged and curling up into the baseboards. It was pouring outside, puking fat raindrops, and the framing company, where John was getting some days under the table, called and said don't come in. Thankfully the second cut of hay was pulled off and in the barn, but it didn't get anywhere near the loft. He'd opted for squares, not rounds, which was more work and could not get wet, but he could get more money for them, maybe from the horse people. And the combine man was coming for the soya bean and corn later in the week, so he took the morning to see what he could do about this bedroom that made him ashamed as a father. Johnny had his feet full of splinters from ripping around the house. John and Polly took turns going at the boy's toes with tweezers and a bowl of warm water. Polly was a nurse and much more persuasive with the tweezers than John and his gnarled hands that were so big and worn he pretty well didn't need mitts in winter.

John pried up the most rotted floorboard and discovered underneath was lousy with rat nests and rat shit. He sat on Johnny's bed and put the crowbar down.

My son sleeps in here, he said to himself, breathes this shit. He tried another floorboard. What'll be under this one I wonder—

perhaps some tuberculosis.

The rain swelled and spat against the window and John looked out as his dad staggered in the dooryard, just like a zombie with a bloody mouth. He was dragging a chainsaw. John ran outside into the rain and yelled: Dad!

His dad turned around slowly to reveal he had blood going from his mouth all down the front of his shirt onto his pants. The rain whipped into his side, made the blood run, and his dad stood there with the chainsaw dangling, looking like he had a touch of the amnesia.

What are you doing chainsawing out here? John hollered through the rain. Dad!

His dad stared with his mouth open.

What are you doing? John repeated, running towards him. Come on, come on inside! He took his elbow.

When his father finally spoke, his voice rattled out slowly, like it was coming in from far away: It was a little alder . . . it just bucked up at me.

In the kitchen John looked at his dad's mouth. It was strange and awful to pull your dad's lip open like he was a child. John saw two bottom teeth were broken and a dark black gash on the lip continued to bleed, full of dirt.

I wish Polly was here, said John. We gotta go to the hospital, Dad—why were you chainsawing alders in the rain?

I'll be all right, his dad said with his eyes sagged and his mouth still open. Someone's been stealing my wood. There's a wood thief about.

John drove the truck into town with wet leaves all over the windshield. His dad was wide-eyed and mute with a bloody mass of paper towel stuck out his mouth like a soother.

Dr. Ayoub, the Younghusbands' family doctor, was at the clinic and had a moment to put five stitches into John's dad's mouth. He was always at the clinic working, or working at his family's pizza and shawarma restaurant, Happy Slices Pizza, and the rare times he wasn't working, one thing he liked was to play slo-pitch at the Guthrie Place diamond, on the Happy Slices Pizza slo-pitch team. He called people "buddy" prolifically; it seemed to him that that's how you were supposed to talk around here. He and John's dad were friends, had been friendly rivals on the diamond and enjoyed their post-game parking lot pints together. Everybody was "buddy" to the kind doctor, sitting on a tailgate, bubbly, loud and jovial in the dirty gravel parking lot.

Jesus, John, he said. Buddy. He squirted more saline in and John's dad spat out pink sawdust. Dr. Ayoub closed the door. Buddy, he said. You should see a dentist about the teeth. He took off his glasses and blinked one eye a few times, something stuck in it.

Oh I don't know, said John's dad, who came from a long line of doctor-avoiders.

Now Dr. Ayoub put his glasses and clipboard down and leaned in close to the old man, now not bubbly, not jovial, and smelling like soaps and antiseptic. John's dad felt ridiculous in a paper gown seated on the stainless steel examining table with his rubber boots hanging off the edge and Dr. Ayoub giving him a schoolteacher's look. He was soaked through, the blood drying down his chin and neck.

I am worried, said Dr. Ayoub. You shouldn't be working. You're showing all the signs of a breakdown, buddy. Like we talked about— now you're chainsawing in a rainstorm. He gripped the cold edge of the table. He grew up in Lebanon during the war, with more and more rockets arcing orange and red every night, snipers in the hotel— pop pop—and bodies on the road, a sandal in the street with the foot still in it too, his own dad gone missing, his five-year-old sister with her little girl's haircut stiff with dust hiding in the cupboard and looking not unlike John's dad, looking bloodied and dissociative. He'd seen every type of clown-shit you could throw at someone. Dr. Ayoub knew the look of a defeated man who couldn't concede. He knew it very well.

John's dad shrugged, which brought a loud crinkle from the paper gown. He wanted to be up on his feet and back to the farm. And besides he had to tell his son something before he forgot, it was important. Something to remember for when he was gone.

John, please get some rest, said Dr. Ayoub.

FIFTEEN

Magnus was at his goddamn poetry recital—or perhaps this was trivia night. Anyway he wasn't home and Anna sat at the kitchen table feeling like the only person in the world. She thought some more about the life Ebenezer had found himself in and then opened her laptop and just gave it to her story, beating down on the keys, showing her teeth with her malice and thinking she could at least fantasize about better lives. Dreaming is free.

I'll write all night, she thought. I'll murder all my characters if they keep bugging me. I can do whatever I want in here.

Ebenezer would free up and then go right back into the shit; she knew it. And she would do the same if she were him. She slapped the laptop shut. She'd choose drugs, money, status, girls over working at the Mega Dollar or hugs and eating cake with teary empath social workers who only got into this business because they were broken themselves. Ebenezer didn't need people like her squeezing on him and his predicaments so they could feel better about themselves through his hell.

Anna dropped a novella an old aunt had given her for Christmas onto the floor. It was the type of book only an old aunt could read. She struggled to be less bitter.

I have had it up to here with these smug, buttery little satisfied sentences, she thought. She imagined letting the poor sentences roam a bit—setting them free across the prairie, out on the line and rabid into outer space, filling them with ands and opening the throttle out, diesel-powered, high-octane sentences, muscular sentences and sobbing free, drop one in the chamber and send it for a fucking rip. She wanted a sentence to explode off the margin, go on for a thousand words, my God a million words over oceans and continents until it finally passed out and died, flatlined into an ellipsis somewhere in the Carpathians—Lord Jesus was she bored.

Just then she looked at her unopened envelope, which she almost ripped open just then but she thought: No, no, no, not ready.

This was exhaustive and foolish, rummaging through everything that happened, trying to be clever and find links, transcribing little things she'd said or someone else had said that Anna thought were smart, good, and worth saving. Oh I'll put that in the story; can I take that for the story? Every sentence trapped in the same plodding iambs, dada-dada-dada pop. Every sentence these days beginning with he looked, or she looked, or it looked. Everyone's just looking.

Recently she'd murdered a character, the poor old abbot, Father Dominic, a man who wasn't quite what he said he was, and she wondered if she'd shown enough compassion or enough personal detail during his sudden gory departure. If she'd earned this grisly murder. Anna sighed and once again dug in, back down to the mines, she squeezed and ripped away at every painful, meaningful, sensitive thing she could plumb out of her private life. She caught her breath and emerged with slow dancing with John Younghusband in grade 9, in the gym at the high school. She put her head down on his shoulder and they moved slow and clockwise in a dark tiny gym, and he held his breath near her ear with his hat pushed back. His hands shook on her waist and he was silent. The song she had in mind was "Crazy," by Aerosmith, of course it was, only that song would work for this memory that hung so far back in her head she could only paw at it. Anna stood up and slowly shuffled clockwise in her Mattawa moccasins, trying to remember. She didn't know what to do with this, but she did wonder how John was for a minute.

Then she thought about fish sticks. She remembered when she was maybe ten and her mother put three fish sticks on Anna's plate with a spatula and then fixed a barrette in Anna's hair while Anna reached for the ketchup bottle. The fish sticks were pressed into identical singed hyperrectangles. So perhaps: Father Dominic ate fish sticks . . . and thought about his mother. Ah frig . . . why fish sticks?

John in grade 9, fish sticks, her mother, Father Dominic's mother, she travelled along this peculiar sequence while staring out the basement window at the feet of the passersby and then got to Ebenezer's mother. Anna met her once when Ebenezer's mother was invited to Centre Saint-Savard to sit in on one of his more ill-fated counselling sessions. She was small and timid, with a short haircut, and she said very little. She had a grocery bag with some candy for Ebenezer and a new blue hat. Ebenezer's file said his mother had a history of drinking and detailed the abuse from old boyfriends that was so horrific Anna couldn't read any more. Anna got up and made a drink for her damn self.

Anna remembered that meeting as the one where Ebenezer punched a hole in the wall. His mother told him from what she knew: his best friend Bernard, the one Ebenezer kept his mouth shut about when he got arrested, had told everyone in the neighbourhood that Ebenezer was a rat-goof. Which was the worst thing you could be in that neighbourhood. And which was an awful thing for someone who was free to say about someone who was irrefutably, spectacularly not a rat, the proof of which was your freedom.

Kids shouted "rat!" and "goof!" and "rat-goof!" at Ebenezer's mother when she was pulling her cart of groceries home and they wrote it on the sidewalk in chalk out front of the housing complex. Bernard pretended like he didn't know her and his mother didn't answer the phone. Ebenezer's sister—who was diagnosed as failing to thrive, and a selective mute as a toddler, and was the tiniest of the tiny family—hadn't said a word in three days. Now she ran home with her backpack bouncing, crying, slamming the door and sitting with her back against it trying to catch her breath, but saying nothing when her mother asked what was wrong.

Ebenezer closed his eyes and put his hands together. Anna thought he was handling it pretty well. Then he got up and punched a hole right through a poster of a calming palm tree at sunset and left. His mother reached for his arm when he passed her.

Anna looked back at her story, unsure how to work these personal details into and around Father Dominic's demise. She wondered where Magnus was and then thought maybe she should do something nice for him. She took a generous sip from her drink, wiped her mouth with her sleeve, and considered. I'll put on something very sexy and just lie here. You know, with seduction. No certainly not, I'll go get some ice cream.

For now, she thought, Father Dominic is going to have to be garrotted, a piano wire slicing into his neck fat and a shower of arterial blood, without a whole lot of context, and we can allllllllll just deal with it.

At the gelato store Anna forgot what Magnus's favourite flavour was. She tapped along the sneeze guard with her house key trying to decide. Surely it wasn't plum-pistachio-whisky. The gelato man looked ill-humoured and she pitied him for having to wear such a silly hat. She got blood orange, mainly because she wanted it. Magnus still wasn't home, and she didn't write all night. She fell asleep on top of the quilt with her clothes still on and the blood orange gelato melting a blood orange puddle on the table.

SIXTEEN

Kirby and Peace were part of a movement called Climate Death Naturalist Society, Fearnoch chapter. Gord, president, Fearnoch chapter, usually held the meetings at his house, one of the new mansions by the river. Gord was downright dashing and Peace didn't hide her crush on him.

He's just a forty-year-old white guy, said Kirby, who isn't bald and isn't fat. With money. I could look like that if I don't get bald or fat, and have money. He shifted gears in the SUV, annoyed and motoring them down Fearnoch Road, close behind a tractor with a hay wagon. Or is it a cheekbone thing? What is it with girls and cheekbones? Loose hay blew off the wagon onto their windshield.

Peace traced a finger along the window at some sheep with their backs painted red.

It's his conviction, she said. That Gordie.

Gord had a foyer in his house, and a tree in the foyer in his house. It looked like a space fortress, built on good farmland too—good by Fearnoch standards. Up-lighted saplings blinded all neighbours at night.

There really was something about him, Kirby admitted to himself. He was very cordial with his guests and he walked around not fat and not bald using two hands to shake everyone's hand. He made his millions in the high-tech industrial parks of west-end Ottawa, developing and selling cyber-security software to larger firms, but that is, perhaps, too boring to even talk about. Now he wanted to give back, and he'd become a community organizer, a community advocate. He could yell and march and be part of something good and it felt superb and he felt less ashamed about all his money. He took over the causes of the less privileged. Reaching out, always reaching out to what he assumed were the less-privileged groups, such as the Algonquin folks up on the rez, and when they didn't respond, or emailed and said politely that they were good on their own, Gord would wonder to himself in his office what he was doing wrong and then vow to do better. Peace giggled when he whispered something to her. Kirby ate a lot of the various dips laid about, wiped his hands and accepted a beer in an impressive goblet.

I read there's good news about polar bears, he said to a lady who was eating a baby carrot. They say there's more of them than they thought.

That is not true—where did you read that? It's not true, said the lady with the carrot. There's no good news.

Okay, said Kirby.

Gord then sat up on the back of a chaise longue. He thanked everyone because he couldn't do it without them and then he got serious.

So some of you already know but there's a right-wing protest, a convoy that's going right through here then to Parliament Hill.

The group members were very quiet. Gord stood up.

And we're gonna counter-protest it, he said with his hands making a perpendicular angle, and he paused.

The group members then clapped. Peace drew her mouth up tight and nodded, and Kirby clapped his one free hand against his chest.

We have to let them know hate is not welcome here, Gord

continued, and the group got louder.

Peace raised her hand and said: What is the protest?

A great question, Peace, said Gord. From what I know it started out west as farmers protesting government regulation . . . he stopped and checked on his phone. Yes, but—it's attracted all the usual hate groups. It's a message of hate. Think they're gonna go dump milk everywhere.

We should do a barricade, said the lady with the carrot.

Gord got very excited, as did his group. Kirby felt the excitement start to creep up his skin, up his sleeves, along his neck, the little inklings and notes of revolution. And Gord poured it on. He spoke at length, getting louder and louder, with a few strands of his haircut falling in front of one eye. He covered everything from Trotsky to a Confederate flag sticker he saw on a four-wheeler to Gaia. He appealed to emotion. To paraphrase him here, he said: And on that subject, I have this to say, which, as we know, is correct.

So check Facebook for updates, Gord concluded as everyone got out of their seats. The event is on the Facebook group—Rosemary is it on the Facebook group? he asked, looking at the woman with the carrot.

Rosemary nodded.

Check Facebook, he said, and he made his hands into guns and did performative shooting motions back and forth at the two people closest to him.

Maybe Kirby would have his revolution. Gord while irksome, was useful in getting something, just anything going. Please, enough with the limbo, the sitting with emails, and gourds, getting beat to shit, beat to absolute shit at hockey. Just something where he could stand up and say, I'm Kirby, I'm still here on this planet and I've got some fight in me. I am not just a worthless civil servant eunuch with shit sperm. What he meant was let's fucking go here. At work they discussed if standing desks were in the budget and whether they should go home at two o'clock not three o'clock on Fridays.

Peace was sombre and bent her head on the drive home. I can't go because of the baby, she said. I haven't been to a protest in forever.

How long before we can tell people? Kirby said.

Oh Jesus a month . . . month at the very earliest. I don't wanna jinx this shit Kirby!

Last go around Kirby told everyone far too early.

Then I—I—will protest my heart out for all three of us, said Kirby. Giddy, he adjusted his glasses, gripped the steering wheel and put the pedal to the floor. The fightin' pride of the proletariat surged in his guts. Peace reached out and touched his ear.

You can wear my balaclava, she said.

Do you ever think though, said Kirby later at home, that Gord might be bullshit?

Peace was back at her beadwork.

Easy now, she said.

———

Mush rumbled down, really givin' 'er heat down John's laneway in a new side-by-side to tell him about the same protest. He'd been out mudding and mud drops like chocolate milk fell out of his beard. He wore large, mirrored-lens goggles which contorted his face into a dazed and imbecilic expression.

So . . . what is it? A rally? said John. His brain was far away, dealing with crop rotation and husbandry, and winter wheat, and wintering steers.

I don't know but everyone's going. They're coming right through Guthrie Place then here on the way down to Parliament Hill. I think it's to tell those fucking nerds in the government to fuck off. Goddamn fucking nerds. He leaned on the side-by-side. Look at the new side-by-each here buddy.

Well that sounds all right, said John, a finger on his chin thoughtfully. Do you want a pint?

Quick beer, quick beer here, said Mush, taking it from John. He pushed his goggles up his forehead. I'm bringing a cow, he said. You can bring some pigs or a cow. Drive your tractor down, that's what the lads are doing, take your combine—

I haven't got a combine, said John.

What kind of a farmer are you?

A poor as shit one buddy, you know that. He stared a long way off down a row of corn.

It's a good farm, a good farm, said Mush, looking around. A curled-over dead elm tree reflected off his goggles and mud continued to rain out of his beard. One of the barns was at such an angle it seemed an optical illusion or some type of backwoods hocus-pocus was keeping it upright. You got some Herefords here? He looked at John's herd. Shorthorns?

Yeah. Look at that one, said John, pointing at his prize calf. Got a bit of Holstein in him I think. Johnny's show-cow there.

Gorgeous. Gorgeous, said Mush. I like a Hereford. No need for these fancy new Europeans you see. I don't even know what's going on any more with cattle to be honest.

My cows eat almost exclusively rotten tubes of hay, John said proudly. He'd sold off all of his good rounds and squares.

Fearnoch cattle eh. Not fussy. Drunk off the silage again tonight, and he raised his pint up at the herd.

But they're all bologna in the end I guess.

They looked at the calf awhile, with their beers, then John said quietly: I'm done, Mush.

Mush thought and then spoke slowly. I'd say, he said, that the day of the family farm is over. But your land will be worth a lot if the city keeps coming. Farming's awful shit brutal work anyhow—you should get into that elevator repair, lad. He sounded like Polly.

I know it's shit but what isn't . . . it's my kind of shit work. But

I'm done, John said again.

Mush drank beer the same way Mush's father did, John had noticed. He'd talk and talk, gesturing around with the full beer, then at some juncture of the conversation he'd recall: Oh shit that's right I've got a pint here, and consume the entire thing instantly.

Mush handed John back the empty bottle.

Then c'mon downtown and we'll tell 'em to fuck off together, he said. This is Fearnoch! He hammered down the gas and ripped up the laneway.

SEVENTEEN

Both Kirby and John, independent of each other, asked Mikey if he would go to the protest or the counter-protest and Mikey told the both of them no.

Like I need any more pain and bullshit in my life, he said.

He had two appointments on one day, and he felt one would have been more than enough. The first was at the community centre to see Polly and the disadvantaged kids. He was nervous but he said to himself, raising one finger at his reflection in the rear-view mirror: A man needs responsibility. The outdoor rink had goldenrods and burdocks stuck up through the pavement near the boards, and past that, past the creek and cattails, a small procession of Highland cattle walked noble and quiet, ancient lords, through all the shit by the creek. Probably kids in Fearnoch weren't too fucked up—just loopy little hicks, Mikey figured.

Polly met him with a crying baby on her hip she was bouncing up and down.

Okay so thanks for coming Mikey, good lad, Polly said, I want you to keep an eye out for Jefferson. He's a sweet boy but he's got a temper, she said looking around the sea of children, presumably for Jefferson.

Jefferson, said Mikey.

Yeah, Jefferson, said Polly doing a shushing sound to the baby. What's that, his last name?

No it's his first name. He's tearing around here somewhere.

Mikey held his hands behind his back wondering which of these little hellions Jefferson could be.

Polly got closer to Mikey and Mikey felt some drool from the very wet baby stick on his arm. Jefferson struggles with FASD, she whispered, looking around to make sure no one heard. Just know that . . . you're not gonna understand some of the things he does, I guess.

What's FASD? Mikey asked, not in a whisper, and Polly's big eyes lit up.

Shh! It's called—Fetal Alcohol Spectrum Disorder.

Oh.

His dad's back in Peru and his mum—Polly looked around some more—you remember Shawna McKenzie? Maybe I shouldn't tell you that.

Oh sweet Jesus, said Mikey. Didn't they lock her up?

The story around Fearnoch was she'd beaten her boyfriend unconscious with a portable phone.

Yeah, well. I shouldn't have told you that. She grabbed his wrist. Forget that, she said.

In any case, I've already forgotten, said Mikey.

Anyway Jefferson's very sweet and I know he'll just love you . . . where the frig is he? said Polly, turning around. Where's Jefferson? she asked an old lady who sat in the armchair by the bookshelf full of donated, under-appreciated children's books.

He's here, said the lady, closing her eyes and leaning her head back in the chair. He's been making lots of bad decisions.

Mikey heard screams then and a boy with long, messy dark hair ran into the community centre carrying a large stick that had a lot of long wet grass stuck to it.

There's Jefferson, said the old lady without opening her eyes. About to make a bad decision.

Jefferson, said Polly. This is the man I told you about. She slowly eased the big, dirty, wet stick from his hands. This is Mikey. She rubbed Jefferson's back and nudged him towards Mikey.

Jefferson peered up at Mikey, his brown eyes large and guarded, a window cut into his ragged hair. He looked like a tiny hockey player with four front teeth gone and scars on his forehead and cheek.

Hi Jefferson, said Mikey. He put his hands on his knees and crouched down to the floor and figured he must look ridiculous. Dump-smell coming off his shirt and trying to pretend he knew anything about disadvantaged children. He stuck out his hand and wondered what to say. How old are you? was what he decided on.

Jefferson recoiled. He turned his head and put it into Polly's thigh.

How old are you? asked Polly, and when he remained mute she said, Seven, he's seven.

Jefferson spun his head around to Mikey and looked up at him again.

Oh, said Mikey. Great.

Why don't you show Mikey your colouring? said Polly. And Jefferson walked over to the table, with Mikey following, and sat on an exercise ball in front of an open colouring book, his page heavy with wax, the black and yellow scribbles. Mikey sat on a small beanbag at the knee-high table and felt humongous.

What're you drawing? he asked.

A bee, said Jefferson. Bumblebee. He pressed very hard and broke his yellow crayon. He looked up through his hair at Mikey for a moment, then re-addressed his bee.

It's beautiful, said Mikey. Have you ever been stung by a bee?

No, have you? said Jefferson.

Oh I've been stung mmm—fifty times? They love me. At the dump.

Actually I have been stung once.

Oh no.

Yes. He got in my drink-box. So I don't drink juice outside in the summertime now.

Oh, said Mikey, with his index finger on his lips. That's actually quite smart.

Do you want a drink-box?

Yes.

Jefferson got up and walked to the kitchen. He was wearing a faded SmackDown wrestling shirt that was too small and jeans that were too big. He came back presently with two juice boxes with the straws already stuck in them, plus a book about Angry Birds.

Look at this, he said, handing Mikey the book. He watched Mikey's reaction to the book and fit the straw into his mouth.

This looks great, said Mikey. Jefferson nodded and sucked on his juice box, the clear straw filling yellow.

Can you read it for me? Mikey asked.

Jefferson took the book. He cleared his throat and said, Angwy Buhds. Fuck, he said. I hate Rs.

I don't like Ds, said Mikey.

Jefferson read, but it was more describing the pictures than reading—this bird is angry, and oh this bird is angry, too—then he stopped and looked at Mikey and started back on his juice box.

Here, I can read a bit for us, Mikey said.

Jefferson brought his exercise ball around and sat next to Mikey. Mikey thought he liked Jefferson very much.

———

Then he had to go into town for his next appointment, which was at the clinic to see his therapist, Dr. Milks. The day sucked out of the

Gatineau hills, the hills bundled up and ran off with the day.

Once I was jolly, he thought. I haven't danced in a very long time.

He loathed these counselling sessions, hated every Kleenex, every concerned mm-hmm, every piece of therapy language. He felt Dr. Milks trying to dig around in his head, and what a funny notion, inviting someone into your brain: Sure, come in please, over here you see is the very deep awful hole and here, have a nice big glass of poison.

No, he thought, no I'm not being honest. It wasn't quite that he hated it, but that it made him feel like a pussy. If we're being honest. They should give his time slots to rape victims or war heroes or people who had to eat rats instead.

Mikey thought about just not going, just driving right past the clinic and into the Ottawa River. But of course that meant his folks might kick him out of the loft and he'd have to look for a job that paid more than fifteen dollars an hour and secretly he didn't even have his high school and he'd have to buy new clothes and get a résumé and LinkedIn and probably have to go to town more and talk to more people.

Maybe he should take a bunch of pills that fucked his liver or pancreas but realigned his brain chemistry and made him normal so he could talk to all kinds of people. Confidently, with lots of enjoyable laughs, and he'd enjoy it and they'd enjoy it. Maybe he could go to a museum gala or something in town.

Hello, I'm Mikey, he would say. I work at the dump and my social skills have taken a big hit and if I have any more than these three beers here there is a chance I could go insane and get pee on myself.

Dr. Milks took her glasses off. Mikey, she said. Mikey. You have to start talking soon. I can't do my job if you don't talk.

I don't want to talk about myself, Mikey said.

She came out from her desk and imposed herself into the leather armchair next to him. Every type of lie she sensed and obliterated immediately.

Can't you be Freud and just tell me about my dreams and everything that's wrong with me? Mikey asked. I'll just lie down in the corner. Look—I have nightmares about Soviet POWs, I think my history books are driving me batty, history comes for all of us, and it always ends in slaughters and famine. Enjoy your nonsense now for the end is coming—these are my dreams. He felt a little bad Dr. Milks had to put up with him. I don't want to talk about myself, he said again.

I don't work like that. Only you can help yourself. I only try to keep you on the road, she said, making a driving motion with her hands.

I d—don't wanna talk about myself, Mikey said. He felt along the brass studs on the handle of his leather armchair.

Dr. Milks glared at him. She looked at her watch then glared some more.

Mikey was a little rattled so he said: Everyone talks about themselves too much and we're none of us as special as we think we are. We're just little bits of something bigger. Mikey thought he was being quite eloquent, actually, and it was something he'd been working over in his head among the rust-heaps at the dump.

Okay so what do you want to talk about?

Mikey thought. The fall of empires, he said.

What about work? Did you get union yet?

No. I don't wanna talk about work.

If you get union in a few years it's pretty good money.

I don't wanna work at a dump. PTSD Ed says it'll make you miserable. But I've been reading about the fall of empires. Like the fall of Rome.

And what do you make of the fall of Rome then?

I think it's the same as what's happening right now. We're as soft and luxurious and fat as fifth-century Romans. Or maybe Romanovs. Or Habsburgs or Seleucids. Or France in 1940. Mikey put his chin in his hand and tried to make the right analogy. No, we're Romans, he said, figuring Romans were the easiest to pick on.

Dr. Milks pulled at her sweater. Mm-hmm. Are we Mikey?

They got sacked, sacked real bad.

Mm-hmm.

The tiniest thing will just flick us over now. We have trouble enough with our feelings—how're we gonna handle barbarians? There's always barbarians.

Hmm.

We live in frivolous times, said Mikey. Christ almighty do we ever.

You know, I've heard this Rome thing before. The world is full of dismal men who think it's all over. Just spend some time with my husband and his hunting buddies.

Mikey was annoyed because he thought frivolous times was his great idea. Well, good, he said. Good. It'll happen, I think.

What?

You'll see one day King Alaric is gonna just walk right in through those gates—he pointed his finger out the window—like a weirdo with a dead bird on his helmet. I dunno, that's how I imagined it, I don't really know what I'm talking about. And we'll be sacked. Because we're lazy and useless. Because we're too comfortable.

Mm-hmm, she said.

Well I'm not trying to say I'm not lazy and useless. I'm definitely not trying to say that. The difference is that I know I'm lazy and useless, so I keep quiet. Mikey folded his arms and looked pleased with his reasoning.

Dr. Milks was old friends with Mikey's mum and she did these sessions at a discounted rate. To her Mikey was the boy ripping through the cornfield with ridiculous poofy hair, covered in mud, with a T-shirt from a museum with pictures of insects from the new exhibit or something like that on it. Curious but too sensitive for the world and crying about how his pixie-dust wasn't working or crying about his Anne Frank book. The world burned a little too real for Mikey.

Why?! Little Mikey said then, with his little arms shaking his Anne Frank book. Why?!

And Dr. Milks thought he had a point then.

Mikey, she said, I think you're taking a little too much pleasure in the sack of Rome and all this death of empires. You're not looking for solutions. Worry about you, what you can do today—not Ancient Rome for heaven's sake.

Heuuuggghhh, said Mikey and his mood went off a cliff. He felt he could see the word spineless projected on the wall, even taste the word, which was like an acrid, overripe banana.

Yes, I know, I know, he said. He scratched his hair. Nothing's fair, not for anyone. I work with a man who ate rats.

Are you taking your pills? Dr. Milks asked.

Yes.

I think this is one of your better sessions, she said, making some notes.

EIGHTEEN

Ebenezer's mother had two jobs, sometimes three, and wasn't home much when Ebenezer was a young lad. Little Ebenezer grew up angry and worried much of the time. Anger and Worry followed him around like two tiny, ragged spirits. Mostly he worried for his sister—she was so small, barely spoke, and got teased. He worried until he could truly and physically feel the worries going down through his veins and vital organs. And Anger always came with Worry. His sister cried silently, like when she didn't want to go to school, refusing to get her snow boots on, or when he wouldn't give her the Nintendo controller. Sometimes he would give in to bitterness back then and he was mean to her because she was the only other person there. And then after he was mean, Ebenezer would try anything to get her to stop crying and start laughing and talking—dance for her or let her punch him on the shoulder. He'd made her toast, and soup, reaching on tiptoes for the plates.

Toast, his sister said, toast again?

Soup then, he said. He only knew how to make toast and soup.

Do the penguin dance, said his sister. Ebenezer put down the can opener and did a waddling, flapping sort of dance that his sister thought was a penguin dance.

His sister cackled and swung her feet under the chair. She

coughed a spume of crumbs.

Like many young men, Ebenezer wanted to be tough. If he grew up in Fearnoch, that might mean getting a lot of penalties in hockey. Or drinking pints and getting in the brawls at the Guthrie Place Fair. With the Johns and Mikeys of the world he could have drunk and drove the Fearnoch side roads, then got a job in the trades, then got a nice gut. But in Ebenezer's world, tough meant gangs.

His job in the gang was to pretty much do whatever Fatty said. Fatty was what Ebenezer could become in about ten years, if he got even angrier, and stayed alive, and gained two hundred pounds.

Fatty gave Ebenezer and his best friend Bernard an old handgun and no bullets.

It's for robbing people, Fatty said. He winced and swallowed, full of peptic acid and cocaine. Don't ask me again.

But there's no bullets, said Bernard. He fiddled with it, trying to open the chamber.

Well I don't have any bullets, said Fatty. He had a lot on his mind. His daughter was sick. The police were on him. A big Blood head was out of jail and on him.

What is this all about? Ebenezer asked, cradling a giant conch he found on Fatty's shelf.

You be very careful with that, said Fatty.

So Ebenezer and Bernard took turns scaring boys from the rival housing projects with the gun. They threatened with the useless gun and they climbed up through windows and took drugs, money, phones, PlayStations, necklaces, whatever they thought of, even a bag of chips. They got in trouble if they didn't steal enough. Sometimes Fatty accompanied them to make sure his standards were being kept, but he usually waited outside under a tree or awning, sweaty as all hell.

There's no way this would work, said Bernard. He pointed the gun down at Ebenezer's head because he was much taller. They were sitting on their bicycles behind the Couche-Tard waiting for Fatty.

Don't point it, said Ebenezer and smacked his hand.

Bernard looked at the gun some more, the gun rusty and short, and then tucked it into the top of his pants and frowned at how it looked. It didn't look at all like something from a rap video, but more like something an old white lady would have in a dresser.

Ebenezer was looking at his phone. A girl from class had been sending him nude photographs all day, from the moment he woke up. More rattled in, lighting up his phone—she was in her room pushing her lips together in a pout and putting two fingers to her mouth, clicking and sending away to Ebenezer.

Crisse, said Ebenezer, looking at this onslaught of soft electric nudity. I wonder if she's trying to send these to someone else.

He wrote: Are these for me?

Let me see that—who is it?! Bernard lunged for the phone.

The response was a whole series of hearts and kisses. Ebenezer was quite pleased about that. Bernard lunged again and tripped on his bicycle, which made Ebenezer trip on his bicycle, both of them to the pavement by the dumpsters behind the Couche-Tard.

No! Ebenezer shouted, stretching the phone away from Bernard.

Fatty was watching them and sweating through the front of his elephantine blue shirt. He walked closer with his shadow preceding him like the devil wings of some fucked hell-falcon riding in to pick off hares. Ebenezer and Bernard felt the shadow and then saw Fatty and saw that he had two older boys with him. Fatty put an arm around each of the boys.

This is Ronald, he said tapping one on the shoulder, and Shitty, he said, tapping the other. They're coming to make sure you don't fuck up like the other time eh là, he said.

Ronald had his eyes hidden by a baseball hat and one gold tooth. Shitty was missing a front tooth. It was true Ebenezer and Bernard had been robbing the wrong places, busting in windows and finding little more than some rolling papers or a single onion.

They were supposed to burgle a home belonging to the parents of a drug dealer with whom Fatty had a tremendous and bloody beef. He wanted to send a message, and Ronald and Shitty were there to take care of things if the parents showed up. Fatty was taking too many drugs these days to make any sort of methodical calculation, shaking more and more coke rocks out, walking in circles and mumbling about getting gunned up or gunning someone up.

Take everything, beat everyone up, he said to the boys. I don't know. If you see Marc-Antoine, cocksucker, just . . . saw his head off. Bring me his heart and I'll eat it.

After this inspiring talk of sorts, Fatty slowly walked away in his flattened flip-flops.

Of all the daughters born in the world every day, he wondered, each one of them with a one-in-fifteen-thousand chance of having severe childhood epilepsy, why for the love of God was it his daughter that had it? Barely been born and sometimes shaking violently for fifteen minutes straight, sometimes two or three in one night. The funny thing was he didn't even want to acknowledge the child and certainly never wanted to see her mother again, but the little creature looked up at him and shook all over the place and his fat evil heart broke.

———

Anna couldn't imagine what committing a robbery or battering someone was like. She could try, one of her characters was a burglar after all, but she couldn't even pretend to know what it felt like, what it sounded like and smelled like for Ebenezer, she couldn't go down his horrible insomniac road with him, and her language always dropped short. She was lying, it was clear, when she described her burglar's robberies. She would write something, get up from her computer to go pee, think of something, write it down, look at it and go off to pee again, and look at it again and still her language was not honest.

I'm not very good at robberies, said Ebenezer. It was the middle of the night and he couldn't sleep so he was up making his Kool-Aid in the kitchen. He had a blue bandana tied on his head and a blue blanket wrapped around him and wished there was blue Kool-Aid. Anna was sleepwalking through another night shift after an evening shift at Café Plus and had ventured to ask him about robbing.

I hope you don't do it anymore, she said. She took a sip of coffee and then scowled at the cup. Jesus Christ this coffee tasted like a pen exploded in it. Oh! I like that. She hunted around in her backpack for her notebook.

What?

Anna had lost another notebook. Ebenezer can you help me remember this? Remember—this coffee tastes like a pen exploded in it.

———

For Ebenezer's last robbery, Ronald and Shitty waited outside while Ebenezer and Bernard tiptoed around and filled up Bernard's backpack.

We're in the wrong house again, said Bernard. He gave Ebenezer an iPad and a fancy heavy watch, then spun around so he could zip them up in the backpack.

Ebenezer explored the house, silent and fascinated. This is how some people live, he thought. Everything was wood, the shelves, the desks, all deep and shiny. There were whole walls of books and he looked at a large painting of a herd of horses charging through a river.

Maybe it's like professor gangsters, said Bernard.

Look at this, said Ebenezer. He put on an immense furry hat the size and shape of a large birthday cake and pointed at it.

This, he said, is a hat.

Bernard nodded, impressed, and then the front door opened.

Bernard and Ebenezer froze and looked at each other with the whites of their eyes shining out. A small and round old white man entered with keys jingling, his top half obstructed by a large potted flowery bush. Ebenezer could see the top of his shiny bald head over the flowery bush and his corduroys and old-man shoes beneath. The man set the flower-bush down by the door.

Phew, the man said, phew, and stretched his back before turning and noticing in his kitchen there appeared to be two Haitian boys, one wearing a shtreimel. The little man looked from Bernard to Ebenezer and slowly opened his mouth. Ebenezer would remember this delicate little moment when he couldn't sleep at Centre Saint-Savard. The man's mouth open and wet, one hand up against the back of his head while he put together what was going on. The hot fur of the hat and the man's corduroys.

But before the man could say anything, Ronald and Shitty came in behind, sent him flying through the door and shut it. Shitty had a handgun that looked like it would work just fine. The man cried out and sprawled down on the floor.

Stay down, said Shitty. Reste—stay there, he said. Ebenezer, which one of you is Ebenezer?—Écoute Ebenezer fuck eh là! Get some rope. Va—stay there! he said with an explosion of spit and kicked the man, who cried out again and covered his face down by the flower-bush.

We're in the wrong house, Ronald said. He scratched himself on the chest.

Yes, said Ebenezer. Bernard stayed behind the countertop staring at the old man, whose hands shook over his face.

Let's just go, said Ebenezer.

Get some rope. Or duct tape, said Shitty.

Ebenezer went and looked for rope or duct tape. He shook, his hearing went in and out and he forgot what he was looking for, so he just looked around. He saw more old books and black-and-white photographs on the wall. There was a photograph propped up on a table of a beautiful young woman standing in front of an olden-days car with her hair blowing and her mouth open like she was laughing. Ebenezer remembered he was still wearing the hat. He took it off and laid it down in front of the photograph. He hoped they could leave soon.

Ebenezer! Shitty shouted again, and Ebenezer went back into the kitchen. Bernard had one of those big packing tape dispensers and was cocooning the old man, mummifying him. Bernard wound it, fed it through the man's jaws and around the back of his head. The man wheezed on the tape and looked at Ebenezer.

Let's just go, Ebenezer said. It's not the right house.

Ronald dwarfed Ebenezer and Shitty squeezed Ebenezer's collarbone from behind. Eh là, he said. He twisted Ebenezer around and shoved him towards the old man on the floor. Take the tape off his mouth, Shitty said.

Ebenezer got on his knees by the old man. He found the end of the tape sticking out beside one ear and twisted the mess of tape off. It was slick with blood and spit.

Don't scream, he said. The man breathed heavily, drooling onto the floor.

I'm eating something from the fridge, said Shitty. Ask him if he knows Marc-Antoine's parents.

Do you know Marc-Antoine's parents? Ebenezer relayed.

The man said nothing, just breathed and stared.

He doesn't know, said Ebenezer from his knees. I think he's hurt.

Ronald and Shitty whispered between themselves in the kitchen. Ronald looked unnerved. A few weeks after this current incident he was shot in the chest and stomach outside a strip club in Laval and pronounced dead at the hospital as Shitty waited, in anguish in the waiting room with blood on his shirt and pants, to hear about his friend.

Ask him again, said Ronald after a moment.

Why would this old white man know anything about Marc-Antoine? asked Ebenezer.

Câlice let me think, Ronald said.

Shitty was more decisive; he didn't need to think, he ran over with the gun out, shoved Ebenezer and held it right in front of the man's nose. Ebenezer cracked his own head off a small table by the door, the man screamed cross-eyed looking at the gun, Ronald paced back and forth waving his hands beside his ears and Bernard started to cry.

Where's Marc-Antoine?

The man shook his head.

Where's Marc-Antoine? Shitty said louder. Are you gonna stay quiet? he added.

Ebenezer steadied himself and rubbed the sore spot at the back of his head, which was hot and wet. He was angry.

Ebenezer—is it Ebenezer?—give him a kick, said Shitty.

Ebenezer shook his head.

Give him a kick.

No, said Ebenezer. Violence was his first language. He had no problem with fights and blood and people crying. Everyone gets the shit knocked out of them sometimes. But he looked at the very old man twisted on the floor in his olive corduroys and old-man shoes. He looked at his eyes and said no firmly.

Fuck, said Shitty, and booted the man.

Around this point in the story, the man, whose name was Mr. Bachmann, around this time he figured he was half-dead anyhow, and his wife was dead and he missed her and he'd had enough. And he figured his parents didn't survive the Holocaust and come to Canada speaking only Yiddish and sew buttons and cobble shoes to put him through law school so that the Bachmanns went from penniless to rich in one generation, just for these young bastards to rob him, kick him and wear his shtreimel.

He shook in his cocoon and began to shout every awful thing he could think of about these boys, Marc-Antoine, whoever that was, and youth and criminality in general. He shouted some awful things about Haiti, where he assumed they came from, and shouted about his shtreimel.

I'm gonna tape him back up, said Ebenenzer, thinking it was the only thing to do.

Mr. Bachmann switched to Yiddish and closed his eyes and continued shouting.

Shitty's eyes went wide behind his gun. I could shoot him right in his brain, he said.

Shhh, shhh! Ebenezer said, back on his knees, with his head smarting, and fumbling for the end of the tape on the tape dispenser. Still Bernard cried and Ronald paced and Ebenezer expected the gun to go off any minute. He stretched out the tape and stuck it to Mr. Bachmann's ear. Mr. Bachmann opened his eyes and bit Ebenezer on the hand.

Ebenezer cried out and struck Mr. Bachmann on the head with the tape dispenser. He punched at the old man, and kicked him, and heard himself scream, felt the blood boiling in his skull and began his lifetime of guilt. He backed away as Mr. Bachmann continued his Yiddish in his cocoon and then there were sirens and the room glowed red then blue, red then blue, and the boys ran.

———

Anna froze, folding dishcloths and washcloths, shocked that Ebenezer was recounting this to her. She wondered if she should call a more experienced staff on the Centre Saint-Savard emergency phone.

You've been carrying this around the whole time? she asked. You didn't tell anyone? No one?

Ebenezer poked his head out from his folded arms.

I kicked him, he said. I hit him. I didn't have to.

Anna sat beside him with the dishcloths folded in squares on her lap. Well, maybe you can talk to this Bachmann. Maybe I can talk to him. She knew nothing of these matters.

Ebenezer remembered Mr. Bachmann's devastating stare from court.

You've almost served your time—you're almost there Ebenezer, said Anna, wishing she had some answer, or anything worth saying at all.

———

When the police came, Ebenezer stayed quiet and didn't struggle when they put the cuffs on. He'd been arrested before, sure, but this one was big—robbery, assault, unlawful confinement. He stayed quiet, said nothing to the police, because you're not supposed to say anything to the police. Ebenezer was, or possibly was, many things: criminal, victim, survivor, gangster, good brother, bad son, bilingual, Haitian, Canadian, Haitian-Canadian, receiver of nude photographs, abused child, murderer, honest, liar. But one thing he was not was a rat-goof. He wanted Anna to take him away to where she came from, where he dreamed there were quiet, dark, empty fields and big horses charging through the rivers.

NINETEEN

Anna wasn't sure what to do about Magnus. He was either a puppy, batting at her hair and trying to kiss, or aloof and unreachable, cold to the touch. He could be two different people. Even his eyes would change shape and colour. Maybe she should dump him. What was all this anyhow—wasn't a relationship supposed to be you like each other, you date, you laugh, you're nice to each other, treat each other well, you have sex, and it's nice and good, most of the time? Maybe things were different here in reality and she was just a Valley hick idiot.

He lost it when she questioned, really just brushed up against the idea that he might not know exactly what he was talking about with such assurance. It was not the right thing to brush against. He stomped around the apartment and said later that he overreacted because he was hungry. Anna herself didn't treat people poorly if she hadn't had lunch yet. He said her writing was too sentimental, too romantic, and then she overreacted and said, well maybe, but if it's not for sentiment and romance, then what the fuck is it for?

Anna buttoned on a plaid shirt with her tongue sticking out the side of her mouth in the mirror. It was a strange tartan of yellow, purple and green, the fabric covered in those tiny little balls that cheap, old shirts get. The shirt was too short—why are shirts all too short and too wide—and she ripped it off and sighed at herself. She wouldn't dump him. She didn't know how to dump someone. He wasn't so bad, and if she was honest, she didn't want to go back to being alone right now. A tiny cold planet again spinning around Montreal, afraid of everyone.

This is hopeless, Magnus said. What kind of a lunatic does this to himself?

He had his pencil in his teeth and was talking about his poetry. His sonnet was a meditation on, or an encountering with, an engaging with, how his love was a ship out at sea. It wasn't doing very well. Every publication was sending it back or not even getting back mostly.

Anna had a stout heart, for the moment anyhow, about writing. We have to respect the words, she said. We gotta cherish the language and not lie. No more corruption of language—that's where the evil comes from.

Where'd you hear that from?

I'm not sure.

Why are you writing a novel then? he asked, letting his hand fall off her shoulder down her back.

Anna drew in a deep breath.

Because I used to be smart, I was smart, then I fucked up in university, because I was weak, and I have no idea what to do about jobs, except to clean shit up off the floor at different places, and this is the only way I know I'm still here. She made a fist and knocked on her head. And to cherish language also, too, she added.

Well maybe one day, with enough work, and edits, and years, there is an outside chance someone might come around to beginning to consider the possibility of taking a look at the first three paragraphs, Magnus said.

Anna laughed. Oh Lord, she said.

Sorry, he added.

All my characters are saying things no one has ever said in real life, said Anna, turning and staring at her computer screen. Disquieted. I am disquieted. That's an odd word, Magnus, eh?

———

At Café Plus, Anna walked in, whistling away with her shirt too short. Yvette folded her arms, all the old tattoos creased over the starchy apron, and nodded at Océane.

Anna, Océane said, Yvette said you are writing.

Anna tied on her apron and looked from Yvette to Océane.

Yes, well, um, she said. A mystery novel.

What's it called? Océane asked.

Cube, said Anna. She loathed titles and had taken to assigning it arbitrary nouns or numbers. Last year it was *Four*. She wanted something hallowed for the title, like something from the Bible or Shakespeare, but hadn't figured that out yet.

I'm also writing, said Océane, pointing at her chest. I'm a poet.

Poetry, said Anna.

Can I read what you've got? Will you read it for me?

Okay.

You can—you will come to my writing group tonight? Are you in a writing group?

No, sometimes I share with my boyfriend or my mum.

Océane reached back and fixed her already perfect hair. Mais non, Anna câlice you need a writing group. It is hell—do not go dere alone! She wagged her finger.

Okay I'll go! Anna loved this new Océane. Thank you, really. I don't know if it's any good.

Océane laced her fingers through Anna's hand and raised her hand up with hers. She shook both their hands in the air with an energetic, devilish grin and then went and smoked darts with Yvette, who also seemed very happy, grinning away with her chipped tooth.

And so that night Anna put her laptop in her backpack, took the metro from Pie-IX to Parc-Ex and met Océane and two of her poet buddies to share and comment on writing, with wine and snacks. It was a lovely evening and all the windows in the apartment were opened high as they'd go with the curtains fluttering and dancing in and they laughed. One of the poet buddies said writing was like that Sunday evening feeling and you hadn't done your homework yet, but forever. Océane said she thought maybe writing was like being pregnant. Sick all over the place and you carry it to term then release it fucked up into the world, and worry.

J'attends un poème là, she said and opened a cracker box. Un poème vraiment cute là.

When it was Anna's turn she got very nervous. She was aware of her face full of wine, felt her face move and heard her voice as she started to read very slowly. The scene she'd chosen for the group was yet another murder scene. This time it was the unheralded downfall of a retired Giant Tiger manager with sleep apnea who was bludgeoned with an old auger by an unseen antagonist at an agrarian venue based on her recollection of Fearnoch Livestock Sales from when she was a girl in 4-H. She had tried to pack in as many strange ideas and words into the death scene as she could, to make it particular. Words she wanted to guide in to shore, like: guileless, gormless, and parishioner. Other words she wanted to eschew, like—well eschew for one, and austere—we're not feeling austere this year. At least have a bit of goddamn fun with it. These poets listened with their wine and their mouths open. Then the former Giant Tiger manager died in ineffable pain, the sun shining onto his opened brain, and Anna said, okay and I'll stop there, thank you for listening.

It was quiet, except for the curtains. The poets stared at her, frozen, mute, and Océane had a tear in a big streak down her cheek.

She sniffed and whispered, tu me niaises crisse. She wiped her face, shook her head, then began to laugh. Anna! she said, and smacked her on the back.

Anna fell over to one side and hid her head in a pillow. She didn't know if she would laugh, cry, or fall asleep.

This whole time you had that, and you didn't tell me, Océane said.

So it's good? Anna had half her face out of the pillow.

It is . . . magnificent, said Océane. Fucking . . .

La poésie, said one of the poets quietly.

Anna rolled her face back into the pillow and said: Oh my God I thought it was shit! And laughed and laughed and started hiccupping. Thank you, thank you, she said.

They all went and sat on the balcony with their legs swinging off, lit the candles, the warm breeze blowing every fabric and every strand of hair around and everything about the world was better and in love. The smells, winds, and atomic transactions, everything glowed and breathed better.

TWENTY

Several of Kirby's colleagues noticed he might actually be shrinking. Stooped, hunched, back all fused up and rounded, looking more and more at the ground, he felt hungover without drinking anything the night before. It was true—he was a tiny bit smaller each day.

His very first day, long ago now, he charged in early and valorous, standing tall in the fresh pleated pants, ready to give 'er. He'd dive into all open files, work through the night if needed, alone, a single light in all the dark brick and glass. Kirby would take on all the files, and woe to the oppressors.

Although each day he was told no, not yet, no, just wait, there isn't a project at this time, just wait. And so he shrank, little by little. All he'd wanted was to help. Now he crawled into work, bent like an old hag, hacking and cursing and stuffed up to the brim with nonsensical emails. When it came that he did get a file, he didn't understand it of course, and felt he missed the acceptable window in which to say he didn't understand it. Then, after it was put on ice, he understood the next file even less. He rubbed the back of his neck and looked and looked at it, trying to will it into some kind of sense. But he was getting the feeling it didn't matter anyway. He took off his glasses and was very sad a moment. He didn't bellyache to anyone but Peace because he was lucky to have a job.

Just tell your boss this is fucking stupid, said Peace, and she probably actually would do that if it was her.

That's not really how this works, said Kirby. He was exhausted, even though he got a good sleep and didn't do anything all day.

Peace was already thinking about something else. She had no time for anything boring. Her mother had raised her naked among the cedars, with no rules, no expectations except love and peace, no shut the fuck up and listen, Peace, child. She wandered away to go and try to organize a potluck.

Kirby drew himself together and spoke with Mrs. Tremblay the next day.

Are there any new files? he asked. Any new big complaints?

I just need you to sit tight, Kirby, she said. How about the POCC? Did you email the TR3?

Kirby had a headache just trying to listen and play along. His chest tightened, even his bag ached. They were going to run out of acronyms. Or start speaking exclusively in them.

I don't understand what I'm doing, he said.

Okay.

I have never understood what I'm doing here.

Ah. Okay—nothing?

Nothing.

You should take some leave, I think, Kirby. You look awful. Mrs. Tremblay let out her breath slowly, concerned, a small scarf knotted at one side of her neck.

I don't want time off! I want to help!

No, I'm going to insist. The leave is there for a reason.

So, I'm on stress leave because I'm stressed about how there's nothing for me to do at work.

Mrs. Tremblay stood up to begin the procedure of Kirby leaving her office so she could get back to work. You're taking some personal time to recharge, she said. Kirby, you're just one piece of a massive operation. You'll have days where you don't think you're making a difference, believe me. Talk to HR, I'll see you in a few weeks, fresh as ever. She patted his arm.

There's a lot of people not making any difference around here, Kirby said, getting reckless. Seems to me there's almost too much government here.

Well you're the socialist, Kirby, said Mrs. Tremblay. You can leave that open, thanks.

———

Kirby went home and he shut the garage door on all his new suburb neighbours and ignored them and they ignored him also. He went on the internet and looked at the news, which really was just a series of: Here's another little story that's gonna make you a little bit pissed.

Then he made chicken because he wanted chicken and forgot for a moment that Peace, while pregnant, threw up at even the mention of chicken. She was out with the rest of the Community Association at the quilting bee. Kirby sat with his chicken on the chesterfield.

What would his heroes of revolution do? he thought. Probably not sit around with chicken, and then he heard Peace cough outside and open the door and remembered about the chicken.

Peace entered like a cyclone, talking before she was entirely through the door.

Kirby dear, you're home! she kissed him on the top of his head. Look at this. She turned and posed, holding her stomach. Getting a gut almost!

She put down her bag and continued, I had some good news, I was talking to Dorothy at the Association and there's a job opening in town—inclusion officer with the vice-equity provost! Doesn't that sound like me? And, you know what my shaman says, or sorry no it was my energy wellness practitioner that says—oh my God is that chicken—and she instantly turned and ripped a gargantuan and bright pink barf across the hardwood.

Then she yelled at Kirby for a long time, barfing more, and fair enough, he thought. Pregnancy was barf and yelling.

Peace ate mainly turnips at the moment. My child is going be almost exclusively constituted from turnips, thought Kirby. He packed up his hockey bag and didn't tell Peace he was on stress leave.

TWENTY-ONE

John was excitable on the drive to hockey. Larocque keep your head up tonight lad! he yelled, shaking his knees.

Mikey wasn't as excited and he drove very slow in the pre-owned sedan, distracted by the sunset. He did wonder why they had to play these French wizards so often. It would be nice for once to run up his stats against one of the shit teams.

Yet a masterpiece of mammoth sky held over Fearnoch. The last summer days detonated and burned mute, lilac cirrus like vertebrae in the east, the deep orange benediction of heavens to the west. And Mikey felt the weight of heaven on the pre-owned sedan, he felt a prehistoric humility beneath glowing guts of clouds bigger than his entire township.

Nothing really meant a whole frig of a lot under these frescoes of painted atmosphere: the thin soils of Fearnoch on the bedrock, fields stitched and hemmed over the hill, Mush exhausted, with the sun in his eyes, ripping Labatts in his work van and his father ripping an expertly clandestine greasy public piss onto his backhoe. The Younghusband log barns with the sheet-metal roofs, Polly and Johnny snoozing before her night shift, the cows licking at roots and each other, the hawks riding up their gyres and the day sneaking behind the silos. There's really only so many ways to describe common sunsets and cows in sunsets, lazy in the sunsets, but it was plain, easy, dull and beautiful. Everything was only a little ribbon, Mikey reflected, but they fit everything they had in there. They filled what they had with their content. They loved each other and hated each other, played hockey and they drank 50. The breeze turned and the trees shifted.

Mikey, said John and he grabbed the steering wheel.

But John was also enchanted now that he looked at the cows in the sun. He wanted to go for a walk down below by the tracks with Polly and Johnny and just stand under all that orange and purple. The world could go and do what it wanted, as long as he and his family had the rectangle of acres under the sky, from the road to the tracks, and he'd put in work, make babies, then die. That was all he needed from his time on the planet. But not yet, tonight—tonight was for the sermons of the hockey barn.

The Lord took his time making Fearnoch, he said, to make sure He got 'er just right. John was being cheesy but he was emotional. He squeezed Mikey's shoulder. Big game, big game Mikey lad, oh we have a new player tonight, I forgot to say.

Well hopefully he knows how to score eight fucking goals, said Mikey.

She.

Oh.

She responded to my ad in the *Weekender*.

You put an ad in the *Weekender*?

Yeah she said she played university-level.

You try Mush?

No, lifetime ban.

Yeah fucking Mush.

———

At the rink there were about eleven people in the stands. A few old-timers in Fearnoch Syrup Kings jackets talked with their twangs, basked in the rink-smell, gestured with large deer pepperettes and beer in old Hortons cups. One Québécois girlfriend sat frozen and annoyed with a blanket on her lap and the tip of her nose red.

Wee crowd tonight! said John. He debated going no-bucket for warm-up.

Kirby filled up the water bottles in the dressing-room bathroom, John put the box of beer on the Zamboni snow, and Mikey went through his superstitions as he dressed. Right shin pad before left, always, tap the goalie's pads twice. And then Stella came in.

Oh Jesus, said Mikey.

Yeah thanks for the invite there Mikey, said Stella in a growl. She put her much shorter sticks with the others against the wall and found a spot among all the Codys and Coreys.

Boys this is our new player, um . . . said John, pausing.

Stella, said Stella.

Stella, said John. What position you like? he asked and handed her a Fearnoch sweater.

I usually go middle.

Okay. Let's try you centring . . . he looked around, a little confused that Mikey was glaring at him. Mikey's line? Shake it up here.

John sat back down next to Mikey, and Mikey whispered, that's the dump-babe!

What?

I thought you said she was beautiful, Kirby whispered.

Look at her! Mikey hissed, pointing at Stella with an elbow pad.

Stella got up, took one of her sticks and started to roll it back and forth in her hands. She stared at the ground, shaking her head and talking quietly to herself.

She looks frigging nuts buddy, said John.

Why'd you put her on the team? said Mikey. This is the one night a week I get to be myself and not worry about shit.

What do you want me to do? John said. We need skaters—she's from Thunder Bay for Jesus' sake! Stella pulled her shoulder pads over her head, blew some loose hair out of her face and nodded at John.

Ready to fucking go, coach, said Stella.

———

And Stella could play. From puck drop, it was obvious the smallest player was going to exert her will on the game. She was maybe even better than John, and people in Fearnoch used to say, when he was about eleven or twelve, John could make the N one day. Stella dangled and toe-dragged all over the place with her braids whipping around, dummied the Pontiac defence, howling for the puck in the corner. The old-timers stopped discussing refrigeration units and how many cows they were milking and they watched. The Zamboni driver by the gate threw his cigarette out the back and came in to watch too. The French girlfriend, who was tired of being called a puck bunny, put away her phone and cheered for Stella. She went down and banged on the glass. John was ecstatic.

Not bad Mikey, John said, and he hopped the boards. Got any more players at the dump there?

Good . . . fucking . . . heavens, Mikey whispered, watching her flat-out fly down the wing.

The Pontiac side got out to an early 2-0 lead, but it would not be a blowout tonight. Mikey dug the puck out for Stella before Larocque pitchforked him down to the ice.

Yes Mikey! Not afraid to take a hit to make a play! Kirby shouted from the bench, beating his stick on the boards.

Stella paused with the puck and drew two defenders towards her before backhanding a pass to John, all alone, and he stepped into it, he really got everything on it and crushed it bar-down, in that sweet spot by the 'tendy's ear. 2-1.

Now angry they wouldn't get to cakewalk through Fearnoch again, the Quebecers started to push back. Larocque was hitting everything that moved, and hotdogger Laframboise in the white skates hogged the puck more and more, trying to score highlight-reel goals without using his teammates.

At second intermission it remained 2-1. The Fearnoch team huddled by the home bench. They wheezed and leaned on their sticks, exhausted but proud they were making a game of it in their barn.

One more period, said John. He waited as one of the Codys spat a huge plug of dip out. Stella, he said, you just keep fucking givin' 'er like that. Mikey—get open, give her something to pass to. One more period. Get to work in those corners. Twenty minutes for one goal boys. And I'll tell you right fucking now, they're not going to get shit past us on defence. He patted Kirby hard on the chest, on the Syrup Kings crest.

The Quebecers collapsed around their goalie, at this point content to defend their citadel and not push for more goals. They sacrificed their bodies, dropping to the ice and throwing themselves in front of every shot. With three minutes on the clock it was still 2-1. The Fearnoch team were peppering the French goal, but every shot was hitting a stick, a shin pad, a skate, an arm, deflecting into the corner or up into the stands. Stella found some room with the puck, spun and wired it on net, but a Pontiac defenceman got in front of it and took it right off the cage. He groaned and rolled onto his side and the referee whistled the play dead.

If you can't take it, stay the fuck out my kitchen, said Stella, annoyed and skating to the bench.

The only Quebec player trying to do anything on offence, of course, was Laframboise. With all the Fearnoch forwards driving the net, no one was paying him much attention. One of Mikey's shots hit a skate, and it was a mighty carom, right onto the stick of Laframboise, who in turn wheeled around hard on his edges and performed an elegant toe-drag around one of the Codys. It looked like he might have a clear lane, a breakaway in on the Fearnoch goalie, who was terrified of this man's deceptive skills.

But as he crossed the blue line, John and Kirby, ferocious and valiant on defence like they promised, held the Fearnoch line. They timed their backwards crossovers perfectly and converged to close the lane. And this was a historic bodycheck, remembered by all who saw it. The rink shuddered with the intensity. Laframboise was airborne for some time, over top of John and Kirby, his white skates flashing above his head, and he landed in a yard sale of gloves, helmet and stick and slid away into the corner.

Kirby lifted the puck out of harm's way, and Stella got it at centre with seconds left on the clock. She carved deep into the ice and found another gear. She chipped the puck around a French player and gathered it on the other side as the old-timers stood up out of their seats. Mikey knew he had to find some open ice, but he had two defenders on him, slashing him, grabbing his sweater. He felt their sticks on his spine, hammering along his ribs. Stella waited. The old-timers looked at the clock, then back to Stella as she stickhandled back in a circle, unfazed by the seconds dying.

Mikey felt an arm draped around him and finally had enough of the abuse. He swung back with a violent elbow, which the ref didn't see, and then he was free at the side of the net. Stella noticed, she noticed everything on the ice and she knew exactly how the play would unfold. She waited stubbornly, relentlessly, until finally the defender in front of her dropped to block the pass, then she went down on one knee and sauced a gorgeous aerial pass to Mikey.

Look at that fucking sauce, said Corey on the bench.

Mikey watched the perfect little delicious black UFO spinning towards him, not wobbling, over all that lay between him and Stella, sticks, legs, ice, refrigerated air, language barriers, screams, old-timers, puck bunnies, hockey haircuts, Scottish-Irish-British-French-Iroquois-Algonquin skirmishes and collaborations, and he knew he'd never been so attracted to anyone in his life. Nothing but the puck mattered for just one second, in all Fearnoch, not people who talked too much or people who didn't talk at all, not people who knew a lot or knew nothing at all, not farms or cows or pigs or Climate Death, not the weather, not the city marching closer and closer, not miscarriages or trying to keep teeth in your kid's head and just hoping he loved you, nothing for a second but the puck and its immaculate journey up, over and down onto Mikey's stick. It dropped right between his skates and merely needed a nudge over the goal line as the horn went. 2-2.

The eleven or so fans of hockey night in Fearnoch ruptured into jubilation. Popcorn and beer from the Hortons cups decorated the stands.

Because it wasn't the playoffs there would be no overtime and Fearnoch and Quebec would have to accept a tie. They shook hands at centre ice.

Tabarnak, who's the new player osti, said Larocque to John.

In the dressing room Mikey handed the pints around and John gave Stella the MVP hat to wear, which was an old beaten-up Fearnoch Farm Supply baseball hat. She looked very happy with the smelly hat dwarfing her head and her cheeks burning pink. Mikey gave her two beers.

Nice finish Mikey, she said, loosening her skates.

When Mikey got home he was too wound up to sleep. He puttered around, thirsty and restless. He gave Robert Plant, who seemed determined to continue dying, a little poke and bestowed on Robert the details of Stella's pass and his finish.

Oh boy I'm getting some dangerous feelings going here, Robert, he said.

He looked at Stella's number in his phone and tried to conceive of an appropriate message. But how to say—sorry I didn't invite you, what a game, you're the best, I'm afraid of you, do you want to go swimming in the river?

Mikey didn't know how to write that message tonight, and dropped the phone down on his quilt. He squirmed in the dark, scuttled around looking at the stars with his legs twitching—for tomorrow was St. Mikey's Day.

TWENTY-TWO

Magnus made supper for Anna as a surprise.

I've got all the things I think you like, he said. There was roasted squash, a salad full of seeds and onions and all that and then Kraft Dinner with wieners. Anna put her hands on her face and stared at the table.

All my favourite things! What is going on—this is beautiful! And she pinched his chin and gave him a long kiss and wanted to kiss more. Is this—why the surprise?

I wanted to do something nice, he said. We've been fighting a lot.

I think so too. Anna put her hand on his knee. You forget about Kraft Dinner eh? Then you're sad and wanna be eight again and believe in something and there it is. She closed her eyes with her fork sticking out the top of her fist. Same old blue box, she said.

She was warm and full and put her head on Magnus's shoulder. She didn't mind his views against having children or for slam poetry right now, and now they were just two more lovers under the moon, full of Kraft Dinner.

Let's go for a walk, said Magnus. Summer's almost done.

Oh I'd love that, Anna straightened up. I really would Magnus, but I'm on a midnight tonight, remember.

———

It was Ebenezer's last night, at least for this stretch, as an incarcerated youth. He was asleep in his room when Anna got there for shift turn-over, which was odd. Anna wanted to see him and tell him a surprise.

The night staff weren't allowed to sleep but they all did. Anna always had trouble with it. Lying on the chesterfield in the common room waiting for a rat to run across her.

Every hour Anna was supposed to check on all the boys and mark down that she did so in the binder. She hated the intrusions, worried she'd knock on the door and open it to find them masturbating furiously or dead with their wrists and eyes open.

In Room #7, Ebenezer was bunched up in his blankets, just a little heap at the end of his cot. At midnight, 1 a.m., at 2 a.m., he didn't budge. Anna watched until she saw this little blanketed heap rise and fall by tiny degrees and could be sure he was breathing. She winced when the door creaked as she closed it slowly.

At 4 a.m., Anna rubbed her eyes and knocked on Room #7, opening it to find Ebenezer sitting up and wide awake.

Hi! said Anna.

I free up tomorrow. Ebenezer's eyes shone big and bright.

I know. Congratulations. Can I sit here? Anna sat on the end of the bed.

Ebenezer tented his knees up to make room on the cot. Anna wondered if he was thinking about drugs, sex and freedom more than not getting shot. Which was exactly what he was doing.

Ebenezer, she said, now you be careful.

Yeah.

I wish you didn't have to go back there.

It's my home.

Anna considered that and felt stupid. Listen, you know, Mr. Bachmann, she whispered.

He turned to the wall. He recalled in heavy pieces the man's hair, house, hat, his ribs cracking, his life they busted in on.

I got his email, said Anna.

Ebenezer frowned.

I thought, said Anna, I'd email him, and we could see if he'd meet you. She exhaled, feeling stupid again now her idea was put out into words.

Ebenezer didn't say anything.

Would you like that? Anna asked.

Yes . . .

I'll email him then and maybe . . .

I don't think it's legal though.

Well, there's no court order against it, I don't think. I'll set it up. Here's my number.

That's definitely not legal I know that.

To talk to you once you're out?

Yes.

Well I'm about done listening to the rules on this one, said Anna, fiddling with her hands on her lap. They pay me seventeen dollars an hour to handle suicide, rats, and shit, and violence. You get what you pay for.

Ebenezer laughed.

Bless, he said.

I'll email Mr. Bachmann then. And you—just don't get killed, don't go around acting hard. We all know you're hard, okay. Can I hug you please, said Anna.

Yes, he said and leaned forward.

Anna was planning on saying something like this, something she'd thought about on the metro: There are people you respect because really you should respect all people. Then there are people you respect more because they're special to you. And then beyond that there's a few people you respect the most because of what they have to deal with and how they deal with it. And you're one of those few people.

But she didn't say it, she only hugged the boy for a long time, sitting on his prison bed at four in the morning.

I was supposed to remember something for you, Ebenezer said.

Oh yeah, said Anna.

This pen has coffee in it, he said with pride.

Oh.

At nine in the morning Anna went home to sleep and Ebenezer completed his outgoing interview then met his new parole officer. He packed up his blue clothes, posters of cars and rap babes and his Nighty Night tea box, and collected forty-five dollars, half a pack of cigarettes, a lighter, and his little necklace with the cross from the office. Into a bloody pink, clouded Montreal morning, he stepped forward, a free man.

TWENTY-THREE

Mikey worked the hot steel, tasting the Labatt 50 to come. It was very hot: summer going with a burning finish. Mumu-bou and Don discussed hunting because Mumu-bou was determined to become a Valley boy. He had a black eye and Don inquired if he had "scoped" himself again, and said he didn't need a gun that size for turkeys. Pete-buddy lectured a young man in a white hat.

No, fuck that, fuck that, said Pete-buddy. You make that engineer money now. I don't want you coming around here without some coffees—and muffins—for the lads. I want you thinking about the lads.

The white-hat was speechless.

Stella ignored Mikey or had too much dump-data to compute. Sweat stung into his eyes and he tried to dab at them with the back of his work gloves, but that got oil and engine grease into his eyes too. He thought how wonderful to drink in excess of four pints, but also felt that scary old thirst awaken down in there.

I'll drink lots of water, he reasoned. Plenty of water and no drugs, oh Lord.

He looked around for Stella as he drove back to the plate-and-structural-steel pile, sweat dripping all over the forklift controls.

—•—

The beavers were damming up the creek by the tracks, which was frigging with John's water table. And the coyotes prowled more brazen and sang louder and louder at night and John fretted about his calves. He'd repaired the fence near the beaver dam each of the last three summers. He dreamed about packing everything with Tannerite, enough Tannerite to afford a small mushroom cloud, filling the sky with animal parts, maybe he'd even get some on Kirby's lawn. But then again he silently admired the beavers' and coyotes' iron will to keep on season after season. They were only doing what beavers and coyotes were supposed to do. Fences tight, thought John.

He called for a taxi, fumbling and annoyed with the tiny phone and hitting the wrong buttons with his swollen early-arthritis dirty sausage-finger farmer hands.

Frigging greasy old hands, he whispered.

At supper Johnny whispered something to Polly and turned to his father with his eyes arched up, his entire face burning with the glee only a child knew.

Why don't you tell Daddy what the dog did, said Polly, eating her butter beans with a spoon and looking like she might fall asleep into her butter beans.

Johnny's face ruptured into a wide and crinkled grin. The honour of passing this vital information to his father was not lost on him.

Puked! Johnny said with a squeak and then covered his mouth with both hands.

Oh Bus, said John. Busty eyed him mournfully from the floor.

He ate some garbage from across the road, said Polly. A deer hoof. Then he came in here and ate some expired birth control—it's been tough sledding for Busty here.

An old Ford Aerostar van, with perfect Os puffing cartoonishly out its tailpipe, came down the laneway then. It was MacKay's taxi, one of the under-the-table pirate taxis that served Fearnoch and the Valley, where the licensed taxis might not.

Well I hope it's a happy St. Mikey's Day for all, said Polly. John kissed her, then Johnny.

And please make sure Mikey doesn't die, Polly called from the door.

I promise, said John.

One of the twelve or so brothers of the MacKay clan drove John to pick up Mikey. John was pretty sure this one was Wayne. The man spoke of horses and cattle and hogs.

Have you been working with horses long? asked John.

Oh all my life, all my life.

And cows?

All my life, all my life. Wayne looked over the wheel into the sky. I don't know what the sky is getting on with these days Johnny, he said. The sky was grumbling up and inclement in the Fearnoch environs.

There's Mikey right there, John said pointing at the house behind the store.

Where are we off to tonight? asked Wayne.

Quebec side! said John. We're going to Hull! And he pointed gloriously toward the river. This was normally more exciting than Ottawa.

Oh a good far piece, said Wayne.

Beers, Mikey said slowly and loudly, putting his seatbelt on.

It's good your generation doesn't drink and drive as much, said Wayne. When I was young—just keep'er between the ditches. He swerved left and right to make his point. City people would drink and drive too if they didn't have the subway and the buses, he said, we don't have buses, we don't have shit.

Wayne then regaled John and Mikey with tales about how he used to drive with his girlfriend up into the Guthrie Place Hills there so they could get the signal for Chez 106 Classic Rock from Ottawa. The man was clearly sentimental and excited, dipping away into his youth. Horses, pigs and hot black summer nights long gone down Fearnoch Road. He ferried the boys Quebec-ward by a bean field plush in moonrise.

——

Mikey was lousy at stopping drinking or slowing down drinking once he'd started. It was a skill he'd never grasped. This frightened John sometimes, how he'd drink faster and faster, even though his eyes were now pointed in different directions. Mikey was thoroughly enjoying his cold, cold Labatt 50s, and they toasted another St. Mikey's Day, this year at a darkened bar attached to an old hotel in Vieux-Hull. There were wooden chairs, light and cheap, good for bar fights, arranged in fours around small round tables, and paintings of cowboys and steers roamed the walls. The regulars mainly played their dart tournaments and had their alcoholism.

Perfect. I love places like this, said John raising his 50. This sort of scenario here is why the good Lord created Cinquante.

They organized the empty bottles to one side of the table. Mikey drank deeply from his fifth beer, savouring the custom of his holiday. He admired at length the shape and temperature of this beer bottle, the beadlets of condensation running on deep amber.

Oh my God it is cold and it is good, said Mikey. It's too bad it's not Wednesday. We could have wings—Wing-nite Wednesday is the heartbeat of the people. I say if you want to understand the real Canada then go to Wing-nite Wednesday. He studied and approved of the wet Labatt 50 label with his mouth full of beer. Sometimes he allowed these judgments outside of his head, to the detriment of his normalcy.

John looked at him and then said, I agree with that.

Mikey had more beer. I think my history books are making me insane there Johnny, he said.

Yes they are certainly, Mikey.

Mikey wished to talk to John about Soviet POWs because he thought it was important and maybe talking about it would be good, but he decided hockey was clearly the appropriate topic. Remember when I scored that goal? he said, aglow now recalling his exhibition-game-tying beer-league goal.

Stella might be the best to ever wear the Fearnoch black and yellow, said John, and he got a little annoyed then. And frig off for getting mad at me for putting her on the team, he said.

Don't make me feel bad, said Mikey. Not on my holiday.

Just talk to her—Oh g'day Stella, great game there, I'm Mikey . . . like that. For Christ's sake look at you, look at your eyes, he gestured at him, you look like a shitty—like a shitty song. John tilted his hat back. Talk to her, he said. Talk to me, lad.

Mikey pulled a fragment of melted steel out of his scalp and set it on the table, with blood and one hair coming off of it.

That's what that was, he said, flicking at it.

Jesus, said John.

Mikey put the fragment in the mouth of a bottle and said slowly: I'm going to be as honest as I can and not lie. Everybody is lying. Okay—it's nice to have a crush. Haven't had a crush in years. I'm not ready . . . I'm terrified really, I want to be slow and safe.

The cowboys, the lonesome desperadoes, sat in their saddles keeping watch all over the walls, with their moustaches, in all the cactus.

Safe is death, said John after a while. The real tragedy, he pointed his bottle at a cowboy, is not being a cowboy. In the one life you get.

Spineless, said Mikey. He drank more.

Eh.

I'm spineless. I'm not courageous.

Well you're pretty courageous at drinking beer there Darling.

Cassie told me—

Ohhh no. John put both his hands down on the table. No, as

you recall, I have nothing more to offer you in any way with Cassie.

You ask me to talk, then get mad at me when I do talk, said Mikey, and he was getting crabby and he bristled. He recounted a story he wished he could forget, about a huge drunk arsehole hick at the Fair who said, all Darlings are faggots, let me touch your poofy hair, and Cassie grabbed at his arm and said, don't do it Mikey, don't let this huge fucker touch your hair.

And I let him! Mikey finished. Cassie's tugging on my arm but I let this goon piece of shit touch my hair. Then she said I was spineless and left. I know I'm not supposed to talk about Cassie.

John crinkled his nose and tensed his hand around his beer. Shouldn't do that, he said.

Spineless, said Mikey.

Doesn't make you spineless. Just don't do that again.

Mikey only drank more beer.

What if I just sat here and said I'm spineless, said John.

You have a beautiful wife, a child and a hundred acres.

You wanna switch? You take dog's barf and the dead farm and I get to watch YouTubes over the garage. 'Cause that's gonna be good for me.

They were un-festive awhile.

Then Mikey said, I don't feel drunk but I've had so much Cinquante I feel like my teeth are falling out. He felt around with his tongue.

You want me to pull a tooth out of my head and set it on the table? Because I can, said John.

Mikey laughed.

Okay, we're happy again now, let's celebrate, said John. You talk to Stella, don't let anyone touch your hair, and we win the championship and it all just fucking works out. He called for more Cinquante.

When it all works out I'm just gonna go stand on the hill and scream until my temples explode and blood fucking cries out my tear ducts, said Mikey.

And I, I will be right there with you. John put his arm around him.

Kirby hasn't been to a St. Mikey's Day in forever.

It probably wouldn't be good for his carbon footprint.

———

Kirby's evening was much different from John and Mikey's. He found Peace's old protesting balaclava and tried it on in the mirror. He ate more turnips with Peace and they read their books on the deck and glowed with all the celestial cinders in the skies.

Fearnoch isn't so bad, said Peace, bookmarking her book and watching the swallows.

They discussed baby names.

Just not a name like Kirby, Kirby said.

My mum let me choose my own name, said Peace. Before that I was Baby.

I don't want to talk baby-talk to the baby. It's condescending and stupid. I'm going to speak to the baby like a person.

You say that, said Peace. But I bet you'll be so in love you'll say all the stupid baby things to Baby.

Do you think it's half evil bringing a child into this world? We already have too many humans. He saw three obese men try to push a truck out of some mud, then took his glasses off.

Oh maybe so, said Peace. She put her head in Kirby's lap. Maybe I'll become a scarecrow artist, she said as she dozed off.

Kirby whispered to her stomach: I'm not gonna be like your grandpa was.

———

Later, in Hull, Mikey's aggressive consumption of Labatt 50 had attracted the bartender's ire.

Ton ami est fucké, she said to John.

Quoi? Eh? said John.

Ton ami là, she shouted and she pointed at Mikey.

Mikey was on the tiny dance floor dancing at a very unsustainable pace under the disco ball with two older women. Country ballads came from the speakers and he kicked his boots up into an ambitious two-step do-se-do. He almost fell off the little stage but gathered himself, hooked his thumbs together and flapped his fingers to somehow manipulate his hands into the illusion of a formidable eagle, and he flapped this eagle up and up to effectively resurrect himself up off the floor. The older women cheered. John was impressed. Then Mikey knocked over a speaker and broke his beer bottle.

Out! Out! Out! said the bartender.

John took Mikey by the arm and they went out into the street. They laughed and tripped on broken pavement and found the only bar that would serve them—a strip club in an old brick schoolhouse with a pink halogen sign that read: Cabaret Le 99. It was mostly empty, with more dancers than patrons.

Bawdy—this place is bawdy, said Mikey. I wish we had drugs.

I would do drugs, said John.

Look at this, said Mikey and he showed John his phone, on which he'd finally sent Stella a message: Do you want to go swimming in the river. What do you think? Not bad eh? He put his phone back in his pocket.

A dancer stood up on their table and slowly took her clothes off. Feathery nylon fluorescent purple garments poured and slid off of her down onto Mikey and John. They stared up at her. She stared away, cold and lonely. John drank his beer and then Mikey looked at his phone some more.

No phone, said the bouncer, who smelled trouble, Anglo-trouble, and he puffed his chest out at Mikey. The bouncer was tanned, bald, frightening, short but wide, and bound with muscle to the point where his arms wouldn't go down by his sides. He had a big leather bracelet that didn't have a watch on it, which John thought was stupid.

Sorry, said Mikey. He wandered away to the bathrooms and left John with the dancer slowly gyrating on the table, eyes locked on John.

Ah frig, thought John.

Mikey came back ten minutes later and gave John a purple capsule.

Take one, he said, have one John—I had two.

What is it? John peered at the small pill in his enormous hand. How do you find these things?

Go on and have it—on y va, faisons du bruit! said Mikey. He slapped John on the back and chattered his teeth away.

Where'd you get it?

Mikey waved at two dancers who sat with their stilettoed laced boots up like they were done for the night. Their legs were lashed up in criss-crossing yellow and pink netting. They both raised their Limon Tornade coolers up at Mikey.

I got it from them, he said. It's MDMA. I think it is.

John licked the pill off his hand. All right Mikey lad I trust you, he said. Christ my bag hurts.

How I see it is that it's only once a year and it has the added bonus of keeping me up long enough so I don't piss myself, Mikey said thoughtfully. Which is a boon.

The dancer on their table sighed, gathered up her clothes and left annoyed. Mikey and John drank the place out of Cinquante and a new dancer climbed up onto their table. She began her dance and clothes, boas and underwear once again flowed and slithered down on them.

Oh boy here we go, Mikey said. The pitch, cadence, the tone of everything in the place shifted and he felt at his face, a slow inquisition of his simmering face. He tipped into the sparkly fuzzy bismuth hold of the pills.

I am absolutely fucked off drugs and beer. How do you feel? John asked.

Mikey opened his mouth as wide as he could and looked at John.

Phew, said John. Phew!

Les gars, said the bouncer. He put a hand on each of their chairs. Will you take some danses-contacts with the girl? Twenty dollar.

I work at the dump, said Mikey.

I'm a farmer, said John.

The dancer swayed, wearing only her boots.

Mikey took out his phone. He sent the same message as before: Do you want to go swimming in the river? The dancer saw this and stamped her boot down on the table beside Mikey's hand.

Eyes here, she said and pointed to herself.

Sorry, said Mikey. I'm expecting a message.

He looked at John and John looked at him, their faces ghoulish from ecstasy tablets and then they looked at the dancer, and everyone really just looked at each other fucked up and annoyed.

I wish the Mouse didn't burn down, John said. He took off his hat and wiped his forehead. There's gotta be something a little more than MDMA in that pill sweet Jesus. Johnny better not do drugs. Oh no—just say no Johnny. He felt like he might cry.

Mikey jumped when he felt a vibration in his pocket. He pulled out his phone again.

Is it Stella? John shouted very loudly and all the patrons and dancers turned their heads.

Mikey held up the phone and slid his finger down the screen to show yes, it was a text from Stella and it was at least twice as long as the second-longest text he'd ever beheld. It simply did not end. Mikey tried to read it but forgot how to read and he felt his face had ignited and was on fire.

Uh, said Mikey. He was having difficulty computing through the information coming at him. This novella of a text message, the cold-blooded glowing blue nakedness, John's sweaty forehead, and Jesus where was the beer?

No phones! The bouncer shouted. He slammed his hand with the leather bracelet but no watch on it down on the table, rattling the bottles.

By then this dancer had simply had enough of these sweaty broke hicks on ecstasy with their phones and their farm-equipment hats. With a well-timed and very violent kick, she booted Mikey's phone clean out of his hand and across the bar. It landed in four pieces against the stage.

Mikey squeaked from this new development of surprise violence and destruction. He got off his chair and bumbled over to his phone parts. The screen was spiderwebbed good and the battery had slid away under something. Mikey thought he was dreaming, and thought: Don't mind me, I'm just in a dream here, no trouble. He swept the phone bits into a little pile with his hands, put what he could into his pockets and then ran through his dream into the hot Quebec night.

———

Take us to Fearnoch, Wayne, John said tearfully some time later to Wayne. Wayne met the two of them at a corner on Boulevard des Allumettières in Hull at three in the morning after receiving John's nearly incomprehensible voicemail. Mikey had his phone fragments in his pocket but he'd already forgotten about it.

Remember it's eighty dollars eh, said Wayne out the window. Mikey considered touching the man's moustache. His moustache looked out of kilter.

John's fly was down and Mikey tried to reach down and do it up for him.

Lemme sort you out here, he said.

C'mon I'll do it for sixty, said Wayne.

What an evening, Wayne, said Mikey. Wayne sped over the vacant bridge under the yellow street lamps back into Ontario. Mikey wanted to ask him if he'd in fact dislocated his moustache.

Do you have any Labatt 50 Wayne? said John. Where are the roadies, Wayner? I think I'll put you on my Christmas card list.

Don't mind John, he's a farmer, he's always worried about something, worried about the weather—look at my face, said Mikey. My face is aflame.

I'd like to put jam all over my face, said John, folding the sun visor to look at the mirror.

My parents gave me an ugly face, said Mikey. He rubbed his arms and checked himself over. I'd feel a lot safer, he said, if I was wearing a lifejacket right now. Yes, I want a lifejacket—a PFD.

Can you play some rock and roll? asked John. We should sleep sitting up back to back tonight, Mikey. To be safe. Like buddies at war.

That's good thinking because there's going to be a war soon, said Mikey.

John wiped a tear.

Jesus Christ what type of evening did you lads have? said Wayne, taking his eyes off the dark road to look from one to the other. Now he was frightening, an autocrat in sunglasses, his grey moustache.

Later and getting back to the dark country, John thought that he loved Mikey very much, even though he'd never understand him, and even loved Wayne at the moment, and he felt good and warm.

Mikey felt the little shift into his sadness, and he couldn't put it off much longer by distracting himself and trying to say funny little things to John and Wayne. Either to himself or to the other two, it didn't really matter anymore, and certainly in no relation to the conversation, he said: Anne Frank doesn't get enough credit for being a genius. At thirteen too. A hundred per cent no-bullshit genius brave writer. No room for bullshit when you're hiding in an attic—Anne Frank rules. She really does rule.

Another half hour more of all that and Wayne gladly dropped Mikey off in front of his parents' house.

Mikey gave Wayne twenty dollars and said, that should do 'er buddy. And a happy St. Mikey's Day to all. He did a big wave.

And then he walked along the gravel road, leaning to one side and rubbing his hands together. Alone in the gravel and dusty sumacs beneath a lycanthropic moon with the beer wearing off. It was very surprising to be conscious, but the drugs blasted consciousness through all the beer, and he would have loved about three beer to settle down. Mikey felt through the garage in the dark, went up to the loft and lay there on his horsehair mattress. Now the Labatt 50 and MDMA ribaldry, the bawdiness of earlier, was decidedly gone and he was sad, and it always went this way. He missed John, and also Wayne. The sheets suffocated, the pillow filthy and bunched, he felt stress, or whatever you'd like to call it, tightening his legs out, then he spun onto his back and opened his eyes. He felt that hole opening up.

We're all just trying, trying to fill that hole, he thought. All us grist down here. Some beer for the mortals please!

Mikey got up, sleep only a fantasy, and he went outside to wander and panic in the dark. Looping, shuffling around the store, under a tree, past the pigsty, to the barn behind his parents' house where the farmhand hung himself during the Depression.

This planet now had more gravity, and Mikey walked underwater in the dark, marooned on a methane lake on his planet, with Earth a dot in the night. He was a lunatic lighthouse keeper visited by rum demons, the devil visiting in on him, whispering him booze-stuff in the night. The devil reminded him about the Soviet POWs, how they marched them back behind the lines, no food, they ate all the leaves off the trees by the road and then each other; they fenced them off by the hundreds of thousands in a field, no food or shelter or plan for them except to leave them there to die. Remember the evil right there never far away in all our souls, the devil whispered. Remember the other side of the fence.

Then Stella's message and how he'd messed that up pretty good hit him hard in the brain, and he thought, no—nice things, nice things here, ponies, piglets, calves, hockey, but what was that sad thing? Oh yeah—Stella—and then the nice things were gone.

He paused in front of the barn, thinking, then lifted the latch on the door. It yawned opened slowly and silently, invited him into the cobwebs, the ancient straw, the must of a century, with the old horse stalls and rusted saws and scythes and all sorts of fucked old barn implements on the walls. He sat in the corner and stayed there until the cracked and dirty window bloomed with a vicious and bleeding sunrise.

This is where the farmhand did it, right here, he thought. He put his hands behind his head and looked up and down the rafters, looking for a notch, a mark or an old bit of rope. It must have been so easy. Like two minutes of not thinking straight, and it's done. Just like that.

Maybe he was supposed to die ten years ago but because of a cosmic error he was still alive. Maybe he actually did die the night he smoked crack with the homeless people downtown but he was stuck on the edge of hell. He looked out the window again, to the punctual sun. This time he saw a ghost and wasn't shocked. The farmhand's apparition floated and fluttered past the window. Mikey saw this and saw that it was good; he felt in the right place now. It was supposed to be so, sad in the barn with ghosts, dying penniless and insane in a barn.

It was so easy Mikey! the farmhand ghost would say to him.

He looked again and saw his mum in her nightie going up to get the paper. Mikey ducked his head and hid in the barn. He imagined his mum crying in her nightie, cutting open another bag of homo milk and pouring it into her cup, sitting at the kitchen table and crying more, with her face in her hands and the fat from her arms shaking.

TWENTY-FOUR

At Café Plus earlier, Anna found Yvette crying in the dish-pit. She tried to hide it, turned and sniffed with one hand on the lip of the sink. Anna rubbed her shoulder.

Je suis correct, said Yvette, in her voice the echoes of a thousand cigarettes. Je suis correct. She sniffed again and smoothed down her apron.

Later she took Anna's hand and said, Promise me you will always talk to your mother, okay? She sniffed and tried to laugh.

Magnus was making an effort to be closer to Anna and said he'd finally come have supper at Café Plus.

You don't have to, said Anna. The food is unbelievably bad.

But he wouldn't hear it and he would eat anything she put in front of him, he said. Yvette and Océane were excited to meet this Magnus.

He came in at six o'clock looking very sweet with a new shirt and haircut. Anna wiped her forehead and waved at him. Yvette crossed her arms and sized him up over the top of her glasses. But Océane stared at him from behind the bar, eyes large and frightening, and Magnus saw her and froze in the middle of the restaurant. He stood there a moment, looked from Anna to Océane to Yvette.

Ah, he said, um. And then he spun around and left.

Océane put her hand to her mouth. Anna was incredulous.

What the fuck was that? she said, running to the door to watch Magnus scurry away down the avenue.

Anna, Anna, Océane came to her in the doorway and crumpled on the floor, her apron a tent around her legs. I am sorry, she said. I didn't know.

Océane had been sleeping with Magnus for months. They met at a poetry reading, they met and they had sex, in a city of two million souls.

He called himself Magsy, she explained. He said he was in an open relationship.

I didn't know we were in one of those, Anna said. She sat on the closest chair and was dizzy. A few patrons paused with their pies.

I'm sorry, said Océane, blinking tears. She took out her phone. I will say to him—fuck you Magnus. Right now.

Okay, Anna said. She thought Magnus must have been with Océane the night she let the blood orange gelato melt everywhere. She felt sick, not exactly angry or sad, but thoroughly humiliated. She felt ugly.

It's not your fault Océane, she said after a time. Don't be sorry.

Yvette came and sat with the two girls. She looked out the door, her face murderous. Anna visualized the old woman putting an axe into Magnus's brain, which wasn't far off what Yvette was thinking.

———

After her shift, Anna rode the metro back to Hochelaga. The empty car squealed around the corners, into the tunnel and she dozed with her head snapping and rolling. Maybe she should cheat. Maybe everyone did it, it was okay and acceptable because this was all one big game of deception. We kid ourselves with fairy tales that say different. She closed her eyes and felt the restless cheating city on her eyelids.

Magnus sat at the kitchen table in her apartment. His eyes were pink. He looked down at his shoe and he fidgeted with his shoe.

Anna, Anna, I'm sorry, he said. Okay, I didn't think you'd be into an open relationship, and well, my needs—I mean it wasn't—

Anna stamped her foot, closed her eyes and put one hand in the air.

No, she said. You're not going to talk right now.

Magnus was quiet.

First of all, Anna began by throwing her purse on the chair, if you wanted to see other girls, just dump me. Why not just dump me? She held her hands out, open-palmed. You can have me, or you can fuck all the other sad poet girls and pretend like you're twenty until you're sixty, but you can't have both. You can't have everything, lad! she said, channelling her mother and that old Berube heart.

Magnus was trying to speak.

No, I'm not done, said Anna.

Anna—

Anna stamped her foot again. I just said goodbye to an immensely troubled fucking ganged-up seventeen-year-old boy, she said, and he's twice the man you are. You are insincere and you're, you're deceitful—no I'm not going to cry—see, this is why no one gets to know the ending of my book. You're not sincere. Probably wasn't going to work out anyway and I really should have dumped you . . . fucking gimme a minute here.

Anna got a glass down from the cupboard, filled it at the sink, drank it all, turned and picked up steam again. Magnus sat there and withered.

Also you don't get to talk like you know everything anymore. She wiped her mouth with her sleeve. And blame everything—it's not capitalism's fault you don't know how to work a snow shovel. She started cooling off at the beginning of her sentences but then got angry again by the end of them, so they had a running sort of lift to them.

I know everyone's doing these poly . . . fucking, these open relationships these days eh, but this is just plain old cheating! And yes, insincere . . . that's why your writing's no good, it's not honest, it's just PR—it's just PR for why people should wanna fuck you—so fuck you Magnus and your, and your . . . cortados, Anna concluded, running out of breath.

Magnus was quiet.

Anna went into the bathroom, locked the door and sat on the edge of the tub breathing in hurried lungfuls. She forgot to tell him his love was not like a frigging boat.

TWENTY-FIVE

John was hungover, that was very evident, but he had his chores. Not much you could do but tuck in your shirt and try to keep 'er all on the tracks. He did all the animals, sweat in his eyes and excited for the day when Johnny could do this shit, and then he spent an hour or so combing the field, that age-old farmer's task of searching for one tiny frigging piece of metal that fell off some outdated piece of machinery that, if lost, or baled up in the hay, could sink your whole operation. He found it.

There was a drought out west this summer, he recalled then, and remembered he was supposed to donate some bales to Hay West. He considered sending them some dirty ditch-hay with old beer cans and garbage baled up in them, as Mush did, those prairie farmers with their oceans of wheat, but that was cruel and besides they were very kind two years ago for Hay East. John set aside a nice stack. And then it was back to the back field to take up the Younghusband struggle again, everlasting, his birthright, to keep the bush back. This was ridiculous, he worked like a homesteader while on the good farms, big farms down the line, they had robots now. The wind sighed through the old farmhouse by the tracks and John had the sensation of being watched by ghosts, squinted and thought for sure that was a ghost shuffling and shimmering by the tracks. He turned back to his task and thought about getting an excavator in there or just abandoning the old field to rot forever. In the bush by the fence, the old threshing mill rusted in the weeds. Old thumb-severing giant, eater of arms, looking like a retired apocalyptic death machine. John went in to see his dad, who was drinking the flat last third of a can of tonic water used to make a gin and tonic the night before.

Jesus us Younghusbands are really out to pasture here, thought John.

Why are you drinking that? he asked. Why don't you pour it out?

John's dad looked at the tin and back to his son, and he reflected. 'Cause I'm Scottish?

John handed his father a flyer. It said: Valley Barn-Wood Restoration.

It was two young lads, said John. They take lumber from old barns you don't want, for a song, and then turn them into artisan . . . you know—city things. They've made a fortune.

Outstanding, said John's dad.

What?

That shows a capacity for innovation and commerce. And acumen.

I don't want them taking our barns. Do they have to frig with every last thing?

Across the tracks, the construction crews were shoving up a house a week, putting another identical crescent around another forgettable and impersonal park with a bench and a play structure with that red tube slide. John's dad watched two framers nail-gun a truss in. Nothing stayed the same. He wasn't angry like his boy—he didn't want to go backwards in time because he'd been poorer than this and poor people don't want to be poor again. One bad year could do a farm in back then, never mind the crooked cow agents, sheep evaluators and Revenue Canada, never mind suburbanization, globalization and corporate farming. He didn't fantasize about his ancestral barns, wasn't ungrateful for new possibilities, and could get near delirious at the plenitude he saw in places like Walmart and Canadian Tire and Tractor Supply Company, after growing up with turnips and farm equipment from the 1800s. The quiet he missed though, and just the stars and their glory. Anyway he didn't remember what John was talking about.

Well, uh—be humble I guess, he said to his son.

I told them to frig off, said John.

John's dad went and stowed himself out of the way by the window with his book, and his pants even higher than normal. The field was getting down: chewed up and begging for rain. He sat by the window, and if that was in someone's way, maybe he'd go out into the rhubarb, and his cucumbers and squash and try to stay out of everyone's road there, with his pants way up.

John was happy his dad was his dad. He didn't say that of course, he didn't know how to talk to his dad like that. And he didn't notice him by the window. All the dads, Mikey's dad, Polly's, Kirby's awful shit father—but his was his.

Kirby's dad used to drive home without Kirby after a hockey game if he decided Kirby had a bad game, and he regularly decided Kirby had a bad game, shoving into the dressing room to say he played like a girl, and so John's dad had a very serious talk with Kirby's dad in the parking lot, which John saw and wasn't supposed to see, he remembered he froze and watched, holding his hockey bag and stick, and the snow fell and twisted in the light over the entrance of Fearnoch Memorial Arena, and Kirby's dad recoiled from John's dad, got in his truck and left, and then after that John's dad took Kirby to the games, fitting him in the middle seat between himself and John.

As for Mikey, now Mikey navigated a hangover he figured had to be a type of concussion. He slept maybe two hours, but sleep wasn't the right way to put it—more of a rustling and sinking into a stressful grey region. St. Mikey's Day might be a terrible idea. Horrible birds, crows or common grackles, the types of morning birds reserved for people coming down off drugs, they cawed and ripped through the garbage bags put out behind the store. There was no grace or magic left in the world. He shuddered, packed with toxins of yesternight, and the sepsis; he demanded a trepanning. He found his phone bits and sat back down remembering about Stella. Then he walked out into the day with one eye shut and called in sick from the payphone in front of the store. Foreman Don said: Feel better Mikey laddie.

Back up in the loft again, and Mikey lay on his floor with his face in all Mrs. MacPherson's old fur stuck in the rug and talked out loud to himself.

Stella. Labatt 50. Jesus Robert Plant buddy what do we do with all this? This is a catastrophe. This is satanic.

In the afternoon, Polly called his parents' house and asked him to come in to the community centre if he was free, and Mikey said he'd go because well that was something good he could try to do, even though he sure would barf.

———

An urgent duck flew with and alongside the pre-owned sedan, so he could almost touch it out the window as he brought the car down the lane to the community centre. Jefferson waited for him, which was something good. The duck climbed up into the skies when Mikey stopped the car. This Jefferson was one busy lad—no moss grew on Jefferson.

Hi, said Mikey.

Hi, said Jefferson. He pulled his hair off his face, tried to tuck it behind his ears and spoke through his hole of missing front teeth.

It's nice to see you, said Mikey.

Um, it's nice to see you, said Jefferson.

They went inside and Mikey's vertebrae clacked together, his skin hurt.

What d—uh, do you want to do, he said very softly.

Wrestling, said Jefferson.

Oh Lord, said Mikey, and already Jefferson sprang, seized his leg and hung off it, spilling out maniacal giggles.

Mikey tried to steady himself, one hand against a laminated sign on the wall that read "Storyland." He stepped on one of several toy wooden ducks on wheels by mistake. He patted Jefferson on the curls, he felt the sweat readying and overflowing the glands under his skin and he looked around for Polly.

Then another boy, this one was Roy, who was autistic and non-verbal, wandered over, maybe wanted to wrestle too. He grabbed hold of Mikey's other leg—Jesus Christ, thought Mikey—and in doing so, knocked Jefferson to the floor. Jefferson fell on his back, with his old poor-kid's shoes up in the air. Roy looked up at Mikey, face bare and affectless.

Mikey was nervous and trying his best not to throw up. And then Jefferson lost it just like Polly had warned he would. His frustration management was poor at best, because when he was a fetus his mother cooked his cells in gin. He pushed Roy down, on top of the wooden ducks on wheels, and kicked, punched, clawed, and cried all the while.

Fuck! Jefferson screamed.

Roy cried silently, affectless and wet on the floor.

Mikey put his hands under Jefferson's armpits and lifted him a foot off the floor. Jefferson swung, kicked, wriggled in the air. Mikey twisted around and set him down, putting himself between the two boys and sweating pure Labatt 50.

He couldn't say: I know you have FASD, Jefferson, and it's not fair, but you can't do that, he's autistic, and that's not fair too.

So instead he put one hand on each boy's shoulder and said: Okay, okay, and tried to get a measure on the scenario.

Later, the elderly lady who read the stories in Storyland told Mikey under no circumstances was he ever to put a hand on a child during an incident such as that.

But he was beating the absolute shit out of that boy, Mikey told Polly.

It's the rules, Polly said. We're liable.

By this time Jefferson and Roy were playing together, setting up a race-car track like they were old friends, with their eyes still puffy from crying.

It's really fucking hot today, said Mikey. He shook his wet T-shirt. Why's it so hot?

After Jefferson and Roy, and Polly and the old lady from Storyland and everyone else went home, Mikey didn't want supper and he sat in the grass beside the pre-owned sedan as it got dark. Hungover in all the milkweed and birdsong, and his senses overwhelmed— he still felt like absolute dog shit but he was happy to get out of the loft at least. And it was nice here, if you looked. He saw the sun fit perfectly behind the domed top of the silo behind the community centre. He forgot about his own self for a while, and he thought only about Jefferson and Roy, and he thought about Stella.

TWENTY-SIX

A nd the next day was hotter still, the corn tall and dry, drouthy, heavens raw, the heat brought disagreeable smells out and pressed its greasy muggy heft down on anything moving. Mikey did go to work but this time it was Stella who was sick. Mumu-bou sprayed Mikey with a pump and hose they'd fitted into the old olive-water drum, all down his neck and back and Pete-buddy commented: Yeah get the old thumb onto 'er Mumu-bou.

PTSD Ed busted open a tin of secret beer behind their water tank-shed and said, something about the heat—makes me wanna be a bad peasant.

They shutterdown and Mikey drove in to see Dr. Milks. John took the old International tractor rattling and shaking down the shoulder of Fearnoch Road to meet with Mush and the farmers' convoy. The radio in the tractor warned about severe Valley thunderstorms when this warm front would collide with a cold front sooner or later. Kirby walked through the field to meet Gord and the rest in the road and he regretted wearing black in this bastard heat. Anna ignored Magnus's calls and met Mr. Bachmann in a coffee shop inside a museum. Ebenezer ignored Bernard's calls and walked free, free and roaming in a clean blue shirt down hot streets full of liberty and babes, and then he went to the dépanneur to buy treats, chips and pop, for himself and his sister.

———

Dr. Milks asked Mikey about romance.

Oh no, said Mikey. Oh Lord no.

Dr. Milks laughed. We all got our problems Mikey.

All got our problems, said Mikey in mumbles. Yes. But what do you do? What do you do? He spent a quiet moment and then said loudly: I'll tell you what you do—you read about the 1943 Warsaw Ghetto Uprising and then shut the Christ up about your problems.

Is this from your war book? Dr. Milks asked. She was curious, knowing what the history books did to Mikey's imagination.

I'm almost done, I'm at the Battle of Berlin. Mikey was in a mood. I want everyone I know to read it, he said, and then we'll convene and work on how to never ever treat people as if they're rats.

What a nightmare, Dr. Milks said and reclined her chair. Why don't you read, oh, maybe a gardening book.

The amount of killing . . . Mikey continued, I mean by the million, Doctor. It's unthinkable! And looks like it happened so easily. Normal people—farmers, frigging students, the milkmaids, kids going to school—piles—piles!—of them everywhere, in China, and Ukraine, and everywhere . . . did anyone think to say, oh maybe we shouldn't murder this whole town?! Mikey put his palms over his ears.

It made him feel sick. No graves, no rites, no proper end at all, the individual caught in this shit and not even an afterthought, and certainly nowhere the luxury of meaning. Only the end. Villages burned and flattened out of history, whole towns crushed in basements, starved, bombed, gassed, raped, shot so they fell into pits, raped and bayoneted and left out in the road.

———

John had hoped the convoy would be some sort of jolly if-you-ate-today-thank-a-farmer day or farmer-appreciation day with face paint and caramel apples, but it was not. Mush waved from his truck. He had his best milk cow in the trailer with Back Off Government painted across her side. The rest of the folks didn't look like they had any face paint or caramel apples. There was nothing jolly about the procession of combines, tractors, cows, pigs, horses, trucks, hay wagons, and men in suspenders and hunting gear that snaked through Fearnoch. John felt he'd made a mistake.

Kirby too was uneasy about his assembly. Several other guardians of the planet rolled down their balaclavas. A lot of these folks were young people, and not from Fearnoch, Kirby thought. One of them had a stick, what looked like a ringette stick, and they attempted a barricade with old bits of fence from the ditch, before giving up, abandoning their battlements and standing around in the split and patched asphalt. Two attractive young women held hands and held a seance or a ceremony of sorts, closing their eyes and humming. This wasn't the Climate Death of retired bureaucrats fussing about loon habitat. It was a different chapter. Gord also didn't know many of these young people but was pleased at the turnout. He wore tinted ski goggles and suggested they sit down and link arms to make a human chain across Fearnoch Road.

Both these sides were very loud and sure, and also bored and restless and miserable, and even though Kirby and John felt and looked ridiculous, they'd been labelled long ago and they stuck to their labels. Only parts of their groups now. It was also entirely possible that—deeper than this—they were angry at themselves. The other side had held up a mirror, put that little idea in their heads, growing away in the back of their heads, that there was a chance maybe, perhaps, horrifically, they were and always had been absolute bullshit. And there is no forgiving that.

—•—

Mr. Bachmann wondered how Anna had found his email and also when she might stop emailing him.

It was right there on the Esposito Gagnon Bachmann Accident and Injury Lawyers webpage, Mr. Bachmann, said Anna. She was wearing her nicest, most professional shirt. She had an ice coffee because the heat was disgusting in Montreal too, like where it feels your face is covered in bacon grease five minutes after stepping outside, and she tried her best to look polite and not like someone who would illegally track down an elderly victim of assault and unlawful confinement.

I'm retired, Mr. Bachmann said. I thought they took me off that. His white hair stuck up at the back and his eyes sagged.

Mr. Bachmann, said Anna as sweetly as she could, I don't think you'd be here if you didn't want to see the boy just a little bit.

Mr. Bachmann felt sorry for this young woman.

He's a sweet boy, he just has no luck, said Anna.

He broke my ribs. I have nightmares. They tied me up in my house!

I know. I know that, I'm sorry, Anna mumbled into her ice coffee and felt insane that she was doing this to a poor old man. They all want Ebenezer dead now, she said.

You shouldn't say his name. This is all highly illegal for several reasons, said Mr. Bachmann. He looked at a gruesome painting behind Anna's head and wondered what on Earth had happened to artistic merit.

I don't care anymore, said Anna very slowly and softly. I'll get laid off as soon as they can't get their funding. I just care about Ebenezer, God help me—he's the only good thing about this whole mess, and her voice was breaking.

Okay, all right, said Mr. Bachmann. What's this Ebenezer like then—what does he like to do other than beat me up and wear my shtreimel?

Well, Anna put her finger on her chin. He likes . . . the colour blue, and owls, and his sister.

———

Dr. Milks spoke, but Mikey didn't hear. He was miles away, long ago and soaring around into memory holes. Sweaty, silent and looking at the beige wall, looking through the wall. Way she goes. Treat people like shit, treat people like shit and get shit endings. He was remembering.

———

Mrs. MacPherson suffocated to death in a Loeb grocery bag. Mikey came home from the dump and there she was on the rug in front of his bed with the bag twisted and knotted over herself—a tight bag full of cat with two pink-padded feet and a tail sticking out. He ripped her head out of the bag, she rattled, wheezed, opened her mouth and caught his eye, then died on his lap.

———

The convoy approached and Gord said into the megaphone: Hate is not welcome.

John heard something about hate, and his tractor coughed and whined. He squinted through the diesel exhaust to see what was going on down Fearnoch Road.

Mush saw what going on, the folks cross-legged and holding hands in the road, and he said: Oh for the love of Jesus—hippies!

———

And then Ebenezer had his bag of chips and pop from the dépanneur and he was slow, dusty and liberated, along the tall weeds behind a glowing lonesome strip mall with a Mega Dollar, an out-of-business laundromat, a Loans-Plus, and a Honduran chicken restaurant. Until his 10 p.m. house-arrest curfew, he could walk wherever he pleased, unmonitored, unattended, just a normal person having a walk and looking good for any girls out there. He saw three boys in a tight alley across the street, which looked a little suspicious, but they were all dressed in blue. Then he saw Bernard in an opposite alley, also in blue, waving at him. He paused but then thought to keep walking. Ebenezer pulled at his own blue shirt and felt the sweat free on his back.

———

The Algonquin, for all their loyalty to the French, then the British crowns, their centuries of bravery squaring off against the Iroquois, the Dutch, the Americans, and whoever else was fucking around down south—they were fucked out of their land over and over, land their ancestors once hunted giant prehistoric beavers on when the glaciers receded, and there were always going to be invaders, there's invaders everywhere, forever, but that didn't mean they couldn't fight.

———

Some years ago Doolan went down with his skidoo and drowned down a dark hole in the ice. A Fearnoch tradition was to try and be the first sled across the river to Quebec with every new winter. Doolan thought finally this was his year, and so he composed himself on the snowbank, he breathed in deep and pinned it, and now this was the best and freest he'd felt in his life that he could remember, full of beer and ripping his sled indomitable on the frozen Ottawa, over and through drifts across bare ice, onwards to the fabled soft patch, tears filling his cow-eyes and freezing and sailing off his cheeks, but it was early, hardly past Christmastime, and then he hit the soft patch. Mikey, John and Kirby were ice-fishing right by the shore with their beers in holes in the snow and they heard the lone engine die into the water, then ran through the dark, drunk, to where one of the MacKays sobbed in an Arctic Cat jacket and pointed at a slushy brown hole and cried: Don't come any closer!

By then Doolan was a kilometre downstream, interred under a ceiling of ice, and they found his body in the spring. Mikey considered a hand pressed up on the ice, wondered how long did he live for, as the current took him, if he had time to scream and punch on the ice, alone in the dark and underwater.

Mikey could never remember the last time he saw him alive. It might have been when he asked Doolan, who was in charge of the bathroom key at the outdoor rink, why all the lights—in the building where you tied your skates, warmed up and peed—didn't work, and Doolan said they did, but they didn't, and Mikey got frustrated and had enough and had to pee and so he peed in an arc in the dark into what he assumed was the bathroom or the general direction of the bathroom and later he saw Doolan annoyed and wheeling over the mop bucket.

Or probably it was when some younger Fearnoch boys were cruel and laughed at the man when he couldn't figure out his Proline ticket at Fearnoch Convenience. Doolan consistently struggled with the math on his Proline and it caused a lineup and annoyed the cashier girl so her mouth betrayed a fast little smile when she heard one of the boys say something about cow-eyes and the others laugh. Doolan knew the boys were laughing at him, with their shitty hockey hats and hockey hair, but he couldn't understand why, and he had thought them to be nice and sweet boys when they were littler. Mikey was at the back of the line not helping in any way. There was no kindness in this store at all, not even from Mikey, Doolan figured out. He was confused and hurt by this, and he looked at the floor between his feet, then sniffed, forgot his Proline at the cash, softly called the boys "foiggots" and left the store, off to go drown. Mikey could have at least said something, instead of just leaving Doolan alone in the unkindness, so he stuttered out: It's a rotten thing to be mean to that man—but it was too late and no one cared.

———

Mr. Bachmann paid for the ice coffee, because he was old and rich. He liked Anna. Her blue eyes were large and wet; she looked like she'd given it her all, left it all out there on the ice, but she didn't get the part.

Anna, I'll just say this, said Mr. Bachmann, leaning forward to put his wallet back in his pocket. You seem very nice. But give up on the boy. He's not your boy. I was a prosecutor for eleven years and I'll tell you—anyone who's seventeen and in the system is too far gone.

He stood up.

The world, he said, is never fair.

———

Since they were little boys, John and Mikey always knew there was a bad, very bad problem between Kirby and his father. They weren't old enough to understand what was happening, but it was there, wordless, and they perceived Kirby's stress and fear, his rattling shaking way of showing he was not good, all the way down to his chromosomes, not good, and John and Mikey felt it as their own. They sat on the chesterfield and played Mortal Kombat and Kirby shook his controller. His dad made a racket upstairs, started yelling, then Kirby dropped his controller and went to hide under the truck in the garage.

Don't tell Dad I'm in here, he said, his eyes wide in the dark under the truck.

They played shinny under the bridge at the one end of Archie McHugo Side Road, then Mikey and John thought it was a good idea to go to Kirby's house because he always had lots of two-litres of pop.

No, Dad's mad, said Kirby. No, no, no.

Later and getting older now, John said: What's wrong with your dad? Is it alcohol? Is he on alcohol? His dad didn't act like this—shouting, and barfing on the Christmas tree. Kirby's dad also vomited a bright blood puddle right in the kitchen. A real awful and dangerous little bald man with rotten little eyes close together he was. But he too had his dead promises of a shit life that he was trying to helm around, such as his own dad drinking alone in the granary to deal with what he'd seen in the war—starving shoeless Dutch ladies in the wintertime, some with their heads shaved over suspicion of them sleeping with Nazis, Kirby said—and beating Kirby's dad, kicking him around the barn, for the smallest of reasons.

This is shit, thought Mikey, this trying to go deeper into why someone was shit. Fuck this man—can I just say fuck 'em, write 'em off? Turned poor Kirby into a communist. He was silent still, and Dr. Milks leaned her head on her palm.

John threatened to kill Kirby's dad. This they all remembered but didn't talk about. Mikey remembered—they were watching *Bleu Nuit* in Kirby's basement; it was one of those nights. *Bleu Nuit* was legendary late-night programming, Saturdays at midnight on the French channel, which sometimes wasn't too fuzzy, and it was cherished by many boys at the Fearnoch Junior High School. Spellbound and undone with all the grainy pink naked women in a bath or the hayloft, then they fell asleep in a nest of sleeping-bags and sofa pillows. Mikey woke up later, cold now in the basement—the TV buzzed with those old colour bars on it, and he saw he was alone. Still in his dreams he heard what amounted to, in his estimation, a monstrous, murderous crab or crawdad scampering and clawing crabwise at the floor above. Chairs squeaking then, and clamours, shouting. He was spooked—this felt very evil—but he worried about Kirby and John and so softly he went up the stairs to the kitchen, lest he seem a pussy. The door was half open and the light over the sink was on. Mikey remembered a little lace doily curtain over the window by the sink that he looked at before daring to turn and look at the rest of the kitchen.

A two-litre pop bottle was on the floor, emptied in a lime-green puddle. Kirby sat in a chair at the table with his face very red, looking down at his hands. Kirby's dad stood, very tense with his mouth dark and blood dribbling down onto his whiskers. Mikey wouldn't forget the man's eyes. It looked like no amount of violence was too far for him here in the kitchen sticky with pop at three in the morning. John was between Kirby and his dad, already a giant at thirteen or fourteen, bigger than the grown man, and only wearing old Anaheim Mighty Ducks boxer shorts. John wouldn't budge and would take and respond to whatever violence was coming. He looked unbreakable then.

You touch him again and I'll kill you, John said very clearly. I'll beat your head in. His bare chest filled.

Kirby looked up, astonished, through his thick glasses.

Not too long after that his dad was good and dead, after a few more savage bouts of vomiting the blood up—thick and brilliant red like paint. He had gotten himself esophageal varices, which meant the veins in his esophagus were distended and bursting from the cirrhosis in his liver. You actually could booze until you barfed your blood out. That was one way to go.

———

Now Kirby felt his phone ringing in his pocket, vibrating again and again into his thigh, but he ignored it. He saw John on his tractor and wished neither of them was there. The farmers' convoy stopped. John was bewildered. Mush was upset. It looked like there could be a fight. On sleepy old Fearnoch Road. With cows everywhere. John figured a fight like this only happened in the city. You're in the wrong frigging place, he thought, downtown's one hour that way.

Still, the belligerents shouted at each other. No one stopped to think they might not really know what they were talking about. They shouted and called each other fascists, communists, faggots, pigs, pussies, hicks, retards and hippies. Old Mr. MacKay listened from his seat on his porch on Fearnoch Road, tremendously annoyed. This is all just really bad manners, he thought.

A farmer with a massive belt buckle got off his tractor and said, out of the goddamn road, and the more brazen counter-protestors stood up, defiant, chests out and arms still locked together. This was the world gone mad, spun up insane in the heat of the day, and it was always going to go this way, a greasy fight in the dust and gravel and thistles. They should have listened more. Kirby felt his phone going off again.

A kilometre and a half of hayfield away, Peace screamed in the bathroom: Kirby come home now!—and she had one of the bathroom curtains balled up in her fist.

———

Across from the chicken restaurant, Bernard shouted—Non! Non non! He stuck out his hand.

Ebenezer looked up, then turned to the other alley but before he could see, he got pitched over backwards and it felt as though his abdomen was on fire. His sister heard pop-pop-pop from the apartment in the housing complex. He fell back into the fence behind the chicken restaurant and didn't understand.

I'm not a rat-goof, he whispered.

———

Sheep bleated, and the horses whinnying and rearing; someone threw rocks and sticks, someone threw them back, projectiles a-clangour off a combine. A farmer tried to drag a young man out of the road by his foot and the young man kicked him with the other foot. The dust rolled. Mush got involved of course, thinking if you wanna fight well let's fucking go then, Gord got excited, then scared, then excited all over again, Climate Death moved like a gauntlet, a humongous farmer almost had a heart attack. The asphalt burned, and Fearnoch Road was tipped down to hell, little abode of devils, and it could be any century really, any squabbling bit of the planet, Mush massive in the middle of it. Someone swung a stick and he ripped it away, threw himself against the gauntlet of Climate Dead and he looked like a large herbivore covered in hunter-gatherers. The revenge of the nerds Mush had been fearing. John rushed to Mush and Kirby slipped in the gravel. Mush's cow spoiled her milk, with the bejesus alarmed out of her.

———

Ebenezer's ears were useless and buzzing, his legs didn't work, his back, eyes, face didn't work, he leaked and burned on his side by the fence. He was falling asleep, or he wasn't at all, he was waking up somewhere else. A fog bank collected on him and he tried to put together what was happening and what he should do, odd as this all was. His spine was full of gravel, holes all through the meat of his back: nothing worked. Squeaking to breathe and wet and hot, he lay in the weeds, pavement and garbage. He tried to roll and cover his face, and couldn't, and he looked sideways at the black sky, could see his mum and sister in the kitchen with supper and homework, could see Anna sitting on his bed, Anna and his sister with a horse.

———

Now they were in it and considering all the resentment and the jingoism, Kirby and John began to enjoy the fight a little. Finally a fight. Dialogue and empathy, compassion, that was all over, if anyone was really even trying to do that in the first place. No, it was time to brutalize and punish, and exact a heavy price.

John saw a two-on-one fight, which didn't strike him as fair, and so he exploded into one of the fellows, manhandled him, tried to wrangle him by the neck and jersey him like in hockey. Enough with these lecturing city people who didn't know anything telling him his life was wrong. John would call on the old clans, summon the old clans out of the hills and into the fray. He'd like to fight naked if he could, as his ancient Pictish ancestors did, tattooed blue with garlands of skinned human heads around his neck.

But Kirby had his psychotic Highland warrior ancestors too and he entered the tumult, he answered the trumpets. He saw his dad's rotten grin everywhere, all through the convoy. He wanted to see some blood. Mush emitted his Fearnoch battle cry and punched Gord's ski goggles in half, sent Gord instantly unconscious down in the road.

Then screams registered out from the dust, an octave above the rest. Screams, these elemental notes of suffering and fear from the deepest tangles of someone's vocal tract. A young woman was cornered, wriggling and squealing, it seemed, for her life. And John stopped right where he was, and thought, what are we doing . . . this is stupid and awful—and then someone suckered him real bad from behind, right in the ear, so he got angry all over again, and turned.

There was Kirby, who couldn't see too well through his balaclava eye holes tangled up with his glasses, who also heard the screaming and stopped and felt like shit too, and shifted his balaclava to see John get clocked right on his ear. It was with horror then that he saw John turn, enraged, and come right for him. John thought it was Kirby who did it. Kirby stuck his hands out.

John—wait, it's me!

But it was too late, John didn't hear, twisted whoever this poor soul was around, cracked his head back and landed a formidable punch right into his throat. John ripped the balaclava off, the glasses fell out of it, and Kirby fell forward into John.

Oh Kirby . . . for Jesus' sake, John said and felt sick.

He pulled Kirby wheezing away from the brawl and held his glasses for him, and again Kirby's phone was ringing. Peace sat on the closed toilet-seat lid at home.

———

Mr. Bachmann gave Anna a drive home, past people sweating and boozing on the spiralling Montreal staircases, and he said good luck with it all, while Bernard called the ambulance from behind the Mega Dollar. And finally Ebenezer cried, he cried like a boy, because he was a boy, and because it hurt and he was in shock, he cried like a small child, hyperventilating with his face scrunched up, huge tears and spit-strands. Then he passed out with one hand across his chest and Bernard held his other hand, and scaled the fence and ran when he heard sirens coming.

———

Mikey spoke slowly so he didn't stutter. When . . . we can't imagine, he said to Dr. Milks, when we can't see everyone else as just like us, just trying to get through their shit, we all are just trying to get through our shit! . . . Well. Bad, bad things happen. He was glass-eyed and drooling like a savant.

But we'll forget, he said, again and again, and again and again.

———

And still the old sky held over them all, full of supercells and piss, clogged black and green to the brim.

TWENTY-SEVEN

The OPP came down Fearnoch Road. Four patrol cars in the road with the sirens and lights flashing into the fight and the fearful cows. The farmers and the Climate Death scattered into a cornfield, down the side road, scrambled back onto their tractors. Kirby ripped his glasses out of John's hand, pushed him away, unable to talk, and he sprinted through the field home to Peace, rasping into the milk-weeds, their heads exploding their floss all over him, grasshoppers springing and flipping into him.

And Peace sat pale and dismal on the porch with her hair in the wind and her hands on her lap. She looked into the distance and spoke slowly without crying.

It happened again, Kirby. It's still bleeding.

Kirby only bent over and panted. He looked up at her and shook his head. It wasn't true—this couldn't possibly be more bullshit. He sat down and Peace moved from where she was sitting on the step, knocked over the gourds and put her face into his shirt.

We should go to the doctor, she said. My fucking uterus is assassinating my children. Then Kirby hugged her and then she did cry, with her face wet against his neck.

———

Anna got a phone call from Miss Natalie. That was how she found out. She was biting her lip without knowing it again and bleeding a little into her mouth and trying to stay busy. She did the dishes, dried the cups and put them back in the cupboard, then cleaned the sink, around and under the sink also. And she got out the grout and the grout-gun from under the sink and took it over to the rotted curling edge of the bathtub but stopped with that futile chore before she'd even started. She packed up old clothes for the Salvation Army—couldn't stop moving, else she'd think too much, think about the circling grizzlies under the circling helicopter in Fort Nelson while it circled her down into their territory, or think about kissing Magnus in a snowstorm, and him and Océane in a bed together, what that was like, about Mr. Bachmann's tired old tuft of old man hair and how stupid she was, about Ebenezer sitting in the hallway, in his huge blue stupid gangster clothes. It would be nice to get drunk, or put on her bathing suit, get drunk and fall into a cold pond. Anna went out on the stoop with *Anna Karenina* but her brain wouldn't rest, not even for a moment, on Levin's cows and his fancies. Then she got the phone call.

Are you sitting down? Miss Natalie asked.

Yes, said Anna, standing.

No are you really sitting down.

Yes, said Anna, and then she sat.

Ebenezer got shot. Now he's still alive okay but it's bad—I'm not supposed to tell you this. But I thought you should know. Don't say I told you this. He's in the hospital in Montréal-Nord. If you need time off work—

And so Anna ran.

———

In the toilet there was a twelve-week-old plum-sized blood-ball, a heartbreaking curled-up little marsupial that didn't make it. Kirby flushed the toilet and watched it spiral away forever dead. Peace was in the kitchen with her head in her crossed arms on the flowery table-cloth. He pulled a chair close to her and put one arm around her back, his head against hers.

And from the kitchen window, John looked in. He'd walked through the field holding his hat and he wanted to apologize for the fight. He stopped at the kitchen window because he saw Kirby and Peace holding each other exactly like he did with Polly some nights, many nights, nothing but two people in a kitchen holding all the hopes and pains of trying to fit your lives together. John walked around to the door, stopped, then didn't knock. He put the knocked-over gourds back up on the porch before he slipped back through the field full of gentle butterflies lifting away.

———

The receptionist looked exhausted as Anna badgered after her, said "Ebenezer" about eight times. The hospital was abuzz with emergencies major and minor.

Please, said Anna. Please please. He got shot! Did you call his mum—is he going to die?! She had one shoe fallen off, her purse on the counter. Leaning forward and begging.

The receptionist asked her to please sit down and get the blue form from over there. Anna turned and walked right into a very tall and handsome policeman. Anna was tired of all this fooling about while Ebenezer was back there maybe dying.

Out of my road, she said. I need to see Ebenezer.

Okay, the policeman said.

What?

J'ai dit okay. Follow with me, he said in a thick Québécois accent.

Anna hurried behind him through the emergency ward doors now with both her shoes off. She didn't expect it to be so easy and quick—maybe this tall cop here was insane? She had to be brave. There was a mop in the hallway with a bucket and a deep, thick disinfectant smell. They had to hide and paste over all the smells from folks shitting out, bleeding out and dying in here. She saw a room at the very end with a chair outside the door. But now she had to be brave.

In Ebenezer's room a doctor and nurses fussed over the bed. The policeman pointed to the bed and Anna was brave and she brought her hands up over her mouth and shuffled closer. She craned around the shorter nurse.

Here is Dr. Kim, the policeman said.

The doctor turned her head and said, Non non non monsieur!

They had tiny Ebenezer very carefully on his side, straight as board. Anna saw four red compression bandages.

Doucement, doucement! a nurse said into her mask, and they put him back on his back. He had a ventilation mask clasped on, and a neck brace, his eyes closed, more bandages and blood, tubes, hoses, valves and clamps.

For God's sake Ebenezer, Anna whispered and she reached to touch his hand.

The doctor grabbed her hand. She had some of Ebenezer's blood on her front.

You can't be here, said Dr. Kim in perfect English. She turned and glared at the policeman as he nodded at her.

Anna wanted to touch his hand. She only wanted to touch his head and his hair and put her head next to his for one minute, that was all. She pulled her hand away from Dr. Kim.

Ebenezer, she said again. Will he die? I just want to touch his hand.

Dr. Kim positioned herself stoutly in front of Anna, who in turn slowly inhaled.

No, Dr. Kim said. He will not die, not on my table. He was shot four times. He won't die but his life will be very different.

Anna didn't say anything but scrunched up her mouth. Without knowing it she had her hand going for Ebenezer's again, under the doctor's arm.

Look, look, said Dr. Kim. Look at my hands. She held her hands in front of Anna's face. I am the best surgeon in the province—he won't die on my table. Korean hands are the best for surgery.

Her hands were gorgeous—tiny, elegant, dainty but strong with short and perfect nails. Steady perfect hands.

Now touch his hand okay, Dr. Kim continued, then you have to go.

Anna finally touched his little hand, covered it with hers. She thought she heard him babble something into his mask. She held onto one of his fingers and tried to be brave.

Just a boy, she said. Just a boy with no luck.

There was shouting in the hallway then, loud and fast and French. An older and shorter policeman shouted at Anna's police-man, who shouted back, then Dr. Kim shouted at the both of them. With the French coming out so fast and frantic, Anna couldn't keep up, she listened and watched, keeping hold of Ebenezer's finger, but it was no use. These Québécois spoke so fast, whipped through their syllables, like the Irish, or folks way up the Valley.

The tall policeman was gentle and took her arm. Sorry, sorry, he said.

The old short policeman had a very stern look for her. Anna let go of the finger and looked at Ebenezer's head stuffed in the mask and neck brace, his eyelids tight, as the policeman guided her out. They went down the hall slowly and then she was alone, exhaled and bent over, tears falling off her chin and jaw, and she covered her mouth so she wouldn't scream.

TWENTY-EIGHT

A nd no relief came, not for the damned. It was Friday then, Guthrie Place Fair Friday, the hottest day yet and the last day of summer.

This is ridiculous, said Peace, with her seat fully reclined and her arm over her face on the drive home from the doctor's, from her flushing and sucking out. This is like the pathetic fallacy, she said.

A man came on the radio in the SUV and said he was from the Storm Prediction Centre down in Toronto. It was thirty-six degrees in the Ottawa area, he said, and going up, and he promised thunderstorms, the thunderstorms of the decade. He said there was a dense cold front from the prairies and northwestern Ontario that was pushing into the Ottawa Valley, which he called a sweatbox.

At the clinic, Dr. Ayoub and Dr. Milks sat in the break room and watched the blistered horizon to the west. Something like a cosmic event or a meteorite didn't feel out of the question with this sickening air, this wet fat plight of ions and joules.

Fucking sweet Jesus, said the man selling corn to the man selling poutine in the gravel parking lot out front of Fearnoch Convenience. Both of them had their shirts off and stuck out their back pockets.

———

Well something's coming down the track, said John. He too took his shirt off, a fetid wet old plaid shirt, which he retired to the garbage. Some more tin had fallen off the barn roof, he noticed, and he should go tack that back up.

He had a present for his dad. It had finally come in the mail that morning. He found him walking with Busty down along the train tracks. John's dad threw a stick a very short distance, which the dog ignored, and the old man walked very slowly with his hands behind his back.

He turned to fix John in his good eye.

I want for to go to Valley Rent Rite, he said. You need anything— I thought barn-paint—

Look at this Dad, said John. He gave him the parcel from the mail.

His dad struggled mightily with all the tape on the parcel.

What is it? he asked.

Seeds! said John.

Eh? Seeds . . .

Yes, see—beans, corn, and—squash. I got it from the Historical Society there.

John's dad shook the envelopes and they rattled.

They're seed strands from the original settlers of Fearnoch. John was very proud to explain the seeds to his father. Last in the world, he said. So you'll be the only fellow with real Fearnoch beans, you know?

The only fellow with the real beans, his dad repeated. He peered into an envelope.

Yeah, said John.

Thanks, that's very special.

You're welcome, said John. And he left, back down the tracks to go tack the tin back to the barn roof.

John's dad rattled his beans some more and poured some of the last seeds out into his hand to have a look.

John, do you think—he said, but John didn't hear him, away down the tracks.

———

At three o'clock the thermometer hit plus forty.

Well this is one saucy hot cocksucker of a day, said Pete-buddy, out the window of a scrap stock car that had its hood busted open but still ran, by some miracle, and which he accordingly drove straight into the scrap pile. Bpppppppppthh, he added, spit flapping out everywhere.

Mikey threw up from dragging around piping hot channel iron and had to go sit in some shade. Foreman Don said to shutterdown. He saw Stella in the distance with her scientific instruments.

———

Kirby and Peace drove to the Fair so Peace could enter her pickles and best pumpkin in the blue-ribbon contests. She carefully buckled the pumpkin into the back seat.

Fuck, she said.

———

Yvette told Anna she'd cover her tables and she could just go sit in the back for a while. Anna sat on an upside-down bucket by the dishwasher and tried to rally herself. She called Miss Natalie but there was no answer, she wondered if Mont-Royal had wheelchair-accessible areas. Then she fell asleep with her face in her hands.

———

Stella noticed Mikey with his head bobbing around under the only tree at the dump and walked towards him. Mikey saw her, checked himself for barf and stood up.

You think it's fucking hot enough to go swimming in the river today? Stella asked loudly.

Yes, said Mikey. It was too hot to think of any lies, so he said: My phone is broken, that's why I didn't write back.

Stella didn't say anything.

You wanna go now? Mikey asked.

She nodded and walked to his pre-owned sedan without waiting for him.

———

Children ran everywhere at the Fair, full and giddy off Beaver Tails, trying to feed handfuls of pellets to piglets and baby goats, they ran in front of Peace and Kirby with helium balloons and released their helium balloons up and forever and then cried. The heavy horse was out on the fairgrounds, the auctioneers were in their glory.

Peace and Kirby walked from the farm end to the midway end holding hands and then Peace noticed an imposing and bearded man waving at Kirby.

Who is that?

Oh Lord, said Kirby.

Kirby! G'day g'day! Mush bellowed. Fucking been a while!

Hi Mush, said Kirby. He squeezed Peace's hand hard and she jumped.

This is Peace, my partner, said Kirby. Peace stuck out her other hand.

A pleasure, said Mush. Carlos is around here somewhere, he said twisting his humongous head around in the crowd. Carlos! he called.

Carlie, Mush's wife, whom he affectionately referred to as Carlos, pushed a stroller over from near the Tilt-A-Whirl. A baby girl with white-blond hair and a blue barrette slept with her head against her shoulder in the stroller.

Oh who is this? Peace asked crouching.

This is Irina, said Carlie. She's sapped.

Beautiful, said Peace. Just gorgeous.

She's from Bolivia, said Mush. He smoothed and fixed her hair, making sure not to wake her.

Belarus, Mush, she's from fucking Belarus, said Carlie, former Fearnoch Queen of the Furrow 2004.

That's right, said Mush.

You adopted her? asked Kirby.

It was expensive, said Carlie. And took years.

My dick is fucked, said Mush softly to Kirby. But look at her. She's perfect.

Kirby was flummoxed: this terrible brute Mush—who was cruel to him and Mikey when they were in school, because it was cool to be mean then, that is until John told Mush to fuck off—he looked like he might cry.

Well maybe we'll see you at the combine derby, Mush continued, and he blinked. You come by sometime there Kirby lad, just to say g'day you know, say g'day.

After Mush and Carlie waved goodbye, Kirby relaxed his grip on Peace's hand.

That man used to beat the absolute shit out of me in school, said Kirby.

Irina, mouthed Peace. I love it.

———

At four o'clock there were a million and a half baby frogs leaping and scrambling along the little spit of gravel and stone-dust, towards the dock at the river. An exodus of baby frogs to the water. Mikey had never seen this baby-frog phenomenon in all his years of coming to the river. He tried not to crush any to death under his bare feet, but that proved impossible.

My phone is busted up, he reiterated. I didn't get to read your message.

Here, said Stella, and she frigged around on her phone for a second then gave it him. You read it. She took off all her clothes except her underwear and walked down the rubber floating dock, along the burning bits of old tires, and had some difficulty balancing with the sway.

Mikey only stared at her on the dock, holding onto her phone. The wind was picking up, hot like breath.

You read it, Stella said again.

Yeah, said Mikey. So he read, first what he said from Hull loaded:

Do you want to go swimming in the river?

Do ypu want to go seimming in the river

The rivr. Yours, mikey

And then Stella's monster message:

Mikey yes I want to go swimming. Are you drunk? I want to go on a date I want you to ask me on a date. I do just ask me on a fucking date Mikey you must be drunk as hell. I think you care too much about what people think. Don't worry don't be embarrassed because everyone is so self-obsessed with their own shit they don't even think about you and your shit ever. Do what you want. Like I'm thinking about my own shit even right now. Most things almost nothing works out but who cares I don't care. I don't give a care. You can never know anything for sure but you still have to act. Well that's what I think anyway. Except math. You can know math for sure everything else you just have to try it out with some faith. You know? Pretty smart I think. But you should know that I'm crazy. Just look at how long this message is. I have borderline personality disorder but I think it's bullshit and it's just from some bad bad things that happened when I was little. But that's the diagnosis. Also I usually date girls these days. I'm lonely. And I'm not a pussy. You know when you meet someone every once in a while who you know is completely not bullshit? That's how I feel. You're not a pointless to know person. I am crazy and I will probably leave you'll see I always do. But when do you want to go swimming and are there lots of weeds? I'll bring my bathing suit to work? I want to watch a horror movie together too I don't care if you live with your parents.

Jesus I wish I'd read that sooner, thought Mikey, holding Stella's phone on the dock with baby frogs hopping on his feet. I am the most bullshit person I know.

What do you think? Stella asked. She turned with her hand on her hip, her freckles making Mikey insane. Not a bad text message eh?

Alls Mikey said was: You're gay?

Stella closed her eyes and let herself fall onto her back into the water.

I'm also crazy, said Mikey. Certifiably, he said.

But she was underwater. He ripped off his clothes and ran off the dock.

———

At 4:15 p.m., John was getting faint and shivery up on the tin barn roof, flirting with the heat exhaustion. The sky was turning bright green. He scaled down the ladder with a little of the tin flapping harder in the breeze. Johnny chased a plastic bag around the lawn, the bag blew out of his reach and looped up in a playful circle.

When's the sap running Dad? Johnny asked. Are we boiling? He wheeled and sprinted after the bag.

That's springtime, lad. What're you doing—chasing old bags? John asked.

Yeah. Oh yeah.

John considered. Pretty good, he judged.

You want to chase the bag too?

Yes. I do.

The wind sucked the bag away over to the fenceline, and there came then an awful sound out of the clouds which made Johnny freeze in alarm: a tortured, sucking, beast-howl, moaning drunk, like the whole lid of the horizon was being twisted off. John had never heard anything like that before and he held Johnny's hand.

———

Stella popped her head out of the water directly in front of Mikey. She plugged her nose and then pulled her wet hair off her neck. The baby frogs made it to the water and swam like tiny experts all around them, the weeds tickled, he felt her leg touch his, the sky—green, maroon, black—whatever the fuck it was, didn't matter, began sprinkling onto them in the river. Her face was very close and she said nothing.

Spineless, spineless, spineless, thought Mikey. Fuck.

The raindrops hopped and burst around their ears and their mouths in the river. Lightning spidered in the clouds. Finally, finally, in the end Mikey was just one Fearnoch lad who was tired of feeling spineless and like shit for so long. And so he kissed her and it was easy and fine, just a kiss, and he kissed her again, longer, and it was, he thought at least, heaven.

———

Kirby and Peace drove home down Guthrie Boundary Road, winding up over the ridge and then straight into the curtain of cloud and snarl. A black thunderhead, kilometres tall, was raised up and inhaling over their town, a black sphinx, a black bear yawning, dark god presiding down on the tiny road, store, barns, homes, hay bales and trucks. The trees were blowing in every direction like they were in a washing-machine spin cycle.

Is this sailor's warning or sailor's delight? What's going on up there? Peace said.

Kirby pulled over and looked up.

———

Anna got off her bucket and put on her apron.

I'm all right, she said to Yvette.

Anna viens icitte. Dere is something on the TV, said Yvette. She looked out into the dining room and wiggled her fingers behind her for Anna to grab her hand.

———

John carried Johnny inside up on his shoulders and ducked under the doorway. He set him down on the kitchen table and the boy wriggled away and ran off.

Something wild out there, said Polly. Something fierce.

John said: The barn's up and frigging falling apart again. He put his hat on the table and slouched.

Yeah, said Polly.

John looked up at her from the kitchen table, his hand and hat dirty on the doily. What are we doing? he asked, then softer: Why'd you choose me?

Eh?

The farm's dying, anyone with sense would have sold long ago, the animals are fucked, the town's dying, dad's not looking great at all. Farming is over. You could have gone to Ottawa, Montreal—

I chose you because of how you are with your dad, Polly said. She sat herself on his lap, even though it was an odd time for a talk, and connected her arms behind his neck, let her shoes fall off her feet. Just how you are with each other. I knew right then. Stupid and sentimental as you are.

Oh, said John. He looked in her eyes and was quiet a moment, then he said: Thanks.

I could give an ass the farm's falling apart. But—you should get a trade, said Polly.

Busty howled and paced outside in the storm. The screen door squeaked and the wind moaned in. Johnny ran out after the dog.

We should go have a party in the basement maybe, Polly said.

———

At 4:25 p.m., Mikey urged the pre-owned sedan 130 km/h up Fearnoch Road. He paid the heavens no attention, the rain swelled into the wipers, and Stella wrapped a towel around herself and kissed his neck. This entire scenario was breathtaking for Mikey.

I'm crazy too, he said. I have to see a counsellor.

In five minutes, they were sitting on his bed in the loft, getting the comforter and quilt wet. Mikey was thankful his folks were at the trailer in Calabogie for the weekend. He dripped all over the old VHS and DVD movies in the movies box looking for a film.

I have one horror movie, he said, making a racket. Here! he produced it: Italian movie from . . . 1971. Ballerina, uh . . . ballerina murders.

Superb—looks great, said Stella without looking. She got under the sheets and wriggled. Mikey heard a slap and saw her wet towel and underwear on the floor.

He got into the bed and reached for her, careful with his cold hands and cold feet. He shuddered and sank down next to her into the closeness, the muchness, the deep tactility of it. His neural pathways flowed and stretched, a deep tremor ripped down into every toe. Stella's wet hair was on his face and she slid one leg over him. He felt her damp river-skin, small shoulders, felt the joy in the shape of her leg, the bend in her arm, felt that he saw God. He'd forgotten. The intimacy came down upon him, and came down with megatonnage. He wanted to be careful with this moment, take a look around and be careful with this moment, keep it in an ode, put it off in a vase somewhere.

I forgot to press play, he said.

Stella kissed him, was on top of him, and she threw the sheets back. She kissed him again with her wet hair all over his face, then she sneezed.

Sorry, she said, and wiped her nose.

Do you want me to put on REO Speedwagon? he asked.

No.

We have to do it twice 'cause I'm gonna be so bad.

Mikey—frigging hush. Stella put her hand on his mouth and held it there. The power flickered. Mikey wrapped his arms around her back. The power went out. She pressed herself on him, then she whispered: Jesus Christ.

And she was looking out the window where a motorboat blew down the road, ripping past on the pavement just as it would on the river.

———

Hail popped in the lawn and in the fields, hail like walnuts and crabapples stung into John's back. The cows, they knew what was coming, and they huddled with their heads all together in a tight circle under their tree. Busty ran away. John caught his boy and hoisted him up to his chest as his hat blew away.

It was the sound of the storm everyone would remember—a heavy-loaded freight train but with no whistle. The wind blew all the spit out of John's mouth kilometres down the way and blew his eyes dry. The hailstones clobbered down.

Maybe I should get the genny out, John thought, and instantaneously saw the generator roll out of the barn and across the yard.

———

At 4:50 p.m. they all knew what it was but it was too late to do anything about it. Every cellphone in Fearnoch and the township got a violent beeping amber alert, the Storm Prediction Centre inter-rupted news programs in Eastern Ontario and Western Quebec. And a tornado walked right down John's laneway.

A tornado, said Kirby.

A tornado! said John.

A tornado? asked Anna.

Tornado, Mikey whispered.

———

It was six tornadoes.

Five of them simply went through the bush, marsh and over-grown fields and didn't bother too many folks. The sixth could have gone anywhere but chose, of all places, to cut a precise diagonal path through the exact centre of Fearnoch's only real intersection. A god-finger pressed down perfectly on where Fearnoch Road and Guthrie Boundary Road met on the map. Rain-wrapped it was, wrapping 260 km/h winds, an EF3 almost an EF4 tornado, three minutes to go through town, fifteen to twenty seconds at any given point, fifteen to twenty seconds to think of what we could lose, fifteen to twenty seconds to salvation or to your life blown up and scattered across the whole Valley. The danger with a tornado is not getting sucked and funnelled up into the sky, but instead getting hit with any one of the million bits of projectile and jargon twisting 260 km/h with the tornado. Cut in two by a microwave, disembowelled with a salt lick, beheaded by a turkey vulture, or any type of madness.

The dump issued its filth in a sixty-kilometre radius. The Young-husband barns, pig houses, chicken houses, ice houses, all the out-buildings ripped free and tumbled one after the other into the woods. Kirby lost a branch from his apple tree, and the internet was out. Mr. Mulrooney draped himself over Mrs. Mulrooney and Angel Mae and he took a blast of granulated shingle and glass to his back, because like many folks, they had all the windows open.

That's my fucking town! Anna said to the TV in Café Plus. Old people wobbling their pie on their forks watched her.

John wasn't sure where his father was. Mikey and Stella wrapped sheets around themselves and ran outside, which probably wasn't smart, but this wasn't Kansas and people didn't know the drill. He held her hand and siding, shingles, soffit and fascia from the store ascended into the sky.

You see! Mikey screamed, pointing in his flapping bedsheet, but no one heard of course.

The sky exhaled pigs, combines, goats, chickens, oats, barley, wheat, animal feed, horses, cows, sheep and tractors. Barns burst, silos unfurled, spread their bits all over the pastures. Up, up and lost forever. Headstones ripped out at the churchyard. The tornado breathed up and carried with it half the school, half the store, the boards and nets from the outdoor rink and an above-ground swimming pool, wrote off the community centre, whipped together everything, quilts, hockey sticks, saddles, wedding pictures, chips, artwork, shovels and rakes, pets, beers, barbed wire and fence posts, supper, the laundry, baubles, ravens, offal, hotdog relish, an old secret Algonquin bent trail-marker tree, a coffee tin with over a thousand dollars in it from Mr. Mulrooney's garage, parts of plumbing systems, Doolan's trailer, John's hat, pumpkins, mittens, and a small tub of spackling.

Mumu-bou hid in a culvert and a round-baler went through the kitchen of his rental unit. The lady who Mikey helped pump gas got slammed into the banister at her house and ruptured her spleen. Mush's pants-boat landed in Quebec. The tornado dodged Gord's house entirely. From his basement window Wayne MacKay watched an oak tree older than Canada halve his pirate taxi-van. Ebenezer slept in the hospital between surgeries, his mum and sister sat on the floor in the waiting room, and Mr. Bachmann sat at home, alone on the foot of his bed with his hands on his knees.

And 166 years ago on this last day of summer the first John Younghusband buried his infant daughter, who died at eleven months. He paused to look for the last time at his daughter, her chin pressed down on the neckline of her white dress, blond curls filling the rough pine coffin, rat-bites down her arm, and she only looked asleep, face like a doll. Trying to be gentle, this was his daughter in the dirt, he closed the lid and pushed the dirt in. And when he thought no one was watching, he leaned on his shovel and sobbed on himself, in about the same spot where John the sixth now looked down at his own child, said into his ear, we're gonna have to run for it Johnny. Johnny's own little greasy Younghusband doll-face that he inherited, he firmed it up with a child's resolve. John hoisted him over his shoulder and ran for Polly in the doorway. A great rogue white pine, thirty metres tall, pirouetted through the pasture, great gouges in the earth and dancing to the end.

Jesus Christ there'll be corpses everywhere, said Mikey. I didn't even know we fucking had tornadoes! But memories are short—in '71 a microburst flattened the curling rink and killed half a prize-winning heavy-horse team. There'd been tornadoes before, there's always tornadoes, though no one remembered.

Peace and Kirby's SUV twisted around on the road so they were pointed back in the direction they were driving. All the windows busted in and the vehicle filled with thousands of tiny violent airborne glass spherules. They held onto each other, come what may. Mrs. Ada Honeywell slept through the whole ordeal. The wooden United church groaned and collapsed. The stone of St. Andrew's Presbyterian held, but the roof and the parish hall evanesced with a whisper. Power lines hung down in the pavement and gravel and dirt roads and the woods. Trees and trucks on their sides blocked the roads. The McKenzies were at the Fair, but most of their farm was now an afterthought or in the road, or distributed in boards and rafters all into John's fields. The tornado even managed to rip up

the topsoil in some spots. The Almanac had not foretold this. Old
Mr. MacKay looked out into the war zone of cratered houses and
spent the rest of the day convinced he was back in Ortona.

I gotta go see my momma! Anna shouted.

She squeezed Yvette's hand, stared at her. Magnus sneaking
around, Ebenezer shot, now a tornado, and Yvette saw that her blue
eyes were wild: bright, absolutely insane eyes. The TV showed video
cellphone footage of a tin granary rolling on down Guthrie Boundary
Road.

Go! Yvette shooed her, pushing on her back. Go go—vite!

Anna called her mum as she ran into the street but the phone
wouldn't even ring.

Anna's mum worried about the birds; Mush and Carlie, who
stopped at Fearnoch Convenience after the Fair, ran out in the furor
of hailstone, vinyl siding and straw bales to Irina in the truck, but
still she slept, unharmed, with a few tiny glass shards on her eyelids.
The shopkeeper commanded everyone into the walk-in beer fridge.
Now sheep carcasses were caught up in trees, a cow died slowly and
terribly, broken against a barn foundation, dead chickens littered the
fields, a pinto mare and foal ran frenzied and gashed with tin, the
fences gone, Busty ran away to wherever he came from, Anna ran
down the crowded sidewalks to the Greyhound station and on
Mikey's bedside table, Robert Plant finally and definitively died.

And still John ran too, John the last of them, with his boy tight
to his chest and pigs tumbling by and a lawnmower, and then a
tornado beside him. John had the sensation of running on angry
molecules, floating and jumping like a dream, like on the moon. Trees
twisted out from the ground, extension cords whipped and mounted
skyward—he had to get Johnny to Polly, get his boy in the door, that
was all, and he screamed for his dad into the snaking rain for no one
to hear. He was almost there, almost to Polly and the kitchen, though
he could feel death on his shoulders, the ending coming, willing him:

come and be taken, come on now because this is how it ends.

But if this was the end, at least it wouldn't be a quiet one. John had enough. He ran on in his rubber farmer's boots with his testicular torsion or his testicular cancer smarting worse than ever, and his boy for some reason not wearing pants and slipping down in his arms, ran right into the wet hell and asteroid belt of farm materials.

Everything pulled away, stripped and blown away down to the bare fact, and John had no control over anything about where he'd found himself in the universe except the only question left, the only real question, which was—well, are you gonna be brave or not? And even then it probably won't matter. Though pull your spirit up out of the shit just for a moment and sing; or die, angry and wasting.

He would give everything—he'd fill a great bucket with everything he had, every minute left, every moment he held onto, sweat, barf, every bone, tissue, and his busted scrotum, his cattle, every handful of the Ottawa Valley dirt, this was everything he had—just to hold on a few more seconds, hold Johnny a few more seconds, for that door and Polly, and to get their boy to her. John gave it all hell and he dove the last few steps, stretched himself across the dooryard and threw Johnny into Polly's arms. He twisted inside, dislocated his shoulder, got blasted with a gust of brush and branches and shit that had flown in from a different township, filling the kitchen and covering his face in blood. He reached with his good arm to slam the door but it ripped out of his hand and away and he never saw the door again, and all John could think of to do was lie on top of his family under the kitchen table, so he lay there on top of them, and he felt around for Polly's hand while that one last magnificent healthy elm tree on the whole hundred acres crashed through the roof and crushed the living room and then just like that it was over and everything was quiet and nothing moved but a tiny sun shower and a peaceful, peaceful breeze.

TWENTY-NINE

Mikey and Stella sat soaked on the lawn and stared at what was at once a soft and pleasant late summer's evening. Stella slowly pulled the bedsheet tight over her head like a hood. Kirby and Peace breathed, covered in glass. John and Polly looked at each other under the kitchen table, afraid to move, unsure if they were alive. The tornado had lived for forty minutes in total, destroyed or severely damaged sixty of Fearnoch-proper's hundred or so homes, bounced over the river and into Quebec, ravaged a low-income apartment unit, and dissipated 140 kilometres away.

Most folks were thankfully still at the Fair, and if the tornado had gone to the Fair, just to the south, it would have been a horror movie. Thousands chased by Ferris wheels: the carny apocalypse.

All Fearnoch was calm for a minute: a quiet, timid, wet disbelief, venturing a tiny peek out from hiding spots. But then soon shirtless men ran all over, shirts off because of the heat and now blown to God knows where, scrambling over trees and tractors to check on their neighbours. A man in his underwear screamed for the Cheesemans, a woman in a bikini-top and flip-flops scaled a pile of brick and rubble, broke a window and shouted for Rosemary. Some held dogs that weren't theirs by the collars and hissing wet cats with their ears flat. A volunteer fireman poked his head into the hole in the side of John's house.

Hello? he said.

———

Mikey felt the sun to the west, a benign and calm sun, and looked to where the community centre had been, then had a terrible thought. He stood up.

Stella we gotta go, he said.

———

On Fearnoch Road, Kirby attempted to turn the windowless SUV back around. He had glass in his hair; Peace had a lapful of glass, both of them covered in dozens of invisible tiny cuts, and they did their best to not touch any more glass than they were already touching. Kirby had to go into the ditch to avoid trees and cows that had broken out, and when the road became impossible with trees and cows and a mutilated hay elevator, they left the SUV in the ditch and walked. They were silent and Peace inspected Kirby's hands because she'd seen blood all over the steering wheel. Their home was untouched, except for that one apple tree bough, and the internet was down. But behind the house—Kirby tried his best to understand what had happened behind his house. He wondered for a moment if they were even at the right house. It looked like there'd been a war. Enormous ribbons of sheet metal, squeaking and lazy in the breeze, dangling from perilous widow-makers; he counted two dead cows, pieces of people's lives ornamenting the fields and flattened fencelines, and one lone horse pawing shell-shocked around the moonscape. It was some time before Kirby could fit the gruesome idea in his head that this was what the Younghusband farm looked like now.

———

Jefferson ran through the cotton-candy forest of insulation behind the community centre. He didn't listen to the Storyland lady or anyone yelling for him to come back, he ran on like a feral child and only wanted to run from whatever that was that had just happened. He avoided a dead duck and ran directly into a wet ghost.

Mikey was down on his knees in his bedsheet and he caught Jefferson in a hug. He could feel the boy's heartbeat and Jefferson struggled until he knew it was Mikey, after Mikey said all he could think of to calm the boy: You're Jefferson, I'm Mikey, we're safe, you like wrestling, don't like Rs, sometimes you get mad . . .

Jefferson gripped Mikey's neck and his eyes were humongous.

Why are you dressed up like a ghost? he asked.

Mikey carried him back to the other children and the volunteers who were doing a head count.

Who's Jefferson? Stella asked him later. They took the pre-owned sedan through the Stygian topography of Fearnoch, hoping they wouldn't find any corpses.

He's . . . my buddy I suppose, said Mikey. He felt like a goddamn mountain lion in the pre-owned sedan, driving around, helping out, with his bedsheet flying out the window like a cape. He drove down a lane in one of the McKenzies' fields to escape the roadblocks and barn rafters on Fearnoch Road.

If the power's out, said Stella, you should check the freezer.

Oh God, said Mikey. He remembered something and turned the car around by an old fence stile.

And I suppose we could put on clothes, Stella said.

At home, Mikey scurried down into the basement, still with his bedsheet fluttering around, and Stella following him. Mikey opened the freezer, dug through hundreds of thawing tomatoes until he exhumed a frosty CCM hockey skates box from the bottom.

Mrs. MacPherson, he said. His cat died in the winter when the ground was frozen.

Oh . . . oh is that—that's not . . . Stella said. Oh no. She shook her head.

We need a freezer or a shovel, said Mikey. He put Mrs. Mac-Pherson half-frozen in the trunk of the pre-owned sedan.

———

Peace and Kirby nearly got lost walking through John's wasteland, so altered the countryside was. Kirby was not doing well—this was a nightmare, he trembled and held up some barbed wire for Peace to crawl under and saw one of the fence posts was blown clean through a tree trunk so it was sticking out the other end. He didn't want to find John and his family dead, hanging on the fences, or a foot poking out from under a hay bale. They were followed by John's prize calf, who met them on the train tracks, and then they heard John calling out for his dad.

Polly sat in the field beside the overturned tractor with her head in her hands. A shredded blue tarp dressed the trees behind her.

He's at Valley Rent Rite, he said he was going to Valley Rent Rite, remember, she said. The truck's not here.

Maybe the truck's been blown into the river—Dad! John shouted. His arm was in a sling and one whole side of his face was puffed out and starting to purple. Some of John's shirts were hanging way up in a tree, still on their hangers.

Look John your shirts are out to dry, said Polly. She wasn't trying to get right down and out. She was always calm in crises, someone you want around in these times.

One entire side of his dad's cottage was blown off and John clambered in and shouted again. Then he saw Kirby and Peace, stopped and said: I'm sorry about the fight, Kirby lad. You all right?

Look at this, Kirby pointed at the gorgeous calf. Not a scratch! We found him on the train tracks. The calf was merry, little frigger trotting in a proud circle.

How—look at that—how did he get all the way down there? John felt a rush of unexpected overwhelming emotion and tried to hide his face. Peace gave Johnny a juice box and sat with Polly.

Maybe your dad's stuck on the road, Peace said to John.

I think he's at Valley Rent Rite. I gotta find Dad, and then the cows, said John, with his arm still covering half his face.

Polly tried calling John's dad on his cellphone that she'd bought him for Christmas which she was very doubtful he used or knew how to use. He didn't answer.

Well there's roadblocks and shit in the roads everywhere so he'll probably be forever getting home, Peace said.

Yeah you're right, said John, and felt a little better. Yeah, stuck on the road.

John you come and stay with us, said Kirby, and then they saw the pre-owned sedan coming in hot through the field towards them, looping around uprooted trees and crumpled farming machinery.

Mikey got out of the car while it was still moving and gave John a long, wet hug.

John was not ungrateful for the hug from his friend. Hi Stella, he said.

Your cows are all over, John, said Mikey. We're here to help you mend the fences. I just gotta go, you know, bury my cat.

———

Anna held her ticket for the Greyhound that was supposed to stop in Guthrie Place just after 10 p.m. and tried calling her mum again, and nothing, and again, and nothing. She put her phone away, then took it back out to try again, but as she was doing so, it lit up with an incoming call from Magnus, which was infuriating. She wasn't gonna answer that and so he sent a message that said: Tornado! Oh my god! I hope everything's OK.

And then another one later: I want to pick up my stuff tomorrow—please let me know if that's OK I'll leave the key.

Anna tried her mum again, and nothing. But then, on the bus somewhere near Hawkesbury, her mum called her from the neighbour's cellphone.

Yes I have no idea where my phone is, probably in the sky actually. We are all okay Anna, the house is fine, but there are about one thousand dead birds, poor dears, she said.

Anna cracked her head off the window she exhaled so hard.

I'm coming home Momma! she said. She curled in her seat and watched the landscape familiarize. And she didn't see it, but an owl, waking up for the night, opened one eye and watched the bus on the dark highway.

At the gas station, which was also a Greyhound station in Guthrie Place, Anna's mum wasn't there yet, so Anna sat on the curb with all the bugs and hay-smells of home coming back to her. A frog pond behind the gas station was deafening and she had forgotten the eternal din of frogs in the country. When her mother got there an hour later, she held Anna's face under the floodlight over the gas station to make sure it was her, that her daughter was finally home, and they sat back down on the curb a while, on the wet asphalt.

You're home! her mother said again. I'm sorry—Christ you need a tank for the roads. But you're home!

With all the roadblocks, police, CTV and CBC vans, cars, trucks, a kilometre of frustrated red tail lights, all the rubberneckers who wanted a taste of tornado-wrath, and then the looters on ATVs, they didn't get to Fearnoch until the middle of the night.

———

In the morning, now it was the first day of autumn, the heat was cut and everything felt very autumnal, and there was a giant Mennonite man in a wool sweater sawing the trees that had fallen onto the Berube laneway.

Hi? said Anna's mother.

I'm Abe, he said. I was sent here to clear the trees.

Thank you Abe! said Anna.

It's my religion, he said. I have to do this. He worked a tiny Swede saw expertly through a chaos of ironwoods. I'm sorry about your house, Abe said.

No the house didn't get hit.

Oh. Abe looked again at the beaten-up little cottage.

Do you want tools? Anna's mother said. I have a little chainsaw there somewhere.

Oh no ma'am. Abe stopped and held up his hands. No power tools please, he said. When he wasn't shuttling around to disaster sites because of the articles of his faith, Abe was famous in the Valley for his handmade masonry tools, and he made his shit by candlelight.

Anna went on a bicycle ride around the town she'd been embarrassed to come back to because then she'd have to give people all her updates. It looked like it'd been carpet-bombed. Already there were volunteers cleaning up the road, sawing trees and looking for pets. Anna saw a group of Sikhs working a wood chipper, Scientologists milling around with Scientology arm-patches on their jackets, the Samaritan's Purse people holding hands in a circle with their heads bowed, Mennonite women pulling wagonload after wagonload of debris out of a soya bean field and looking like something from the last century. Anna wrote her name and email on a clipboard to volunteer with the Samaritan's Purse. Big Albert Cheeseman was in charge of the administration of new volunteers and he sat at a card table in front of the Fearnoch Convenience and gas station plaza, which looked like Baghdad. He remembered Anna from the 4-H Club and he didn't want an update, he wasn't upset she wasn't rich and

famous, he only said, Anna! You're home! I wondered . . . fucking
twister eh, a fucking twister, rip the ass right out of our town . . .
how's your mother? Things like that.

Kirby had been up all night answering calls for the Community
Association about insurance and disaster relief, then he helped serve
a hot breakfast to the Red Cross volunteers in a pavilion tent set up
on Fearnoch Road, then he went to John's to help with the fences,
then he got the flu he was so exhausted, and still he didn't stop.
Mush and Gord took a break from clearing the fields to have a cold
beer, sitting on the road with their legs stretched in the ditch, side
by each, each wearing orange Helping in Jesus' Name T-shirts, each
with no idea who the other one was.

Fucking Fearnoch Strong, buddy, said Mush with his cold, cold
beer.

Fucking amen, said Gord, big swig of affordable domestic ale.

Mumu-bou, Pete-buddy, and Cassie, who came home to help,
also wore the orange Jesus shirts, and they worked together to free a
lamb from the rubble. PTSD Ed held a dusty and crying puppy against
his impressive stomach and looked on. He saw two boys climbing on
the church rubble and relived a horrendous memory from his tour in
former Yugoslavia. Dr. Milks and her husband gathered someone's
family photographs that had been blasted down into a gully. Larocque
and Laframboise and the rest of les boys from the Pontiac wore
their hockey sweaters and went around with ladders and chainsaws,
offering help in broken English. With them were some fellows
from the Algonquin reserve up in Quebec, that Larocque knew from
hockey, and they also wanted to help. Dr. Ayoub brought one hundred shawarmas for volunteers. Mr. Mulrooney gave Anna some
farmer-gloves and together they filled a trailer with huge barn-wood
splinters they had to tug out from where they'd speared into the

ground. How one of these evil splinters hadn't gored right through someone, Anna couldn't understand.

Do let me know if you find an old blue coffee tin please, said Mr. Mulrooney.

Farmers took their tractors, if they still had them, to help the police and Team Rubicon—a group of demobilized soldiers who helped in times of disaster—with clearing the trees and carrion out of the roads. Fearnoch was trying to get up off the mat.

———

At John's farm, Kirby and Mikey weren't sure where John was. Probably out rounding up cattle if they'd wandered to the creek. They acquitted themselves well on propping up the fence posts and cutting away the mangled wire. Kirby had a coughing fit and managed to not throw up. Then he saw the Mennonites, who were everywhere at the moment, clearing brush from the train tracks.

Why don't we switch? he said to them.

No sense wasting a Mennonite's fence-building skill on some brush. The Mennonites were happy for the change, and so Kirby took Mikey, and Peace and Stella, and some of the orange T-shirt Samaritan's Purse people, over to the brush piles.

Stella and Mikey got on like they were completely in love and annoyed all the other volunteers.

You should've had to try harder to find me, said Stella, with her arm around his waist. Apps . . . or something! I just show up at a dump and boom.

We had sex in a tornado, Mikey whispered and looked full of mischief. How about that? He clicked his loppers.

Ninety-five per cent of tornadoes in the northern hemisphere rotate counter-clockwise, Stella said, spinning her finger.

Mikey was fascinated.

Would it be a deal-breaker, Stella asked, if I had a unibrow? She bent to drag a tarp covered in brush.

No, that's fine, said Mikey. Moustache is also okay. Would it be a deal-breaker if I joined ISIS? Or—wore cargo shorts.

Stella put a hand to her chest.

Oh please don't, she said.

——

On the tiny TV in the hospital room there was a news program that showed video of wrecked barns, police cars, a dead milk cow, cows in the middle of the road, then an interview with an old and very large man with suspenders, a tiny baseball hat, and a huge sagging face underneath. It said: Fearnoch, Ontario across the bottom. The old man began to cry. The program cut back to the newsman at the desk and the bottom of the TV now said: Attaque de Tornade dans l'Est de l'Ontario.

Ebenezer was doped and drugged to shit, fantastically so, on all the fancy hospital meds. He watched the TV and drooled. Something was occurring to him. His sister sat in a chair next to the bed with her feet curled under her, and she took advantage of Ebenezer's state to borrow his phone and look at videos.

Bless, said Ebenezer, softly to the TV. He scrunched his eyebrows and drooled some more.

Bless, he said again, and his sister looked up.

——

Down the tracks then it fell to Peace to burn the burn piles and keep the fires cooking. She sat in an armchair that had landed down there and poked at the fires with a long piece of quarter-inch rebar. Some of these stumps would burn for days. The east wind rolled down the tracks, on through the ghost lands. Peace got the shivers and she stood out of the armchair when she saw a dreadful figure coming in, phantasmagoric through the smoke. It was John. He was piteous and filthy. He looked like absolute shit, and he could hardly see or hear. He was thinking about pigs.

After the big pig escape when John was a young lad working on the fence, after they'd loaded all those poor pigs up, the McKenzies' old farmhand spoke with John's dad, and then offered John payment—which was really just some loonies and toonies on Fridays— to slop the next litter of pigs and clean out their pen. They were happy and friendly animals, happy and wee and filthy. He named them after hockey players: there was Mark Messier pig, Sergei Fedorov, Rick Tocchet, and Dale Hawerchuk pig. John swore they had big human smiles and they'd laugh and run over to see if there was food. They were affectionate and knew who you were. One day when they got big, the men came for their teeth. They came and ripped their largest teeth off, the canines, and the pigs cried and John cried. And then another day, the men came back for their testicles. John gave the pigs apples while the men got behind them, held the animals down, seized the testicles and either cut them out, or simply squeezed them, clamped them until they burst. The pigs' eyes lit up wide and they screamed like people as they processed almost indescribable pain. Young John sat later in the grass beside his hyperventilating, exhausted and castrated pig-friends and felt the pain in his own bag. And then the pigs got on their truck and didn't escape.

John recalled that feeling often and easily over the years; he felt the trapped hopeless pain that goes nowhere.

John, Peace said. There you are . . .

He stared and held a flashlight that was still on although it was noon.

———

Mr. Bachmann shuffled along the hospital hall and almost turned around. He was shy and afraid; Ebenezer's mum said it would be okay to visit. Anna had some effect on him, and he thought about her sitting there pleading in that café, and then he thought about the boy too, while he was having supper by himself, or going to the swimming pool by himself in the morning. She made him feel awful and he decided—what was he up to anyway?—sitting alone and listening to an old sad record—decided it wasn't acceptable, in his estimation, to ignore her wish any longer. He could at least see. He went through all his contacts from his law days, and an old police captain said: Oh yes I know him well, he just got shot up.

And so Mr. Bachmann panicked and bustled down to the hospital.

He saw Ebenezer lying there broken in the hospital bed, plugged into bags and machines, and he saw his sister, who was startled at this old white man in the doorway.

Hi, he said.

Ebenezer turned, high out of his mind, and addressed Mr. Bachmann like an old friend.

I think that's Miss Anna's town. Look, he said, pointing at the TV. Tornade in Anna's town.

———

Anna sat on a hay bale on the side of Fearnoch Road and had half a sandwich her mum packed for her lunch. Then she lay down on the hay bale. With burrs in her hair, scratches up her arms, sweat cooling on her lower back. She was spent. Back in the country with her Shur-Gain Feeds hat sweaty and the hay scratching her through her old farm-girl flannel shirt. Across the field, through the devastation, she spotted a great old Clydesdale cantering down the lane, thump-thump-thump and jangling along. She turned on her side, holding the other half of the sandwich, and watched as he ran tall and mighty, carefree like nothing had happened, he was just out for a canter. The tornado never got him. Anna's phone rang.

Probably going to get fired, she thought. She hesitated, would rather watch the Clydesdale, but then answered it, no clue what this area code was.

Hello is this Anna Berube? A man's voice.

Yes. Hi.

Hi—this is Steve Cruz. I'm from—I'm a literary agent. In New York. He spoke calmly over the din of sirens and a truck backing up.

You what?

Um . . . this is Steve, I read your book. You sent it to my agency. I'm an agent in New York.

New York City? I'm talking to someone in New York City right now? Anna was looking at the Clydesdale cantering through wreckage in her town that no one knew and taking a monumental phone call with someone in New York City.

Yeah, New York City that's right.

Oh, said Anna.

Yes okay, so. Anna. Miss Berube. I got a call from, um . . . Magnus, I think he said.

Oh.

Now he said he opened the envelope I sent you and he called me and said to call you. Because you were never gonna open it—is what he said. He said you're a great writer. Anyway . . . Hello?

I'm sorry I didn't open it.

That's okay, that's okay. Let me say I loved your manuscript. I loved it, Steve repeated very slowly.

Anna saw stars. She thought she might black out.

I just loved it Anna.

Anna only nodded, hyperventilating on her hay bale. She couldn't talk and she lay back and let her tears run down into her ears. Deliverance. Maybe this was what a triumph felt like. She wanted to get up and run with the horse, manically with the horse.

Where are you now? Canada?

Anna held the phone away and cleared her throat, trying to pull it together. You wouldn't have heard of it, she said. But then she considered, and said: Actually you might see us on the news. We just got hit by a tornado.

I'm sorry, that's awful. My God.

We're okay. It's a miracle really. Some people lost some livestock.

That's good . . . anyway I love it and I sent some edits, which I need you to look at—now there's a lot of edits okay but that's how it goes. Don't get discouraged.

Thank you, said Anna. Thank you, thank you. Yes I understand—so you're gonna publish it? Can I go to New York? You're gonna publish it?

Steve was quiet. Then more sirens and lots of honking.

You all right there Steve? asked Anna.

Well, said Steve. He didn't have the heart to tell her now that he had no idea at all, he didn't know anything. And he'd since been let go by his agency and was trying to get on with another. He'd been walking for an hour, avoiding the flattened paper-thin rats, and was somewhere off Fulton into Bed-Stuy, with the wheelie kids wheelie-ing past again, and he wasn't quite sure what was going on. Well I wanted to say loved it, he said. You let me work on the rest.

Yes, Anna said. How's New York City?

Can we do email? It's a tough time in the industry. Please look at the edits. Please open mail from now on. New York City is wondrous.

I will, thank you Steve. This is really . . . just really great.

Just keep going. And write something new. I know it's insane, you just gotta hold on Anna, fuck everything. Of course, he was speaking to himself as much as Anna.

Yeah, said Anna.

You gotta tell me, though, said Steve. Who did it? Just tell me. It was the cuckolded jockey, wasn't it?

Anna sniffed and bit her lip. It would come. And she could feel it, and she watched the Clydesdale running on down jangling through the glen, the last Clydesdale, still out there, fuck it all.

THIRTY

John couldn't find his dad. He never came home. John tried to explain to Peace what was happening.

Polly was talking with the police to organize a search party, he said. The man at Valley Rent Rite said no, Mr. Younghusband never came in. The McKenzies said they saw him, they thought, staring at them from way out in the field at dusk, when they finally made it back from the Fair. Polly thought she saw a plaid shape skedaddling to the treeline and investigated but found no one. Peace gently eased the flashlight out of John's hand and clicked it off.

And so it went that all night John had been out with the flashlight splashing into swamps in the dark and tripping over logs and dead animals and all these awful new features of the hundred acres. He wiped his face and blew his nose in his shirt and fell over again. The hours got darker and then it was just John and the ghosts out. If his dad was dead and mangled up in a birch copse or a ditch, he didn't know if he had the courage to handle it. He imagined his dad broken on his side, in his plaid shirt, work pants and workboots, he saw his face several times staring out at the flashlight from the ruins. John was talking to himself but he didn't know it.

Dad, he said, he whispered or yelled. I bet he doesn't recognize anything, I don't recognize shit, everyone's forgot about old Dad, I wanna see him before he dies, I miss my dad!

On he stumbled, hopeless by the tracks, the barn roof blown up against the bush, the old ghost-house missing a lot more bricks. The door fell off when John climbed up into this house his dad was born in. He scanned the kitchen with the flashlight, over the broken lath, peeled wallpaper, the rusted wood cookstove with an old pot of dust—then he jumped, but it was a dead pig, blasted through the window, the poor pig.

About dawn he found the truck upside down and in a pond, covered in hay bales. His dad wasn't inside. John continued, wringing his hands and the sun getting bigger and higher, recalling pig castration, until he was aware Peace was talking to him and taking his flashlight.

———

Hundreds descended on the Younghusband farm. Volunteers from Fearnoch and volunteers from the city. There were police on horseback, police on four-wheelers. Folks reacted in different ways to the crisis. John was guided by the belief, perhaps fantastical or deranged, that his dad was fine because it wouldn't end this way for his dad. While Mikey was convinced at any moment he'd step down on the old man's body, hidden in the hay, and he had to be there to support his friend when the moment came. Polly was steady and was promised helicopters.

The plan was to make four groups, one in each corner, then comb through and meet in the middle. In the northwest, in the coyote-shed-swamp-dead-cow area, went Mikey, Stella, Mush on his side-by-each, the Mulrooneys, Dr. Ayoub and some of the Climate Dead. Over near the ghost-house was John, with Polly, Mumu-bou, Pete-buddy and the lads, with some Mennonites, Sikhs and the

Scientologists. Starting at a pile of barn and silo pieces by the road was Kirby with Peace, several McKenzies and Clan MacKay, some farmhands, some of the Samaritan's Purse. Then up by the gate and flattened cedar fence went Anna with her mum, who, peculiarly, brought a humongous bowl of potato salad, and police officers with German shepherd service dogs tugging on the leashes, Dr. Milks, hockey players, and Gord.

In this way, John, Mikey, Kirby and Anna walked slowly through all of the shit until they were the four of them standing in a circle looking at each other in the middle of the sunny tornado-wreaked cow field on that afternoon. All four of them, together in the end, in the field.

Anna looked at her old high school friends for the first time in ten years. The boys saw her walk out of the past and right up to them. They were quiet.

Then John said: Anna!

Anna? said Mikey. Jesus!

Hi! Anna called, and she sidestepped around the twisted pieces of the old manure spreader and hugged John. Her head right against his muddy shirt and one strand of her hair fluttering in the wind.

You're home! said John.

I'm here to help find your father, Anna said. She straightened up and patted his arm.

John, Anna, Mikey and Kirby continued to stand in their circle and no one knew what to say. They all wanted exactly the same thing, which was find John's dad, then lie down in the soft flat field and sleep.

You look great, said Mikey.

Thanks Mikey, said Anna.

Hi Anna, said Kirby.

You're home, said John, who was pretty out of it. He took his hat off and didn't know what to say other than that.

I'm home, said Anna. She stretched her arms out in the Fearnoch cow field.

Let's find your dad, Kirby said.

Remember, whatever happens, Mikey said, well . . . here we are.

And Mikey looked at the others and thought about how much he'd miss everyone if they'd all been blown up in the goddamn tornado. How they'd miss each other. And we should just try to remember that, he thought. Nobody really knows how to explain themselves to the next person anyway.

John put his elbow up on Mikey's shoulder to steady himself and then they could all hear the dogs begin to bark. Mikey saw John's eyes light up huge when a police officer shouted: Found him. And John charged through the field.

His father now crawled like an old beggar down the fence-line. The dogs flushed him out. The tornado had spat him and a wagonload of hay bales into the bush and he'd been wandering ever since, a lost ghost, not sure where he was or what had become of things.

Now it was horrible to look at him. The old man stared, it looked like he was blind, and his mouth was wide open. A cut was open on his forehead, one leg mangled and awful in the tattered pants. He looked haunted. There was his son, there—there was John, his boy. And he had to say something to him.

John helped him up and held him up and felt his dad's old frame against him, unable to stand on his own. John's dad looked from face to face and seemed like he was trying to say something, but had lost the ability. Polly put her sleeve against the dark blood collecting on his forehead.

Peace whispered: Oh no, he's lost it, and cried into Kirby's shoulder.

Dad, John said. Dad.

His father looked at him, looked at the ground and back to John. He tried speaking again but made a choking sound. His eyes got wider and his mouth hung open still as he bent over and couldn't say one word.

Dad. Dad.

ACKNOWLEDGEMENTS

Thank you always and forever to my family: Mum, Dad, Annie, and Teddy.

I stole your words and stories, I'm sorry, I loved them too much, and I put them all in here. Now Andrew Otto, Diana Kuiper and the young lad Henry. My grandparents, all gone.

Thank you to Rebecca, Rhonda, Nicole, Lisa, and everybody at Breakwater Books for their faith in me.

To Jessica Grant, who made me see stars, to Claire Wilkshire for her patience and care, and to Lisa Moore for starting everything.

Thank you Phil Moreira and Conor McMahon, whose words are also all over the place in here. And Blake Watters too, and the old fellow we met in the hotel bar in Arnprior on that cold night.

Thank you to the MUN English Department for the funding and support when this was a thesis, to Nancy Pedri, Rob Ormsby, Jennifer Lokash, and others. And *Riddle Fence* and SPARKS Literary Festival.

To farmers.

To the old-timers, like George Kennedy and David Carroll.

Thank you Tim Helliker, Brock, Guthrie, and the masons and labourers at the locks, down in the lock-juice.

Thank you early readers: Nick Bon-Miller, Sarah Wright, Terry Doyle, the Bollingers, Kluke, Hillier, many aunts—I know I'm forgetting some, I'm sorry. Also needing acknowledging here are Hertwig, Levesque, Hannah Dean, Heidi Wicks, Bridget Canning, Laura Hillary, Darrell Daley, the Mousseaus, Alexander MacLeod, Mark Jarman, Rod Moody-Corbett, Amelia Schonbek, and Kat Lear.

Thank you to my great glorious collection of buddies across the land who've helped me whether they know it or not, from Carp and Constance Bay, from Quebec, to St. John's, Cupids, to Saskatchewan, Edmonton, 100 Mile House, to New York City, Ireland, and Mongolia. It has been an honour.

To Andrew Harvey.

And to anyone who was in Dunrobin on that day in September.

JIM MᶜEWEN grew up in Dunrobin, Ontario. He is a graduate of the English and creative writing master's program at Memorial University and winner of the Cuffer Prize (2015) and the Leaside Fiction Contest (2019). This is his first novel.